GUEST

SJ Bradley

GUEST

SJ Bradley

All the best!
  -SJB

dead ink

68/100

dead ink

First published in Great Britain in 2017 by Dead Ink, an
imprint of Cinder House Publishing Limited.

Paperback ISBN 9781911585053
Hardback ISBN 9781911585077

Printed and bound in Great Britain by Clays Ltd, St Ives
plc.

www.deadinkbooks.com

For Ricky.

For Richer

LEGAL WARNING

Part II, Criminal Law Act 1977
As Amended by Criminal Justice and Public Order Act 1994

TAKE NOTICE

THAT we live in this property, it is our home and we intend to stay here.

THAT at all times there is at least one person in this property.

THAT any entry or attempt to enter into these premises without our permission is therefore a criminal offence, as any one of us who is in physical possession is opposed to such entry without our permission.

THAT if you attempt to enter by violence or by threatening violence we will prosecute you. You may receive a sentence of up to six months' imprisonment and/or a fine of up to £5,000.

THAT if you want to get us out you will have to issue a claim for possession in the County Court or in the High Court, or produce to us a written statement or certificate in terms of S.12 A Criminal Law Act, 1977 (as inserted by Criminal Justice and Public Order Act, 1994).

THAT it is an offence under S.12A(8) Criminal Law Act 1977 (as amended) to knowingly make a false statement for the purposes of S.12A. A person guilty of such an offence may receive a sentence of up to six months' imprisonment and/or a fine of up to £5,000.

Signed
The Occupiers

N.B. Signing this Legal Warning is optional. It is equally valid whether or not it is signed.

I.

Samhain waited in the dark hallway, restless. Carrying a rucksack of things that might have looked, to anybody else, like the tools a person might use to break into a place.

'No – no – no – no – no...' Frankie, bent as a folded card, sorted through hasps and screws. Gorilla's palms: hands that gripped drum sticks, and shifted guitar cabs. Fingers that fixed, cooked, nursed. Rattling now with loose lock mechanisms, and keys that didn't fit.

'You know what this is like,' Samhain said. They'd got in through a window at the back, and whoever had been in this grand hallway last had boarded over the top glass. It may be midsummer outside, but it was night here. If Frankie would only step out into the day a moment, he could find what he needed right away. But Frankie never wanted to open the door to the outside. Not until they were standing with lock and key and screws laying out ready, to secure the squat. A superstition that had grown from Frankie once having been thrown out of a place, only ten minutes after breaking it.

'That time you hid in Endra's wardrobe because her boyfriend came home.'

'No.'

'No? I guess you were in your pants then. Hang on, this could be it boys, this could be it.' Frankie's silver shaved head tilted down; he winked to a brass Yale right in the centre of his life line.

'Cells at New Cross, jizzlip.'

'Ah.' Crinkled envelope eyes: a smile with one molar missing. That was the smile. The one that had seen Samhain through hangover after hangover: the smile that, seen first time, had started the longest friendship of his life. Eighteen, young and stumbling, with head throbbing and the gig room rolling around him like a head of lettuce in a salad spinner, Samhain had looked into that face and taken Frankie for somebody he already knew. He'd thought Frankie was the same man who'd lent him a balaclava and scarf in Genoa. Firm hands had dragged Samhain up from the sticky social floor, and he'd started saying, 'I love you,' before he'd even made it to his feet.

'Steady on,' Frankie had said.

On their second, more sober encounter, Samhain had realised his mistake. But those first few words had been the start of something. And now here they were.

'Seen enough o' them. Wood Street Wakefield – Doncaster – Hammersmith – New Cross – could be any of 'em. Police cells are all the same, mind. You ready?'

'Yep.' Samhain had one hand inside his bag, his heart beating like an idiot with a set of saucepans. Touched a hammer, a wrench. Fingers brushed the crowbar, before he found what he needed. The screwdriver had wriggled its way

4

all the way down to the bottom, and was nestling under his other shirt. 'Open it up.'

Heavy door. All chains and sliding bolts. The swollen wood and metal mechanisms had oxidised red and rusted shut. The whole thing stuck. 'Haven't you got a hammer there, dreamboat?' Sweat poured off Frankie as though he'd been oiled. 'Don't just stand there, do something with that bolt. Not my hands, dickhead! Mind my hands.'

Samhain started hitting, working away at the bolts. Blows exploded along the door. Across the floor: he felt every hammer-fall in his shoes.

'Right,' Frankie said. Then he had a hand on the knob, right in the centre of the door. 'Ready? Let's get this thing open.'

Two sets of hands, working away. Hauling at it, pulling a truck's weight, until at last the door came open. Just a nick at first: enough for a golden hair of light to run down the right-hand wall.

'Nothing's ever simple, is it?' Samhain could already feel the beginnings of a morning-after ache in his chest and shoulders. His belt chafed with salt sweat. This was a solid door, a thing built to keep intruders away.

One last wrench, and it came swinging like a backhanded tennis racquet.

Sunlight. Liquid amber on wall and into eyes. Samhain blinked: he was looking out into a tangled bower of blooming pink roses, white trumpets of bindweed. Leaves brighter than new peas. Twigs and stalks twisting in an arch, branches and boughs in a person-sized nest. And there in its centre, wearing slacks and a golf sweater, stood a bald and cheerily-smiling man.

'Hello!' he chimed. 'Are you the new neighbours?'

Samhain had dreamed of a home like this. Abandoned, bay-fronted, a Georgian thing with double rooms, and en-suites. The

Boundary Hotel had a faded sign facing the road. It promised tea-making facilities, and a TV lounge. Samhain had been riding past it on his bike every day for months. He had wanted to check that it really was empty.

Life in the slum had made him filthy as an animal. Eight of them in a place with only three bedrooms, and only one bathroom, all of them living on top of one another. He had become obsessed with the idea of white sheets, and of making tea and coffee in a room where you never saw another person's face. Floor space enough for a person to tread freely, without needing to step over somebody else.

The slum had only ever meant to be a house for three. But things got crowded when Sam had started crashing there following a break-up, and Frankie rolled up after being evicted from another squat. He'd brought two others from the same place with him. Soon, there had been a mattress in the living room, sleeping bags in the landing, and they were all always keeping their elbows in no matter where they were in the house.

The sides and back told you this was a working hotel. The sign made it look that way. The windows. The car park. It was only when you really stopped to look, through the exact spot in the unruly twigs-and-sticks privet, that you could see. A door black and heavy, and always, forbiddingly, and very finally, locked.

'It needs a fair bit of work,' Frankie said. 'But we're hoping to be open for business by the middle of next year.'

'Wonderful!' David bounced on his toes, head swivelling. 'Me and Barbara have always said – that's my wife – that it would be ever so good if some enterprising young lads, like yourselves, would get this place up and running again.'

The long hall. A dusty reception desk with papers, opposite the bar archway. This opened into the velvety, syrupy catacomb of the guest bar.

'This place was always such a grand success – always full. It was ever so sad when the Evanses had to give it up. She was ill, you know. Cancer.' David lowered his voice: 'They never did come back.'

'I'm sorry to hear that,' Frankie said. 'We hope we can do them proud.'

Samhain could choose a room first. He'd found the place, so he could decide which part of it was his. That was the only rule they had. 'Nice to meet you, David,' he said.

He had aspirations for the top of the house. A place right up in the trees, closer to the moon and sun, with light flickering through the greenery. Almost like being outdoors. 'Sorry to leave you,' he said, 'but we've got a lot to do, and I'd better get started.'

Hand on the bannister. His skin met a fine coating of dust, which stuck to his palm like fur from a moulting cat.

He looked into the gloomy, twisting staircase, and started up the stairs.

2.

Things had been left tidy. Bed corners squared and grimy with dust. Four UHT milk cartons, spiderwebbed and politely perched on saucer sides on a tea tray. A dead house spider, legs curled inwards in death, crumbling in the cup.

Samhain might have been in a tree house. Branches stretching in dancers' arms over the Velux, the sky a searing blue behind a fluttering confetti of new leaves. He opened the window to let out the scent of decay, and heard a lawnmower.

The scent of trapped life had been stronger with each step he'd taken. He'd pushed open this last door half-expecting to find a museum. Oak furniture, an old Grandfather clock. But it was more like a Premier Inn. White walled, all one piece. Everything covered in a dust so fine it formed a coverlet like dryer lint.

He glanced around, and ditched his rucksack on the bed. His shoulders felt strangely light without it: he had been carrying it a long time. Tools, his hoody, a t-shirt. Things he couldn't manage without, when things were so easily lost. He looked in the mirror, and realised that somehow he had ended up with a cobweb in his buzzcut.

'Sam?' Roxy's voice had the tone of a rusted gate blowing loose in a gale. She appeared in the doorway, in her work clothes, her tattoo a vibrant splash of green and blue. 'So this is it, huh?'

'Great, isn't it?' he said. 'Our new home. At least, for now.'

Something in her expression made him think of a laboratory beagle. The way they didn't know what to do when the clasp slipped to let them free – looking at both sides of their cages, uncertainly, the only life they've ever known. 'It's great,' she said. 'It's so big.'

'We should keep it for just the three of us. You, me, and Frankie.'

She nodded, and stepped closer. He could smell last night on her. The taste of whisky in her sweat; her top thin enough that he could see her nipples.

'So, this is your room – is it?' Her smile was wary.

Sudden silence from the lawnmower. Quiet, and the noise of cooing pigeons overhead.

'Yeah. Well, there are plenty to choose from. It's not like any of us need to share anymore.'

He saw her harden, and turn away. 'No. We don't need to share. I just thought you might want to.'

In the next step, she moved to an unexpected distance. Out of reach and curving backwards, too far for him to touch. 'Roxy,' he said. 'Come on, don't be like that.'

'I'm going to choose my room.' She receded into the darkness of the stairway, and started hopping down. 'Just so you know, I'm on a split – so don't expect me home early. Tommy and me might go out after closing.' Pausing at the curve of the stairs, with one foot hanging over the next step. 'Did you hear what I said?'

Samhain didn't answer right away: he didn't know how to. Anything he said was going to be the wrong thing, anyhow. That was always the way with Roxy.

'Forget it,' she said.

It was as she hopped around the bottom corner, that he suddenly remembered. They were without electricity and gas. Somebody had to sort that out.

'Hey, Roxy?' he called.

'What?'

She paused where she was, already on the second landing, and didn't look happy about being stopped.

Reconnection in a squat was easy. Frankie had taught him how. First step was to find a call centre worker lazy or gullible enough to send a letter to him at this address, which he could use as proof that he lived here. Only, Samhain couldn't make phone calls. He'd lost his Nokia in a pub a week or so ago, or maybe in the street on the way home, and had no idea where to start looking for it.

'Can I borrow your phone?'

3.

The woman behind the library desk had a face like the gallows. Moping her way around, rattling the pencils as though this place was a funeral home, and these books the skeletons of her dead children. 'Yes?' she snapped.

'Can I book a computer session, please?'

She sighed, and beckoned. 'Card.' Clawed hands, the hands of a darning woman.

The computer room was off to one side, and full of clicking and typing. Screens open to Yahoo! Mail, or the kelly green of the Total Jobs website.

'Start at ten past,' she said, sliding him a pencil-written code. 'This will only work today, so there's no point keeping this slip and trying to log in with it again tomorrow.'

'I know,' he said. He was in here all the time. Daily, when he'd been living in the slum. He knew the rules.

'If you're trying to access certain websites and getting an

error message, chances are it's blocked by our central I.T. system. We can't do anything about that here.'

'I know,' he said.

She gave him a sharp, shrewd look. 'Current session finishes in ten minutes. You'll be able to get on after that.'

The branch library had been a better place than home, until he'd moved into the Boundary Hotel. Its hush: people spoke in whispers, and nobody ever asked you to move. Cushioned seats around the reading table. New newspapers every day. It was a place of calm, with a familiar smell of carpet tile and public buildings.

It was in this library that Samhain had started trying to set up a European tour for the band. Frankie had contacts, and Samhain had contacts – they were both all over the Europunk message boards, and all over MySpace, trying to pull something together.

Nothing about it was simple. Trying to get the gigs to line up, to avoid having to drive all over Europe and back – the whole thing was a nightmare. But this, Frankie liked to say, was the best thing about being in a punk band: the 'ravishing, dashing uncertainty,' as he called it, 'makes you feel so alive!'

Samhain sighed, and looked at his MySpace. He spent half of his outgoing messages apologising for being British. *We don't agree with those imperialists Bush and Blair* and *We don't support the war in Iraq*, to avoid any doubt. They were giving any benefits from the sale of their CD to Médicin Sans Frontière, and he always mentioned that too. It was the only thing they could do to help in a situation where they felt totally powerless, where they'd been taken into a war against a protest of millions, a protest he and Frankie had been involved in. They wanted to show the sincerity of their intentions; they wanted to get more gigs. But until the gig collectives started replying, lived chaos. Samhain was waiting on replies from three different sets of people. He sat on the lumpy library chair, clicking refresh.

Message from: Marta
Subject: Re: re: re: re: re: re: re: re: re: re: re: re: re: re: re: Guitar

Marta had been looking after his guitar for weeks, ever since things had taken a strange turn in the slum. When new people had started living there, people he didn't know. He hadn't felt safe having it around. His guitar was the only thing he had that was worth anything, and he couldn't replace it if it went missing. Better for it to be with her, in the flat she shared with her boyfriend, than in the slum, where anybody might pick it up.

They'd been chatting back and forth, on the same message thread, ever since.

Samhain,

Been sitting here half the night wondering how to start this message. If it doesn't come across right, I'm sorry, Samhain, I really am.

A friend from CopWatch sent me an article today, and I thought you'd probably want to see it. Because of a story you once told me about your mum.

Mart. Beautiful, dependable Mart. She'd changed her profile picture so that it showed her sitting in the sun somewhere, bare shouldered and golden, auburn curls tumbling over one eye, at a picnic pub table. Looking at it made him realise that he didn't see nearly enough of her.

It was just like her to see an article and make the connection between that and one of her many friends. Just like her to remember a story he couldn't even recall having told her himself.

You probably already know that a lot of Deep Green Resistance groups were infiltrated by undercover cops in the 80s, right? The DGR movement was crawling with them in the early 80s. Loads of climate groups and deforestation activist groups all over northern Europe and South America were affected.

My friend Sky had a kid by one of them. She thought the guy was an activist too. Long story short, she found out he wasn't. He was a cop. Some of the other activists found his real passport. It gave his real name and listed a wife as next of kin. Turns out the guy already had two kids, aged 6 and 8. Sky's son must be about 22 now.

He couldn't give any real explanation for the passport when challenged, and then Pete vanished from camp, poof! Gone! Just like that.

Only a cop could have managed to pull off a disappearing act like that. God only knows how he managed to get away so quickly. They were in a camp right in the middle of nowhere, accessible only by foot or bike.

Samhain knew camps like that. He'd grown up in them. An infancy spent in sandy soil and tree houses in climate camps all over Europe. Memories of his boyhood weren't of solid walls, or of a nursery, but of canvas and placards, and chain-link fencing and tents; of dancing and wildfire; of dirt, of earth, of bicycles and yurts, or bearded men serving meals foraged from the woods; of minty tasting herbal tea, drunk out on a huge, expanding earth, that stretched endlessly out towards the horizon.

Cider always made him tell childhood stories. In drink, he'd tell anybody who'd listen.

Turns out she's not the only one it happened to. It happened in a lot of DGR groups in the early 80s. Sky said she couldn't even look at her little boy for weeks. Bear in mind he was only about a year old when she found out. No way would she have ever knowingly got into bed with a cop, never mind have a baby with one. She said it was like being raped by the state, twice.

Sky is working with a group of women to try and bring it all out into the open. If they can get enough together they might bring a legal case. She did say that some of the women this happened to were so traumatised by it that they left the movement altogether.

Didn't you tell me that your mum suddenly quit Deep Green Resistance when you were a little kid?

His last day at camp. Flores had come to get him, clean streaks running down her face. A strong hand on his wrist. 'I've had enough, Samhain.'

She'd turned to one of the other women – a face Samhain couldn't recall, because there were always different women there, they changed all the time – and said: 'I'm done with this shit. For good.'

Something she'd said often. Hundreds of times, since Samhain was tiny. 'I'm done with this shit' usually meant a couple of days in the yurt, playing with toys, together. He remembered the warmth of her face, round and brick-warm, glorious, in those moments when he had her all to himself. Not sharing her with all of the other women on camp, or with some job that needed doing: a padlock to be closed, or a bulldozer to lock onto. Turning brightly coloured pages. Pushing wooden trucks over the uneven ground. Smiles and cuddles. Her undivided attention. It never lasted long. A few days later she'd be opening up the tent flap and saying, 'Come on Sam, time for the weekly consensus meet.'

That last time, it had been different, the sobs harder and deeper, as though she were a quarry being remoulded by shifting tectonic plates.

She'd put him into the bike trailer, gathered their few

possessions into a knapsack, and cycled them both over to the nearest coach station. A long bus trip through Germany, Belgium, France, followed. He remembered her silence. Face ghostly, reflected in the bus window.

On the other side of the Channel, Flores had abandoned the bike. Left it leaning against a railing at the station, for anybody to take.

A week later they were living in a house, and he'd started school: a strange place, with brightly coloured stacking toys, where everything fitted onto shelves and into boxes. Things happened at certain times of day. A bell rang, and that meant you could go out onto the cold concrete for playtime. You had to sit at your table when the teacher said, choose toys when you were told to, eat lunch when the bell went – you couldn't just leave your desk any time you liked. The other children already knew the rules, and he struggled to pick them up. Samhain sat down when he was supposed to stand, went wandering when he was meant to sit still, talked when he should have been quiet, and shouted out when he thought things were unfair. The teacher sent him out into the corridor often. He spent more time sitting outside the head's office than he did in class. He never could get the hang of school.

Flores got a job in a garden centre, and was always quiet. There were long periods of silence. Hours when she drank beer, and gazed out of the window, and didn't say anything at all. Moments where she glared at Samhain with what seemed to be hate.

Maybe your mum quitting DGR had nothing to do with any of this. She might just have got burned out. Lots of people do. Not easy living in camps all the time, going on actions, taking part in the cooking and cleaning rota. It can't have been easy, especially not with a young kid. You'll know more than me. Could be she got worn out and wanted an easy life. Can't blame her for that.

If your mum was affected by infiltration, I thought you'd probably want to know. CopWatch are doing their best to make sure it all gets out. I thought you'd rather hear it from me than read it on a blog. Didn't think it would be right if you heard it from a stranger.

Might be that I'm wide of the mark here. In which case I'm sorry. Ignore this message if you want, and I won't tell anyone. Not even Jeff. Call me if you want. Mart x

He sighed, leaning back in the chair.
Another message came in – a postscript.

PS. How can you call me when I've got your phone! Found it on the floor in the social last week. Tell me where your new squat is. I'll drop it over. See you. Mart x

An old lady struggled by the library door, dripping under a rain visor, shopping cart wheel caught in one corner of the mat.

'Here, let me.' Samhain pulled it loose, pushing the door open, and she darted out.

Rain thundered, drumming the roofs of passing cars. His shoes drenched instantly, by weather which threw itself almost horizontally into his eyes.

The water struck him over and over, every drop an insult. He was carrying the library copy of *Maus* in a carrier bag, and that was getting rained on too. Soaking cotton clung to his shoulders before he'd even reached the corner.

All thoughts of restarting the electricity forgotten, Samhain started the long wet walk back to the squat.

4.

He dreamed. The lightless, wood-panelled hallway of the 97 Ash Grove squat. Reaching for the light switch, and nothing. Darkness whichever way. Everything was empty, the way it had been the week they'd moved in. Empty apart from Frankie's coat, hanging over the lower bannister.

Water dripped from the sleeves. Drip, drip, drip. Into a puddle on the hall floor.

Samhain's steps creaked up the stairs. Looking not for Frankie but for his mother Flores, hoping she'd be somewhere here.

The upstairs became the second floor of the Boundary Hotel. A narrow carpeted hallway led down to a recessed window. There was a note on one of the bedroom doors, like the one he'd had on his room in Ash Grove: *This is not a communal room. Knock first. People live here.* He had something he wanted to ask.

Then without knowing how, he was in the old Ash Grove living room. Wooden floor, the three mismatching chairs. Seats they'd found in bin yards, or out on pavements in the student area. Those, and the coffee table, were things they'd scavenged anywhere. *Your trash is our treasure.* And in that treasure, the pervasive smell of damp.

Discarded things from which they made a life. Samhain had no money, and lived like a prince. He didn't have to work. Other people wasted hours of their lives in jobs they hated, or got into massive debt buying things they didn't need. Not Samhain. He was free. Living behind found fabric, in a subterranean womb of deep, mossy green. This was the place where Samhain really belonged.

The fabric clung to the window, in the grip of thick condensation. He could hear the outside's rain dribbling down the panes, through the sills and down onto the floor, drip, drip, drip. She was in here, somewhere, Flores. Must be.

He called for her, and woke. In that sleep-wisping moment, remembered – Flores was on a retreat in a rural part of Wales, somewhere without a phone line or internet connection.

There was a knock.

Samhain levered himself into a sitting position. Freezing cold. He had fallen asleep the way he'd come in, jellyfish-wet.

'Jesus dickhead, what you been doing?' Frankie came in. 'Having a shower with your clothes on?'

Sitting, confused. Wet shirt clinging to the coverlet like velcro. He tried to make sense of it: a white door, the laminated sheet with a fire evacuation procedure stuck glossily on its inside. That was right – the hotel. 'No. I went to the library.'

'You don't look right. Maybe you should get out of those wet clothes.' Frankie pointed at the knapsack. 'I need to get a few things done around here. Alright if I use your tools?'

'Look at this place.' Frankie was already behind the bar, manhandling the ancient spirits. 'Old Navy Rum – Captain

Morgan – Taboo... Galliano! Wonder how old this is?' He pulled out a bottle with a swan-shaped neck.

'I wouldn't be drinking that.'

'No.' Frankie put it down, giving it a reluctant glance. 'Well, maybe not until you've had a couple of others first, anyway.' He pushed the cap back off his head, and scratched his scalp. 'Look at us. Living the dream, eh?'

Plush banquettes, round tables. The windows looked out into an overgrown garden. Through mottled glass Samhain saw greenery. Coloured glass streamed cathedral-bright onto polished tops and patterned carpet: it was like drinking in paradise. They were literally living in a pub. This, right here, was the squat jackpot.

'You can thank me later.'

Frankie was getting into something beneath the bar shelves. Rustling, rifling, looking for something – anything. This was always one of the first things Frankie did when they got into a place.

'For finding it? I will. You know, our mate next door reckons the woman who ran this place died. He wasn't sure, though. Says there was a "For Sale" sign for a bit, then it blew down in a storm, and nobody came to fix it. Then after that – we came.' Frankie stopped rifling, and emerged wearing a grin. There was a pair of sherry glasses resting between his fingers. 'So the story, right, is that we bought it. We're trying to refurbish the place and open it as a legitimate business. He doesn't need to know we're a pair of dirty punk squatters.' He clinked the glasses together. 'Look at these fucked up little things. What's the point in having a drink that small?'

'You moron, there's a squat notice on the front door. He's bound to have seen it.'

'Oh, that.' Frankie shrugged. 'Well, he didn't say anything about it. Anyway, we can always say there were squatters here, before us. Problem solved.'

'Not bad. Hey, I got this weird message from Mart earlier.'

'Sexy Mart? She still got your guitar?' Frankie worked at one of the pumps. Settled a hand around it, and pulled. A film of dust sputtered out. 'You should ask her to teach you a thing or two.'

'I'll teach *her* a thing or two.'

'I bet you would. She'd never let you, though.' More dust; Frankie coughed. 'Christ, I thought there might be beer in this thing. You phone up about the electric?'

'Not yet.' Samhain pulled Roxy's phone out of his pocket, and started pressing the buttons. 'Listen to this. Mart said, she's got a friend who had a kid by a cop.'

'Fuck that.' Years of laughter settled into the crinkles around Frankie's eyes. That smile took Samhain directly into the heart of the very best of times. A disastrous tour around Austria and Hungary in the back of a van whose engine ran mostly on old tights, and the crossed fingers of everybody in it. Sleeping in the back of the van, doors open, and waking to the silence of the mountains, seeing hundreds of empty miles of distance in either direction. The sun, the air, seeing civilisation down there in the valley, and being too high up and too hungover to call down to it. And laughing. Always, ever, no matter how much it hurt, always laughing. 'Never be able to relax, would you? Little fucker probably came out with a badge and number already attached. No offence to its mother, like. But still.'

'She didn't know he was a pig. She thought he was an activist, like her. Turns out he was an undercover cop.'

'Christ. Like the McDonald's two?'

'One of them was a cop?'

'No, idiot! So they were fighting this libel action, right? That McDonald's had brought against them for handing out these leaflets telling people not to eat the burgers, right? Their support group were helping with the case – legal support, moral support, bringing them food and baby clothes and what have you. Anyway, turns out – one of their support group "friends" was an undercover cop, and one of the other support group "friends" was a snitch for McDonald's.'

'No way!'

'Seriously, there were more undercover cops in their group than there were genuine activists. Ugh.' Frankie drank old whisky from a dusty tumbler. 'Thought everybody knew that. Anyway – never know how many of those traits are genetic, do you? Take you, for example – wearing patchwork skirts and gurning at festivals. Part hippy. Just like your Mum.'

There was a sound like the old tour van trying to start. Mid-pitched squeal and whirr, something turning, catching on a stuck hose. 'What is that?' Frankie looked down, puzzled, beneath his feet. 'I start something by trying to work that pump?' He stamped on the floor as though trying to put out a small fire.

'If you've fucked this squat already...'

'I haven't, I swear, I haven't. Probably just old pipes. Nothing to worry about.' Frankie stopped for a moment. 'No harm to the mother, like, but I couldn't live with a kid who was half-cop. Always be watching your back, wouldn't you? In case it snitched. "Hello, is that Crimestoppers? My Daddy's come home from a war protest talking about how he'd like to assassinate Bush." You'd probably end up in Guantanamo Bay.'

The whisky was thick, slurry coloured. 'Anyway, reckon I'd have to give a kid like that up for adoption. Now do me a favour, clart, would you? Go up and get changed. You look like you're about to drop nearly to death.'

5.

He wrote:

I know it wasn't your fault and I don't blame you but you should have told me. Some time when I was little. About him being in the police. Boys should know about their Dads, even if they don't know them.

I've got all sorts of questions now and you're not here to answer them. That time when–

The banging in the basement had stopped, and now there was somebody knocking at the front door. A heavy, blooming thunder rumbled right the way through the house.

'Hello?'

Looking out of the top window, Samhain couldn't see much – just the top of a bald head, shining, with filaments of silver either side. The neighbour. Night was falling now, and who

23

knows what the guy wanted.

He decided to leave it to Frankie to sort out.

—I asked Panzo whether he was my Dad. Because he was always around, taking me out somewhere. Panzo was the one who got me clothes. It was Panzo who got me my library card. He was sometimes around more than you were. But when I asked, you said, 'No, he's not your Dad, and he never will be.'

The thing is he used to get me ready for school sometimes, when you were ill. I kept hoping you'd change your mind, about him being my Dad. There was a boy in my class who got a new Dad and afterwards he was always saying Stephen this, and Stephen that, because his new Dad got him a Mutant Turtles jumper and new trainers, and always remembered his birthday in the way his first Dad hadn't. It was like he grew six inches when his Mum married Stephen.

Anyway I didn't dare keep bringing it up because of that time—

He stopped, scribbled the line out.

Right at the bottom edge of the page, no paper left to write on, not that the letter had gone in the direction he meant it to.

Samhain got up, and went into the hallway. There was still no power: he felt his way onto the stairs by keeping one finger against the wall.

'Oh, yes.' David's voice was floating up the stairs. 'You'll not be short on customers – the Evanses never were. What are you planning on doing in here? Will you keep it all the same, or put in new carpets? My son-in-law was telling me the other day, that a lot of the bars don't have carpet now – just bare boards – all varnished up and polished… that's the fashion now, he says, though I suppose you'll have your own ideas.'

'We don't know yet,' Frankie was saying. 'We'll have to see what condition the floor is underneath, won't we, Sam?' He turned, winking.

David peered down the hallway, his hands clasped. 'Every time I've looked at this place, I've thought, what a shame it is for a beautiful old building like that to lie empty. It's a crime, really it is.' He glanced back at the doorway, where the squat notice flapped in the breeze. 'When a group of young lads like yourselves could move in and make a living in it.' This last part sounded like a question.

Frankie slapped a hand against his head. 'Samhain, why don't you show David around?'

'Oh!' The neighbour took a step in. 'I don't mean to intrude. I can see you're busy.' But his face had lit up, and he was already half into the hallway.

Samhain's torch was upstairs, in the front pocket of his rucksack. Going back up to get it seemed more trouble than it was worth; instead, he pulled Roxy's phone out of his pocket, and used the screen as a dim blue torch.

The glow of light showed glasses, mirrors. A stamp-sized electronic square moving across dusty bottles of whisky and gin. 'This is the bar,' he said.

'Bigger than it looks, isn't it?' A seasickening blue lay on the crest of David's cheeks. 'I mean, from the outside. You'd never guess there was all this in here.'

'I'll show you upstairs. Mind your step.'

Out of the bar, and up to the tomb of the hallway.

Frankie was around the back of the stairs, doing something with the fuse box.

'Just keep a tight hold on the bannister, and you'll be alright.' Samhain didn't want the old fellow falling down the stairs.

'So,' David said. 'You live here, do you?' His breathing had a weight to it; he sounded like a torn accordion. 'I saw your sign.'

'Hang on, David.' They were nearly at the first landing. Samhain grabbed a chair from the nearest doorway, and quickly checked that it had four legs. 'Sit there a minute – get your breath back.'

'Oh, dear. Dear me. Dear, dear me.' Hand right over his tank-topped heart. 'Not so young as I used to be. Soon pass.'

He leaned against the back wall, looking down the length of the hallway. In the end wall, a window showed constellations of stars.

'We've no stairs at all in the bungalow. I'm a bit out of practice.' His breath seemed to still. 'So – this is a nice place. A very nice place, indeed. Will there be more of you coming?'

'No.' Samhain knew what this man feared. A constant, smelly rat-pack of drunk punks, spilling out into the yard and maybe even into David's garden. The incessant noise of banjos and shouting and beeping, bassy techno. Everything on into the early hours. He half-feared it himself. 'It's just the three of us – me, Frankie, and Roxy.'

David nodded contentedly, closing his eyes. 'Good. Well, it'll be good to have you here. Sometimes I think this crescent's too quiet.'

The Ambland Road squat, a place with bedrooms the size of whole apartments, and ceilings the height of Glasgow tenement flats, had been a home for anybody who wanted it. Dozens of people had lived there, the place full of their tat and squalor, and broken bits of drum kit. Its house band had been every band that came through the North. Groups would play at the social club, then come back to Ambland Road to sleep, but first they'd play in its living room again, usually at one or two in the morning.

Samhain had never got too much sleep whilst living there.

Frankie had liked to say they were living the Anarchist dream, in the Ambland Road squat. No landlord, no need to work if they didn't want to. Everything decided by collective. If they wanted to put on an art exhibition or a gig or anything else in the living room, they could. It was free living, in every sense of the word. Eating misshapen bagels hauled out of the industrial bins behind the bread factory, punk stew made from vegetables thrown away by the restaurant suppliers on the outer ring road. No money ever changed hands, and nobody had to pay rent. You could do what you wanted, providing it didn't bother anybody else.

He used to compare it to 'Ungdomhuset in C-Town,' a legendary squat in Copenhagen where he had played with his old band, once, and which he kept on bringing up in conversation, years after the fact. 'We're Europeans now, Sam,' he used to say. 'Every punk and crust band in Europe can make this place a stop on their tour.'

And true enough, Samhain had heard every language. Arguments in Finnish and Magyar, drinking songs in Swedish, German, Flemish, French. They used to have these parties – he'd known they'd had one from waking with a leaden head and dry mouth, although he never could remember even half of them – they went on for days, sometimes. He remembered lying awake on a mattress, where he could feel the floor underneath him, listening to a crowd of people in the living room downstairs. Mouth still burning from absinthe, feeling their voices tingle in his bones and in his spine. Talking as the light came up and through the curtains. Mumbling, laughing, sudden bursts of anger; somebody was drumming against the wall. An uneven paradiddle that never settled to a steady rhythm.

There had always been something happening, something to do, somebody to talk to. And so many girls. New ones, all the time. Ones with interesting names and interesting tattoos under their clothes. They'd appear once, crawling into his sleeping bag for warmth or conversation and other things, and then, in the morning, be gone.

It had been a shame when that squat had got overcrowded. Some parts of it he still missed.

'Well.' David was getting up. 'I should really go home. Barbara will be wondering where I've got to.'

'Let me show you one of the rooms before you go.'

Samhain opened a door at random. The nearest. The bed was made with tucked corners and tight sheets. A haze of moonlight lit the centre of the bed, hopefully.

'Very nice,' David said.

In another slice of moonlight, landing on the sill, winged insects lay, their limbs folded as though in sleep.

When Samhain closed the door again, the hall seemed even more dark. They might have been picking their way through a ghost train after hours. 'Let me run up and get my torch. Help you down the stairs.'

'No need. Absolutely no need, Sam.' David had a serious handshake. He squeezed Sam's hand as though trying to force water from a lump of clay. 'Nice to know you. I'll see you again soon.'

6.

'Here's your code for logging in.' All in grey today, the librarian. Everything on her drooping forward – skin, hair, clothes. Her dress hung like emptied carrier bags.

In the seat beside him sat a woman in a worn blazer, shiny black, with the life ironed completely out of it. She looked tired in the face, as though she'd been a real person once, and then something had happened to wash the good fortune away.

He clicked over onto the Red and Black news blog. Every other day now, he'd been coming here, to look for the news story. His big fear was that it would appear one day, and that somebody would connect the dots, the same way Marta had.

Click here for news on the radical Guatemalan Coffee Co-operative - now taking orders for international delivery!

He breathed out. The site hadn't been updated for a month.

Red and Black, run by volunteers, sometimes went for months without being updated at all. It covered whatever radical news stories its opaque, backroom operation were interested in. Samhain had learned much from its paper newsletter, which had once slid out from between a fanzine's pages and into his hands at a gig.

The first one he'd ever read had been about Tesco supermarket. That farmers were being forced to sell their fruit and vegetables to the supermarket giant for less than they cost to produce; and that Tesco zipped produce from all over the world into UK distribution centres the size of a hundred football pitches. No food was stored anywhere for any length of time. It went from the trucks to the distribution centre, and in under a day from there to the supermarket shelves. There wasn't two days' worth of food anywhere in the whole supply chain. If the lorries stopped, the whole country would be hungry and rioting in under a week.

Red and Black had written about Tesco a lot, in those days. When he had first started reading the blog, there had been a story about them pretty much every single day. Then slowly, slowly, it had started to stop. Samhain was still interested, but it seemed that the volunteer who'd been writing these stories wasn't. Either that, or he'd gone off on tour with his band, and forgotten about Red & Black entirely.

The coffee farmer story was accompanied by a grainy, pixelated picture of serious faced men and women wrapped in black flags, forming a straggly blockade around their crops.

We need your solidarity, Comrades! Revolution Coffee available to purchase now!

There was an address for sending money orders. But nothing about the activist women and their children, and nothing about

Deep Green Resistance.

Samhain breathed a sigh of relief, and opened another tab for MySpace.

Mart,

My mum's away at the moment and I can't reach her, so I haven't been able to ask her about all this. But I think you might be right. Now that I think about things, it all seems to add up.

I haven't told anybody about all of this, and I don't know if I will. Would you mind keeping it to yourself for now?

Sam x

PS Squat is in the old Boundary Hotel off Fox Lane. Either me or Frankie will always be in. Come round any time.

PPS. PLEASE don't tell anybody where the squat is. We don't want it turning into a party house.

On his email, there were a couple of messages about the tour.

Hi, I am sorry. The person in our collective who used to set up gigs has gone away on activist activity, we don't know how long, or when she will be back. The rest of us are no good at organising gigs and it is best that we don't try and fuck it up. You might have some luck with Lukas who lives in Hamsaft (50K away) and puts on bands sometimes. His email address is...

The second message read:

Samhain, yes we can put you on. We will put on a punk / crust alldayer around the dates 18th August. With bands you, Fuck Destroyer, Big Boys Small Room, Simone DeBoudoir, and others as well. This will be our sixth year of putting this festival on now. It is always popular and we can pay you plenty of Euros for the trip. You can stay here also, there is lots of room in the squat.

Just down the road (about 100Km from here) there is a new squat and social centre too. Their email contact is thrashthrashthrashthrash@yahoo.com. Contact there is Janka, she listened your demo at weekend and likes, please get in touch with her.

He started typing answers, and felt a tap on his shoulder. 'I'm afraid you'll have to log out in one minute.' The droning, church nave voice of the librarian. 'There are lots of people waiting.'

There was no time to write anything but, 'Thanks,' and 'I'll be in touch soon.'

Then the librarian's hand again, soft on his shoulder, a falling leaf, and Samhain shoved his notebook into his rucksack and pulled his rucksack onto his shoulder, and walked out of the library to go home.

'Frankie?'

Samhain pushed open the heavy door.

The hotel was quiet, but he could hear his friend scratching away somewhere. The slow scrape of sandpaper, its rhythmic fizz.

'Frankie, you there?'

There was no need for light, but he tried anyway. Flicking the hallway light switch: nothing. Samhain stood looking at the fixture as though he might solve the problem by staring hard enough at the bulbs. On, off. On, off.

Roxy wasn't home. He knew that coming past the first bannister, and seeing that her bag wasn't there. When she was in, she left it in the hallway. Always left things lying around, even though he had told her a thousand times not to. Roxy didn't believe that even in their community, there were thieves. To Roxy, all things were communal. If something went 'missing', she would say, it had most likely been taken by somebody in greater need of it than she was. Roxy had always been too trusting. It had been one of the things he'd liked most about her, at first.

He swung around the next rail, and it came off in his hand. Screws and plaster exploded free from the lower end, and momentum alone carried Samhain up to the next landing, where he landed against the wall, face to the artex, wondering what the hell had happened.

Bottom end of the rail stuck across the hallway like a train station barrier. It leaned diagonally across the stairs, pointing. You, it seemed to say, to whoever might come and try their luck next. You. He stood a moment, looking at it. Then he thought he heard somebody in the front yard, and took the final set of steps at a gallop.

His door was open slightly, a way he hadn't left it. That was no surprise, from living with Frankie. He'd probably been to borrow tools, knowing Samhain wouldn't mind.

But there was something else, when he went forward into it – a heat like a baker's back door. This was a problem Samhain hadn't known about when he'd taken this top room – the broiling. He wilted, and leaned against something. Went into a cloud which gathered, sticky and stuffy, touching all four corners of the room.

Samhain's face dripped. He wiped it, and started ditching his bag on the bed.

Then stopped, still holding on by the strap, bag dangling at arm's length.

There was a cat. In the spot where his bag normally lay: a black, white and tortoiseshell thing, laying on a nest of band t-shirts, licking its paw as though it had always lived there. Belly distended and stretched with soft white fur, a womb that was fat and hard, and obviously full with young.

It paused in grooming to look at him with cockleshell blue eyes. As though saying: What are you doing in my room?

'Frankie!' he shouted. 'Frankie!'

'I don't know how it got in.'

Frankie was at work on the back door. Sanding, he explained, to make it close better. He answered Samhain's questions with the sweat of the day on him and wood dust on his brow. 'Nothing you can do about it, mate. Just settle where they settle, don't they, when they're due to drop.' Frankie put the sandpaper in his back trouser pocket. He was wearing a wicked grin, as though he knew something Samhain didn't. 'Better get some cat chow in, eh? You won't be able to move her now.'

'You left the bloody door open.'

'How else do you expect me to fix it?' Frankie said. 'Been in and out of the back all day here, trying to get a few things done. Somebody's got to fix things up. Cats, right, they can sneak in quick, if you're not looking. And I didn't know I was looking out for a cat – see?'

Another pocket full of fuses. Frankie had them out, squinting at them in the light coming in from the back door. 'They say they've switched this power on. But it's still not bloody working. Why don't you phone them, and see what's going on – eh? Pull your weight, like the rest of us.'

'She looks like she might have them any minute, Frankie. I don't know what I'm supposed to do. What if they all die?'

'Don't have kittens about it! Look at you, bringing life into the world, when you can't even hardly look after yourself. Won't remember the time I had to ask Russ where you live so I could get you home, will you? Carried you all the way back there myself. Thought to myself, now *there's* a guy who knows how to party.'

'That's not even true.'

'Isn't it? Know how you got home after watching Against Me, do you? Remember catching the bus, walking home, all the rest of it?'

'No, but–'

'Course you don't. That's because I carried you. Like Jesus, in the story.'

'Dickhead.'

'Ah! There's the fucker.' Pinching a nine-amp fuse between thumb and finger. He looked at it the same way a jeweller might eye a diamond. 'That was only the second or third time we met. Course, you wouldn't remember.'

A knock.

'That'll be Mart with my phone,' Samhain said. 'Reckon she'll know anything about looking after cats?'

Frankie mumbled an answer. Sounded like: 'You'd better hope she does.'

7.

Marta steered her bike into the hallway, glinting. 'Wow,' she said. 'Is this it – where you live? Mind if I bring this in? I don't really want to leave it outside.'

Her gaze made its way around full ceiling height. Cobwebs in the cornicing; slow dust, lit by lazy beams of light through the top window. 'Who's here – just the three of you?'

Samhain tried to think of a good explanation for leaving the rest of the rooms empty. 'We've only just got into it,' he managed. 'We're thinking of installing a bike rack outside.'

'Sorry.' She started back down towards the bike. 'I didn't realise.'

'Ignore him, Mart.' Frankie was up on a chair by the stairs, with a torch between his teeth and a screwdriver in the fuse box. 'That boy was dragged up. He doesn't know how to treat a guest. You leave your bike where it is.'

'So what happened to the owners?'

She walked down the hallway towards them, holding Samhain's gaze with those large, espresso eyes. Up close she smelled faintly medical. Antiseptic, the scent of doctors and nurses.

A click, and suddenly light.

'He's done it!' Frankie shouted. 'By God, he's only gone and bloody done it!' He jumped down, clapping his hands. 'Now, for the important bit. Anybody fancy a pint?'

'In a minute.' Samhain turned to Mart. 'Want to go upstairs?'

*

Things looked different with the lights on. Anaemic light, pale yellow, but light all the same. By the shy buzz of lights in their fittings, he saw dust on the door handles, on the bannister, an amount of shored-up silt that he hadn't noticed before. There was a layer of it on the picture frames in the hallway.

Mart had this way of stepping quietly, like a museum visitor. A foreigner with backpack worn chest-forward and an eye for wonder. 'This is some squat,' she said. 'I've never seen anything like it.'

'Come up.' The cat was still in the centre of the bed, curled up with her eyes tight closed, paying neither of them any attention. 'Now what am I supposed to do about this?'

'Hello, beautiful.' Mart took a spot gingerly on the bed, and scratched the cat in a spot behind one ear. 'I didn't know you had a cat.'

'I didn't, until about four o'clock today. She just came in and made herself comfortable.'

'Lucky you.'

'What are you meant to do when they give birth?'

'You'll probably need towels – for all the goo and blood, when she has them. And to keep them warm. You'll have towels

37

somewhere – won't you – this was a B&B, right?'

In eight days he hadn't thought to look. 'Towels. Yes. I'll find some. Then what?'

She put a hand softly on the cat's belly, and it rubbed its cheek against her wrist. 'Ah, you've no collar on, poor thing.'

'What if I make her a really soft bed on the floor – in a box? She might sleep in it.'

'You can't move her, Samhain. Look how much at home she is. She's comfortable. You're the one who might have to sleep on the floor.' She glanced around the room. 'Probably should get her a litter tray and whatnot. Some food. Poor thing's probably starving.'

'The whole point of moving into a squat with lots of bedrooms was so that I wouldn't have to sleep on the floor. And now–'

'Come on, it's only for a couple of nights.' Scratching the purring cat on the back of its head. 'Maybe not even that. She looks fit to burst.'

He started backing out of the door. 'I'll see if I can't find those towels,' he said.

The linen cupboard was on the first floor.

A mouse family were living inside one of the sets of sheets: they'd chewed a hole the size of a two pence piece. When he stepped inside, he could hear them rustling around inside it – the sound of living things making themselves at home.

Samhain pulled a towel from the shelf. It came unfolded, scattering moths' wings to the floor, and the next one was the same. He took six altogether, all billowing with dust.

Samhain came back to Mart cross-legged on the duvet, a little way from the cat and his phone, dead, laying on the sheet in front of her.

'My phone.' Scrabbling through the gritty darkness inside his rucksack. It had a depth he'd forgotten existed. 'Got my charger in here somewhere.' Fanzines obscuring things with bent bat-wing covers; these had been new once, and not long ago, either.

'Sam.' A reluctance in her voice.

Guest tumbler on the table. Wet edges, leaving a ring on the letter he'd been writing. Flores. Suddenly, inexplicably, he was thinking of her, and of a summer spent at home, aged seven. Panzo had said they could go to a seaside and stay in a youth hostel to keep it cheap. But Flores had said no, and Samhain had felt the things he'd been promised slip away. Playing Outrun in the arcades. Flying a box kite on the cliff top. Chips salty enough to shrivel your cheeks. He had cried tears that had hurt him with their sourness, and hadn't understood why. 'You and me don't need a man in our lives,' she'd said.

It was one of those times when she'd sounded less certain. And, maybe sensing a crack, a crack he could get his finger inside and pull wide, Samhain had kept on about it. He had been old enough to think he could talk her around. By mentioning the things he knew she liked. A day to herself, as promised by Panzo. Evenings in the real ale pubs all the way along the main street. Where she and Panzo could go and have a few drinks, while Samhain stayed at the youth hostel, looking after himself, like he always did at home.

Samhain had kept on washing away at his campaign, and thought he was seeing her weaken. He followed at her heels up the stairs, up into her bedroom, talking about it. One last reason, he'd thought, one more reason to go, and then she'll cave. Getting away from the estate for a few days was his strongest sluice yet: he was just about to deploy it, expecting her to say, 'Well, alright then, we'll go,' when she'd turned, grabbed him by the shirt, and slapped him hard in the face. 'I don't want to hear about this again,' she'd hissed.

At last, his hand was on it. The curved, heavy black plastic, the three prongs.

'Sam,' she said again. 'I'm sorry about your mum.'

He plugged it in. Boxy screen and buttons glowed the colour of sickening larvae. 'What's there to be sorry about? Don't worry about it.' The numbers were mostly worn blank with use.

Texts from Roxy, days old.

Come and meet me from work?

Then:

Never mind. I'm at Matty's now. Probably better if you don't come.

Then:

Memory full. Messages waiting. Open text message folder to select messages to delete?

'Big thing to get your head around.' She was standing on the bed, shaking towels out of the window. 'Unless you already knew about it?'

'I didn't know.'

'No?' She turned, knelt on the bed, rolling the towels into tight cylinders. 'Here, girl.' The cat let itself be propped forward, while she wedged a towel behind its back. 'She's big, alright. How many do you think she's got in there?'

He touched the cat's tum softly, the way he'd seen Mart do it, and felt around. 'Three?' he said. 'No, four. Definitely four.'

'Look, my friend goes to these meetings sometimes. It's a sort of – support group. For the women affected.'

'Women?' Mama Cat had her claws out, sharp. Resting them on the back of his hand, as though experimenting with the idea of hurting him.

'Yeah, mostly.'

'I don't know, Mart.' He drew his hand away. Somewhere around the cat's shoulder, their hands touched. Her skin was papery. Thin, from being washed too many times. 'Who goes to it?'

'My friend. Her friends. I don't really know them. It's sort of – half support group, half information and political campaigning. They could tell you more about your father.'

'He's not my father.'

'Well. Ok. But you could go and meet them, at least. Aren't you even a little bit curious?'

News spread fast, that was one thing Samhain did know, in their tiny, interconnected world of gigs and political protest. Keeping a secret was almost impossible, and this one – about being fathered by a cop – was something he could hardly even admit to himself. He was afraid that if he thought it too loudly, even, somebody might figure it out. 'Where is it?'

'I don't know. I'll find out for you.'

'I'm not going if it's at the club.'

'Why not?'

He shrugged. 'Don't know.' Turned back to his Nokia, looking at a backlit folder of memories.

Sure, what time?

And:

Are you in now?

And:

You about? Get down to Sainsbury's big bin. They're throwing out some good salads.

Delete. Delete. Delete.

'What if it was at somebody's house – would you go then?'

'I don't know. Maybe. Thing is, I'm not as bothered, Mart. Didn't know my dad growing up, don't know him now. I don't need to know anything about him. He was obviously a dick, and that's all I need to know.'

'Sam... oh, hey! I can feel one of them moving. Quick, give me your hand.'

The full scrape of her skin, palm barked by disinfectant, and then something tiny under the fur, wriggling. Penny sized paws kneading against the belly. Mama Cat slanted in discomfort.

It was there, right under his hand. Life. Fighting to get out. 'Wow, Mart. That's amazing.'

'Didn't I tell you?' In a moment, in those dark eyes, a gleam like stars. 'Listen, Sam–'

The door opened with a bang, jolting the end of the bed.

They all three looked up: Him. Marta. The cat.

'Whoops.' Roxy was framed in the doorway, hand on hip. From the way she was standing, he could tell there was something he was meant to notice about her. 'Didn't mean to open it that hard.' There was a lot of wear in those clothes, as though she'd come home in the same ones she'd been wearing yesterday, and probably the few days before that, too. Hair sticking up all directions.

'Hello, Marta,' she said.

8.

'Here's a little thing for you,' Frankie said, handing him a glass. 'Drank half a bottle of this yesterday, and lived. Cheers.'

Brandy, old. With a snakeskin of dried pink lipstick on the rim. 'Frankie, that's gross.' Samhain was making stew on the one working gas ring, in a pot the size of a truck wheel. The other rings were all gummed and stopped up: when the heat rose, it brought with it a smell like warm corpses.

Frankie looked through the open door into the bar. A Roxy shaped zoetrope paced across the bar arch, staring angrily into her phone. She was wearing the look of a thousand fighting men on a hillside. 'Listen, mate. Tell you something.' He lowered his voice. 'They're not worth the trouble. Look how much bother you're in with this one.'

'I haven't even done anything.'

'I know.' Frankie laughed softly. 'Maybe not. But let me tell you. The only way to not get involved with a girl is not to get

43

involved with her. See? You can't go cuddling or–' He screwed up his face, waving his glass in the air. Made a pinchy-grabby motion with his free hand. '–anything with them, anything at all, and *definitely* not sex. It leads to all sorts of trouble. Guarantee you they take it the wrong way. So take my advice, lad. You want a hassle-free life, don't go sticking your knob in things.' He drained off his glass.

'But I like–'

'No!' Frankie's words snapped around the hallway like a pop-gun. 'I don't want to know what you like and what you don't like. Look, if you really must get into it with a girl, at least always use a condom. You'll be in even more trouble otherwise. Sometimes they say they're on the pill when they're not, or even...' Frankie scratched his crotch, and pulled a face. 'You see? Look, a boy like you, you need a firm hand. You've got all these girls throwing themselves at you, God knows why, I suppose they find you attractive for whatever reason, and it's hard to say no, right? But no good can ever come of it. Listen to this, right. When I was your age – and I've never told you this before, so listen carefully – I had these two girls on the go, this smart little blonde one with a mind like a sewer, though you'd never think it to look at her, looked like butter wouldn't melt she did, and then this gorgeous one from Yemen, Sophia she was called, beautiful dark-eyed thing with lips like a bouncy castle, you know what I mean?

'Anyway, the one of them lived in Derby and the other one here in Bradford. I thought to myself, I'm onto a good thing here. Got these two girls on the go and neither one of them knows about the other, and they'll never find out, neither. Well. They soon did though, didn't they?'

'How?'

'Well, they only both went and turned up to see me play in Sheffield, didn't they, when I was playing with Ivor Cutler

Heights? Sophia turns up and she says, Frankie, I wanted to surprise you, aren't you pleased to see me? Well, it was a surprise all right. I went off to get the guitar cabs out of the van and while I was out there, Emma turned up as well.

'So there they both were, while I was out there bringing in the drum stands and the guitar heads and all the rest of it. You can't stop women from talking, that's one of the other bits. They like a good yap. You can't stop them from talking, and you can't stop the angry ones from putting their keys through every single one of your drum skins. When they tell you having a girlfriend is expensive, that's what they're talking about. Because having one girlfriend costs one amount, and having two costs you more than twice that, know what I mean?' He lifted his glass, and went towards the bar in search of another. 'Anyway, so the last bit of it is, everybody was supposed to be using my drum kit. Three other bands, including this Crust D-Beat band from Sweden. Well, they couldn't use it after that. Whole gig cancelled, and everybody mad with Frankie, not just the girls. An entire gig, all ruined by me and my stupid cock. Needless to say, they kicked me out of the band. Ended up going home on the National Express by myself.'

'Bloody hell, Frankie.'

'Yeah, well. If you ever want to read about it, Sophia did a whole article about it in her fanzine. It was her best-selling issue ever.' Frankie lifted a bottle off the bar, and started pouring. 'So, all I'm saying is, if you've got to have two of them on the go at once, right, at least be careful how you go about it. Don't end up like old Frankie here – banned from every venue in Sheffield.'

Roxy stared out of the window, looking as though she were trying to cause David's car to explode with her eyes.

Samhain rattled amongst the bottles behind the bar. Most were syrupy-sour; the whisky and vodka were both nearly empty – he looked around them, and found a bottle of dark rum. This, and the stew, went down him like a damp firework. He'd thrown half a bottle of oregano in the pot, yet all he could taste was twigs.

Every time he made stew, he had a fantasy that it would turn out like the one he'd eaten in Genoa in 2001. The nineteen-year-old Samhain, all in black, arriving in Italy with a bust card in his back pocket, and the idea that anything was possible. He had arrived hoping for a protest like the one he'd read about from G7, the previous year – where protestors had trapped delegates from the World Bank inside their meeting rooms.

He joined groups who had set up in a school building. The air smelled of garlic and tinned tomatoes; dogs ran around trailing string leads, drooling happily on their bandana collars, making pals of all new arrivals. Sam heard snatches of languages he didn't even know existed. Hard-sounding vowels, a music of slippery consonants. The main hall sang and muttered with groups, planning in constant circles. Every classroom was full of people and their bags. Samhain had looked around at it all, and had known himself to be more at home here than anywhere.

A woman with a loose vest and no bra had a map of the centre of Genoa, a blurred thing that looked like a photocopy of a photocopy. Too small for them all to see it at once, so they passed it around the circle.

'You're new?' said a man, with a sympathetic smile behind his whiskers. 'Here. Wear this when we go out.' He gave Sam a scarf for covering his face, and a pair of cheap swimming goggles. 'You'll need them, if the police use gas. Which they probably will. You've got a passport?' Sam nodded. 'Leave it here,' the man said. 'They can't charge you if they don't know who you are.'

They protested the next day, and Samhain somehow got separated from his group. He walked out into a street of thousands: you couldn't even see the buildings. It took him a moment to take it in. Banners stretching street-side to street-side. From the stairs, all he could see were head tops, millions of them, bobbling in a hirsute ocean. No space, not anywhere, just arms and shoulders and faces and whistles, all crushed together by force of their sheer number. He looked at it all for a minute, then looked around for his new friend; to say, 'Did you know it would be like this?'

Samhain had never seen a protest like this, a sea of a city. He looked around for the bearded man, but the stairs were empty. His friend, along with the rest of his group, had already vanished into the crowd. Everybody was in green: he had no hope of finding them again.

He went down the stairs, and was thrust into a crush of warm and wiry bodies. All around him started the Samba band. Timbales thundering in front and to either side, cowbells hammering every off-beat. Somebody gave him a whistle and a cowbell; he put the whistle in his pocket, and hit the bell every offbeat.

'Just joined?' The woman beside him beat her drum with good humour, and spoke to him without missing a beat. 'Just follow us. To the city square – where we'll stop.' She paused, and joined the syncopated rat-at-at-at tum-tum fill. 'And bring the city to a standstill. At least, that's the plan.'

It was a little disappointing to miss the action he'd planned, but Samhain liked this nearly as much. The vibrancy and hilarity of it. The idea of stopping, not with weapons and banners, but with maracas and cabasas. He thought: nobody arrests a man carrying two musical instruments. 'Great,' he said.

Elbows. Ribs. Everything so close to him. A squashed pit, like being at a gig in the club. There was a pause, while the music stopped, and applause rose around. Then he heard the tap and snap of the drums starting, and almost without thinking, put the whistle in his mouth.

'Here,' the woman said, holding out a spliff. Her face was lined, aged, but he had a feeling she was probably no older than thirty. 'There must be millions of us here. They can't ignore us this time.'

She joined a bloom of song. Women's voices: 'This land, is our land. It belongs to you, it belongs to me.' People dancing in whatever spot they could find, matching the melody to the samba rhythm. He was caught up, and started to sing too, with tears in his eyes.

'This your first time?' she said. A hand on his arm, softer than expected. 'I know, boy. I know. What's your name?'

Hours moving at the pace of penned cows. Still singing but trapped, stuck on all sides by the weight of their own protest. The band weren't able to get to the crossroads when they were supposed to: they were still shuffling the streets by late afternoon, when the trouble started.

Crowd bucking in waves. Bodies thrown against one another like mussels in a pan. The singing had stopped, and in its place, screams. Samhain got up somehow, and saw a line of shining black helmets. The crowd was being crushed – pushed back into itself, trying to go back the way it had come.

A drum in his back. He could feel metal at his spine, the wing-nut pressing his vertebrae. He could have drawn it from that feeling.

'Where are we supposed to go?' she was screaming. 'Where are we supposed to go?'

'Get on my back,' he said.

He ducked down, and the woman climbed on his shoulders. She was much heavier than his travelling bag, and he couldn't see a thing. There was somebody standing right in front of him, with his back pressed right up against Samhain's chest. He had his nose in the man in front's hair, breathing in a smell like undipped sheep.

She was saying something to him, but he couldn't hear what it was, and then the crowd suddenly gave way, and his lungs filled with what felt like glass dust. He was coughing, eyes shut and streaming, clutching for something to lean on, not wanting to fall and knock her off. Couldn't see a thing and didn't know where he was; the air around him was full of the sound of hacking. People gasping for breath. He fell to his knees, and landed with his hands on something sharp. Just before she fell off his shoulders, she sprayed a stream of warm piss all down his back.

Somebody grabbed his shirt, using the back of it to drag him to his feet. Rough voices in Italian – a grip from which he couldn't struggle free. He spent what he thought was probably two days, and two nights, in a cell. Sometimes a cell and sometimes an interview room, which was slightly larger. In both rooms they bruised him. Once, in the interview room, an officer barrowed him off the chair from behind, and Samhain's face hit the desk on the way down. While his eyes were closed, two men beat him with steel bars.

In the quiet moments, a tall, good-looking young officer with neat hair and tanned, Scandinavian-looking skin, kept on saying: 'We know you were with Martine,' and 'Come on, you might as well tell us. Who else was in your group? What was your action plan when you came here?'

Back in the cell, Samhain ached whichever way he lay. Breathing hurt like a hundred grazed and open wounds inside. He knew it was a waiting game. Once they realised he knew nothing, they'd let him go.

Yet he was struck by the cop's persistence. The guy asked the same question a hundred different ways. By the end of it, Samhain started to think – maybe I do know a Martine.

They let him go on what he thought was the second day.

He stepped out of the police station into drizzle and half-light. It was early morning, and they were already sweeping the streets. A street bug made its way towards him, with kerb brushes the size of tractor tyres. Mist landed on his hood in a light rain, and he thought: aw hell, I've missed everything.

Also, he realised that he had no idea where he was. He did not know this city, nor any of its landmarks. Samhain looked both ways up and down the street, then went to the nearest crossroads, and looked both ways up and down there; then he picked a direction, and started walking.

Three hours' walking in a tightening circle, pausing often, brought him back to the old school. The smell of herbs still hung in the air, but the room was already mostly empty.

A woman appeared from a doorway. She saw him, and jumped slightly. 'Were you here before?'

'Yes,' Samhain said. 'I've come for my passport.'

'And you're British, so...'

She held out four with red covers.

'Did the police take you?' she said.

'Yes.' He searched around the floor, found his bag. Everything was still in it. His fanzines, and his screwdriver and socket set. 'They kept on asking me about somebody called Martine.'

She started laughing. 'Martine!' she said. 'Who the fuck is Martine?'

'I don't know.' The pain in his ribs was like the batons all over again; he didn't want to laugh, but found he couldn't stop. 'I don't know. And neither do the police, probably.'

'Well.' She gave him a banana, and two apples. 'That shows you what the fuck the police know. Still, it's too bad they took you in. You're the – well, I lose count – but you're not the first person I've spoken to today, who got arrested just for being there. This is a new tactic they seem to have. They take people in, and keep them in there until all the protests are over. Bastarding Carabinieri.'

That time had left Samhain with marks on his ribs that had scarred. He showed them to anybody who said protest should always be peaceful.

'Jesus Christ, lads.' Frankie had emptied his bowl. He was sitting with the duck-chested brandy bottle beside his glass. 'Anybody would think somebody had died. It's like a morgue in here.'

Roxy chewed silently, face all bundled up in a frown. She sighed, and threw her spoon down into her bowl.

'Tell you what we need,' Frankie said. 'Some music. If we could get these speakers working...'

He got up and wandered away.

Samhain threw a mouthful of rum down after the stew, and it tore a Catherine wheel down his chest. 'Roxy,' he said. 'It's nothing for you to be mad about.'

'So you say,' she said, stirring her drink, a clear thing. She was drinking from a pint glass, full of ice and mint leaves. It had two straws, though he'd never seen any in here. Roxy always had been a resourceful girl. 'But that's because you don't care about how I feel. You don't and you never have.'

'Roxy...'

'Shut up, Sam,' she said. 'Look, do whatever you want. Hold hands with Marta if you want to. Hell, hold hands with Frankie. See if I care. You do what you want, and I'll do what I want.'

'I never said you couldn't.'

'No, I know. That's always your get-out, isn't it? Everybody doing whatever they want, all the time, no matter who it hurts. Because that's punk rock, right?'

'I never said you were my girlfriend.'

'Fuck me.' She stood up suddenly, and threw her glass right across the bar. Heavy and spinning, it emptied half across Samhain's shoulder, and shattered against the far panelling. 'You and Frankie are as bad as each other. Can't believe I agreed to live here, with you two... dickheads. I could have moved in with Danny and Felix. They asked me to. I must have been mad to say no. Or stupid, or something...'

'You probably still could move in with them.'

'It's too late now!' Her voice cut him in half. She was red, livid, shrieking, a boiling baby. 'How the fuck do you think I'm going to move into a flat with them *when they've already signed the contract?* Christ, Samhain, I don't know how you think the world works sometimes. It's like you think everybody's sitting around, holding places open, operating on the same weird, lazy, not knowing the month basis as you.'

'I'm not lazy,' he said.

'"Come and live with me," you said. "I've found this great place," you said. "It's got loads of room and it'll be just you and me and Frankie, and it's massive," you said. Then we got here, and you couldn't get away from me fast enough.'

'Let's not fall out over this,' he said. 'This is still a great place to live – you don't have to leave.'

'Don't be a twat!' Now she faced him, devil-red. 'Don't you get it? I can't stand living here and I can't stand looking at you. Every day. Christ. People warned me about you. Girls – all of your exes. Pretty much everybody you'd ever slept with. Your friends. Stick. Paulie. Stevie. Marta, even. They said I should be careful and I said no, you don't know what you're talking about, Sam is a great guy, you don't know him like I do...'

'Roxy, please,' he said. 'I'm going through some stuff right now.'

'Stuff? What stuff?'

'Never mind. I can't say.'

'Huh.' She stopped pacing, and continued, talking almost to herself. 'I told people you were a great guy – that you were just confused, that's all. But they were right. Every single one of them was right. And I should have listened. Christ, I was naive. To not even listen to Charley. When she knows better than anyone exactly what you're like. No wonder...'

She stopped.

Swallowed carefully, whatever she had been about to say.

Frankie had been right, he realised. Girls could be vicious when hurt.

Samhain picked up the empty glass, and turned slowly towards the bar.

Speaking every word with great regard, Roxy said: 'No wonder she disappeared on you like she did.'

The dusty, grimy glasses. Samhain asked: 'Do you want another drink?'

9.

Fingers on Anaglypta. Samhain was in the dark, blinds closed, somewhere after-hours. Shoulders and spine on a hard wooden floor. Wooden legs around him. He was in the place he belonged – sleeping under a table.

Then he was up. A fortune cookie crumbled to dust in his mouth, and he was holding the slip of paper. *Some things are best left alone.* He turned it over: the other side read, *You and disappointment are lifelong friends.*

Snack grit on his fingers.

He woke sweating, and wondering where he was.

Still floor. Stiff boards. He looked up. Less than half a metre away was a bed. He could see the underside of the divan. It was whiter than anything he'd seen in any punk house. Sun blared in through the Velux and he blinked, grasping the edge of his sleeping bag. If he was away, then he must be on tour. But where, and which country?

The polyester made a soft crumpling sound beneath his fingers as he tried to remember where he might have left his guitar.

He heard a movement on the bed, wedged himself painfully into a sitting position, and saw the cat. A triangle of ear, soft ginger and chocolate, fuzzy with the light. She was grooming herself – and still pregnant.

Samhain made his way downstairs, with the feeling of a passenger trying to disembark from a sinking ship. There was a sour taste in his mouth, to go with a sour feeling. Rum and brandy and god knows what else, something with the taste of rotten peach. However the rest of the night had gone, he knew it hadn't ended well.

'There he is,' Frankie called. He was by the bar, pouring thick black coffee from the jug. The sound system was almost working – loud, enthusiastic folk-punk, all scratching violins and good-natured Midwestern shouting, blared from a single speaker. 'So, how is she – has she had 'em yet?' Frankie looked as though he'd been dragged out of the canal.

'Not yet.'

The music sounded scooped-out, half of it missing. No mandolin, and no double bass. Over by the window, the second speaker was silent – save for a whining, trapped-insect sound.

'What happened last night, Frankie? I had this really strange dream.' Samhain forced himself up onto the banquette, holding a screwdriver.

Outside, hundreds of white towels blazed. They waved on a drying rack and on a washing line, a thousand flags of surrender, and suddenly something came back to Samhain. Coming down from the airing cupboard with his arms full of towels, to set the washing machine running. He had found mouse corpses amongst the linen, whole families curved stiff-still with their paws curled, and their empty eye sockets still open; how, looking at them, the enormity of life and death had hit him, and he'd cried over their hard, clawed little bodies.

'You shouldn't have let me drink so much,' Samhain said. 'Christ.'

'Who am I to stop you?' Frankie said. 'You're a grown man.'

Something else. Samhain reached into his back pocket, and found a matchbook, with a picture of the hotel on the front, and a phone number along the friction strip. A cheery message on the back read, 'Thanks for being our guest at The Boundary Hotel!'

'Jesus,' he said, looking at it. 'I must have been pretty far gone last night.'

At some point, he remembered, he'd stopped bringing the towels down, and gone to look around the place for matchboxes. He had wanted to give the tiny mouse-tenants a proper burial. But these had been all he'd been able to find.

He had held one of the mouse bodies in his palm. A grey-streaked thing with white ears. He had been thinking, I must put these out of reach of the cat. This had happened while he had been standing in the doorway of the laundry cupboard. He had lined them all, slowly, slowly – every one along the shelf, neatly, in a row.

'Me too.' Frankie looked regretful, and sorry for himself. 'So, come on then, last night. How much you remember?' He stared into his cup, and took a loud slurp.

Another thing. Roxy shouting and red-faced, eyeliner sliding all down her face in a coal seam.

He forced the Phillips-head into the speaker bracket, and noticed a furniture-moving bruise on his upper arm. There were others, too, fist-sized. Now he remembered: Roxy had done that. When he had tried to calm her down.

'Impressive beer injuries, lad,' Frankie said. 'Things got pretty heated, didn't they? For a little while, there.' No sound but the noise of Frankie turning a teaspoon over and over, over and over. He looked like he had something to say, and no good way of saying it.

Samhain knew that look. He'd seen it before, when they'd had to ask Matty to leave the band. He loosened the bracket, and brought the speaker down to chest height. 'What is it, Frankie?'

Frankie opened his mouth, then closed it again. 'Erm,' he said.

'Come on, douche canoe.' Samhain stuck the screwdriver blade between the back plate and speaker front, as though he knew what he was doing. 'Out with it. It can't be any worse than Tallinn.'

'Complete blackout? Nothing at all?' Frankie left the spoon on the surface, went behind the bar. Turned the taps on. Picked up a scourer, a bottle of spray cleaner. Like he was going to clean everything. Scrub it all down. 'How...' he started: 'How much do you remember?'

'Well, obviously, I remember doing the towels. Something about dead mice. Having an argument with Roxy.' Wires and screws spilled out onto the table; he started making a pile of the bits that looked useful. A shining circuit slid away from the back plate, and another memory suddenly came. Looking at something on Roxy's phone. A tiny, pixellated photo. Samhain's eyes had been woozy; he'd clapped a hand over one eye, to try and help him make sense of the faces.

He quickly felt the sensation of freewheeling a bike towards a cliff edge.

'We were looking at a picture.' He laid the screwdriver down, and sat.

Frankie was scrubbing away at the bar, nearly strongly enough to make the top layer of varnish come away.

'Yes. Keep going.'

It was some effort to take himself back. The phone blazing with light in her hand. Roxy's face, lopsided with triumph, lit ghoulishly by the screen. This photograph had been her last word in the argument they'd been having. Evidence of his irresponsibility, his selfishness. To show him how much his other exes hated him, too.

Thinking about it, he realised he must have found the mice after this, because it was this moment with Roxy that had made him cry. The picture. A smiling girl in a red dress, standing in a garden of sunflowers. A sturdy toddler that was half-him and half-Charley.

This was the girl that Roxy had told him Charley didn't want him to meet, that he would never get to meet, because he had shown himself over and over again to be the kind of selfish, self-absorbed loser, that would never achieve anything good in life, and could never be a positive influence.

She had won that argument, all right.

He wasn't sure exactly what had happened after that. Other than that he had cracked into a bottle of something else – that would account for the taste of rotten peaches – and cried, talked to Frankie all night probably, and that at some point Roxy had gone. Now he knew why his elbows were sore: he had been resting them on the bar for most of the last part of the night. It had been one of those awful, black, alcohol-stolen nights, where nothing is fun, and everything gets forgotten.

Most likely, he would never know what had been said in the early hours of this morning.

Frankie said, 'Coming back to you now, is it?'

Her name. Samhain stared into a large circular stain on the carpet. Black where red wine had once been spilled – bloody. What was her name?

'Two types of Christ, Frankie.'

'Yep.' Frankie poured more, looking more into his cup than at Samhain. 'Knew it'd come back to you eventually.'

'A little girl, though. Mine.'

'That would seem to be the case.'

His head hurt, as though it was all concrete inside. All things heavy and stuck, and nothing moved.

Trying to remember when he had last been with Charley. They'd still been a couple when he'd gone on tour to Estonia and Latvia with Patrick Stewart The Band. That much he remembered, because of the girls in Tallinn. A wild-eyed thing with a ripped shirt had climbed into his sleeping bag and rubbed herself all over him, and then the morning after had kept on saying: 'I'm going to come and visit you in Bred-ferrrd,' and he'd said, 'No, don't come – England's a hole, you won't like it.' But somehow she'd got his landline number and kept on calling.

It had been hard to keep it from Charley, because they'd been living together in a tiny flat by Bradford College. Though in the end, it hadn't been the Latvian that had split them up. It had been somebody far closer to home.

In those days, Samhain had hardly known Roxy. Distantly at first, only as the girl who house-shared with Frankie, until he started to get to know her a little better. Long late nights spent with her, watching poor quality VHS footage of bald, bleeding chickens in cages. Roxy cared about animal rights. It was her passion, the only thing she wanted to talk about, long after Frankie had gone to bed. When she got onto something, she'd lean forward in her chair, cheeks flushed and knees slightly parted. It was on one of these nights that she told him about the male chicks. They could never lay eggs, so they were of no use in the battery farms. Boy chicks, a day or two old, were run through the industrial mincer. That was the most efficient way for factory farms to destroy them.

'Christ. I'm going vegan,' he'd said.

Roxy had hardly been able to hide her pleasure. 'Good. I'll teach you everything I know.'

She had been vegan for years, so knew all about it. What to eat, and how to cook it. There was a lot to learn. Before too long, he was spending two or three nights a week with her, learning new recipes, trying to absorb everything Roxy already knew.

Charley didn't like it. She used to call him at one, two in the morning to ask where he was. Accuse him of all sorts, and demand that he come home. It made him feel exactly like one of the chickens from the videos: trapped. During one of these phone calls, Roxy went out of the room to get more Red Stripe and when she came back, all legs and shoulders, he'd taken one look at her and made a decision. Since Charley was so sure they were humping anyway, and since nothing he could say or do could change her mind, he might as well make taking all of the shit worthwhile, and fuck Roxy for real.

They hadn't moved out of the room. Roxy slid her vest straps down, and spread her legs right there on the sofa. She was hairy as a badger, and wet as a pot of Vaseline. Samhain knew he shouldn't have been doing it, but it was too late by then to do anything else. He was hard and inside her, and too turned on to turn back. By the time they finished, he was already regretting it.

In the morning, he went home to Charley and confessed. She cried in a way he'd never seen before. Awful and red-faced, the tears spouting in a never-ending stream. Beautiful eyes made froggy with grief. It was a face that he'd caused and now couldn't escape. 'I knew it,' she sobbed. 'How could you do this to me? How? How?'

He and Charley certainly hadn't been together then, or afterwards. Two years ago, the day he'd moved out. Saying sorry and trying to leave quickly. Not wanting to stay with that face any longer. Ten minutes to grab his bag and go. Screwdriver – hoodie – notebook – address book – a couple of zines. Everything else, he had left behind. He realised now, thinking back over it, that while he'd darted in and out of rooms, grabbing the few things he couldn't bear to leave, as he had taken his door key off the ring and left it on the side, apologising again and again and again, as he had closed the door behind him and gone out into the hallway for what he knew would be the last time, that she must have known then that she was pregnant.

'I can't believe it, Frankie,' he said. 'That she's kept it secret from me all this time. What am I supposed to do?'

10.

Today, in a shackling heat, the librarian was a thin man. Samhain handed over his library card, receiving in return a slip of paper with a login code.

There were four floors in the central library. Cool, stone stairs whose chill filled the air with quiet; as he came to the second floor, the babbling from general lending faded away.

Flores had left a blank space on his birth certificate where his father's name should have been. She'd once told him that if she could have put her own name there, as well as in the mother's name space, she would have. But the registry of births, deaths and marriages didn't allow it. 'Fucking bureaucrats,' she said.

On the third floor, the research space, the long floor was tiled with sienna and burnished oak. Walls lined with long shelves, leather-bound spines, gilt lettering. *St Augustine's Parish Magazine, 1980-81. Headingley Examiner, 1985-86.* Bound copies of local minutiae: he ran his fingers along the spines as he walked down to the reading room. Soft, and warm to the touch.

Then the reading room. Soft carpet, long wooden desks. Old men reading newspapers on sticks.

'Can I help you?'

The girl wore a loose beige jumper, her face clumsy and wan, with a nose that didn't seem to fit her face. She studied him with keen, fox-coloured eyes.

'Maybe. I'm trying to find out about my Dad.'

She held his gaze for a moment, maybe too long. 'Ok. What do you know about him so far?'

'Not much. Hardly anything.' Samhain fixed his look on the pile of scrap paper beside her on the desk. 'I know he was in the police. And that he spent some time in Europe, in the seventies and eighties.'

Fox-Eyes didn't flicker. Sympathy perhaps, like a drip of water running over a stone. 'In the police – in Europe?'

He was surprised. 'Yeah.'

'Undercover?'

'How did you–'

'Here.' She scrabbled in the pile of leaflets, and pulled one out.

CopWatch support group, it said. *Legal support – information – open to all.*

'You're not the first to come in here, trying to find stuff out.'

'Thanks.' He took the leaflet.

'Somebody I know runs it. A friend. Listen – there are loads of ways to find somebody, even if you don't know very much about them. You'd be surprised.'

She pulled the scraps towards her, and her sleeve caught on the desk, riding up all the way to the elbow. Spiny capillaries of black ink networked her forearm: leaves, branches, the shape of a tree. 'All people leave traces. The police have got an advantage on using them to find out things about you, because they've got access to more things than you. But that doesn't mean you can't do the same thing back to them. It's just a matter of knowing where to look.' She scribbled a bluebottle's flight pattern with her biro on the paper, then drew a box. 'Birth certificates – marriage records – mentions in the local paper. Nobody goes anywhere without leaving a trail. Once helped a woman find her long-lost father when all she knew about him was where he'd been born.' She looked up at him, expectantly. 'I mean, it took ages. Lots of detective work. Hours spent in the registry office. Referencing, cross-referencing, finding the original marriage certificate...'

'You did all that?'

'Yeah. Well.' Embarrassment crept over her neck like a red scarf. 'I like a project.' She started scribbling away again at the page. 'So. Shall we get...' she cleared her throat. 'Have you tried the Salvation Army?'

'No. I hate religion.'

'Me too. All that tambourine-waving. Always trying to get you to go to their meetings. So. What do you know about your Dad? His name? Whether he was ever married? When or where he was born? Anything might help, no matter how small it may seem.'

There was so little. Samhain had been so young, he didn't even know which country they'd been in when they left; he didn't even know the fake name his father had been using. He told her all this, and Fox-Eyes nodded, softening.

'Man, they really screwed you over, didn't they? They didn't give you or your mother a thing. No money, no information, no apology... have you even got a photo of him?'

Samhain shook his head. 'My mother must have got rid of it all.'

'Christ.' Fox-Eyes cast a glance around the room, then picked up a key on a large wooden fob. A thing the size of a door wedge. 'Let's try and get you sorted. Follow me.'

At the back of the reading room, a door was hidden by a rack of leaflets.

She led him inside, into a cool, dark corridor. 'We're not supposed to let customers in here,' she said. 'But my manager's off today, and I think you need help.'

A short flight of creaking, wooden stairs. Up five steps, then a dusty room, and the smell of sawdust.

In the centre of the room were three tall, hooded machines, with sides of jaundiced metal. 'You ever used a microfiche before?'

She pulled two heavy binders off the shelves. There was also a computer, one which looked about the same age as the machines. Fox-Eyes dropped the binders on the desk, and switched it on. 'Well, don't worry. It's easy. Just look through these binders to find the newspaper stories you want, and take the names and dates, and I'll get the films for you. Use the computer as well, if you like.'

She stood at the top of the stairs a moment. 'The report's probably a good place to start. It'll give you a bit of knowledge about which groups were infiltrated, and which years. Try cross-referencing those years with mentions of organisations like Greenpeace and your mum's group, if you know it, in the news. You might be surprised how much you can find out, from not knowing very much.' The stairs made a noise like a stuck door as she descended. 'There are some things I can do, too. Sources. People I can talk to – records I can search. Don't worry – between us, we'll find him.'

The rattling of the microfiche took him right into the past. He looked into a tiny screen and read newspaper stories twenty, twenty-five years old. Soft light inside it, like candlelight on parchment. *Activists protest against new road in rare frog habitat.* An action he could barely remember, though he knew from reading the date that he might well have been there. *Police clear women's protest at Menwith Hill.* The films turned and clattered inside, wheels and bobbins.

Menwith Hill. That, he did remember. A chain-link fence, tents pitched in the shadow of huge, terrifying devices they called 'the golf balls.' He and Flores shared a tent in the heather. Drums beating: women dancing in overalls and leggings. Staring and shouting at the grey, man-made planets right there on the English hills. They were bigger than the Death Star and yet nobody really knew what they were, or why they were there.

He remembered Badger with her guitar, leading them in a song towards the concrete. Nuclear war was on everybody's lips. There were enough bombs to persh the planet three times over: anybody not killed right away would die in the nuclear winter that came after. They said you might as well not build a fallout shelter. Doors alone couldn't stop the radiation.

He didn't sleep easily, in those camps. Nightmares: a flash whiter than lightning, a boom loud enough to break your eardrums. He woke screaming, imagining he could feel the flesh melting from his bones.

The newspapers blurred and merged before his eyes. He still had his finger on the button, pushing the pages forward. They had been in those camps for peace, not violence.

There had always been music and dancing. He wasn't even supposed to play with sticks – Flores didn't like it. If he wanted to play war, he had to do it in a place where she couldn't see. And this, too, being in here, looking for him, was a betrayal. Flores had told him nothing about his father, her ex, because she didn't want to be reminded.

He would keep it quiet. All he wanted to see was a face. Only that. To see, to know, where he had come from. He went on searching, with the dust thick on his fingers.

The state had hidden him well, whoever he was.

In one news report he thought he saw a face. But the photo was old, grainy through the microfiche screen, and he couldn't be sure.

More recent reports kept the women, and the police, all anonymous. Only one woman had chosen to give her name, and she was somebody he'd never met.

A text from Frankie: *When are you planning on coming back? I've got to sign on today.*

Badger might know more. She was one of the few friends Flores had kept in touch with from her activist days. She might know the fake name his dad had used, maybe even his real one.

The only trouble was loyalty. She had more of it for Flores than she did for Samhain.

There had been a time when she had lived with them. For how long, he wasn't sure. He just remembered coming down one morning, all ready for school in his shirt and tie, and finding a purple-haired woman asleep on the sofa, with one arm scrunched up under a smashed-umbrella face, and a leather jacket draped over her torso. His first thought had been, I'd better go and tell Flores her friend's here. But then the woman had opened one witchy eye, looked at him as though he were a bird hopping across the sand, and said: 'Don't you look the proper little man?'

Those were days of good food and laughter, lots of it. Flores got up in the mornings, and looked more alive than he had ever seen her. It must have been summer, because he remembered the sunlight, orange and flaming onto the back yard, long into the evenings. Also, missing Sports Day, because Flores wrote a note and let him stay home.

They were always sitting in the backyard together, Badger and Flores. Drinking out of bottles, Flores in sunglasses, and Badger squinting into the sun. Samhain went out on his own, circling the estate on his bike. Around and around the park, sometimes along the canal tow path. Over the motorway bridge. One night, bored, he called for Graeme, and Graeme's mother had answered the door, and told him not to call again. 'Don't you know what time it is? You ought to be in bed.'

He had gone home afterwards and Badger had told him, slurring, that he was going to grow up to be a good man. Looking at him kindly, though lopsidedly, with smoke escaping through her teeth. She was a soft-haired dragon with scaly tattoos. 'You're going to be a good man, Sam,' she said. 'Not like the rest of them.'

Flores: 'Despite everything.'

A warm, beery embrace. He had crawled into Flores' lap as best he could although, by the age of nine, he was getting too large to sit on her knee.

'You're my boy,' she'd said. 'My very best boy.'

Badger's MySpace profile had a picture of her standing gleefully, blurrily, in front of a cauldron in the middle of a field. Trees and camper vans in the background. He tried to figure out by looking at her face, lined now, and the hair mostly grey – when had Badger become an old lady?

The next picture had Badger and Flores together. Arms around one another, faces streaked with blue paint, their pupils pencil nibs. Both standing in a field, in front of a scattering of tents. Their hair was wild, as though they'd been awake all night. The date said it had been posted two weeks ago. He and Frankie had a couple of pictures pretty similar to this one. Photos taken after a night of outrageous nonsense. Arms round each other, brothers in trust. You could share a lot over the course of a night. Say all of your secrets, stretch your skin inside out, almost. There was just that one person who saw you for who you really were. If anybody knew his Dad's name, it would be Badger.

A red notification appeared on the screen. *Badger*

NoneOfYourBizznizz likes your photo comment: 'Don't Do Drugs, Kids.'

That small, red circle, told him something else: that he couldn't ask Badger, not now. She was Flores' friend, not his. Anything she knew had been told to her in confidence, and he couldn't ask her anything without going to Flores first.

His phone bleeped again. This time, it was Mart.

Hey there. How's the animal sanctuary going?

'Find out anything?'

The librarian was at her desk, stringy pieces of lettuce falling into her lap. She was eating a sandwich, and making a clumsy mess of it.

'Nothing.'

'Here.' Swiping crumbs from her fingers: 'Give me your notes. I'll keep on looking for you.'

'Really?' He looked uncertainly at the single half-page of unintelligible scribbling, including a drawing of a cat in the bottom corner. 'There's not much to go on.'

'Doesn't matter.' She pulled a scrap from the stack. 'You'd be surprised what things can come in useful.'

He handed it over, and he didn't even know why he was doing it.

'I might go to the meeting as well.'

'Yeah?' A bit of falafel gathered on her lip. 'Why not? Tell them Alice sent you.'

'That's you?'

'Yeah. I help out when I can. Not by going to the meetings, but by helping people like you find information.' She shrugged. 'It's my one small way of saying F-- You to my manager, who thinks this library should be turned into a coffee shop.

'Write your number on there,' she said. 'I'll maybe see you at the meeting.'

II.

'There you are.' Frankie came out, with a paintbrush in a jar of turpentine. 'I'd nearly given you up for lost.' He'd dragged one of the picnic benches out into the yard: its tops and sides were glossy with new varnish. 'Mart's here.' The bike was gone from his hands, as quickly as if he'd left it unchained in the town centre. 'Better go – don't want to get sanctioned again. See you later.' Frankie rode away, bicycle bell ringing.

Mart's bike leaned against the wall in the hallway. She'd chained it with a long rope lock, to itself. Anybody wanting to come in and steal it would have to lift it up and carry it away.

Samhain glanced through the kitchen door at the mess. Pans crusted, all sitting inside one another. He pushed the door open further to get a better look, and something darted along the top. A thumb-sized thing with a long pink tail.

Something in the cupboards. Onyx-bright eyes, a chewed hole in a catering-sized pack of stuffing mix. A mouse stared out.

It had dust and suet on its whiskers. Samhain closed the door carefully, and went up to his room.

Marta was in there, sitting on a clean towel from the linen cupboard. For a second, he thought what he was seeing were hairballs.

'Well,' she said, 'she's had them.'

Helpless, eyes-closed things in shades of ginger and coffee. Mama Cat had its paws around one of them, licking its head, its neck; and the kitten, no larger than an egg, was submitting to it.

'So I see.'

Four. Five. Or four? A mass of ginger lay curled in the towel, all fur with no beginning or end, and he couldn't tell whether it was one kitten or two.

'Lucky that I happened to be here. Thought I'd pop round – see how you were doing.' She wasn't looking at him, was just doing something with the edge of the towel. Folding it inwards, then straightening it out again.

Mama Cat paused in her cleaning as he sat down on the bed. His eyes still swam with newsprint. *The protestors... A source said... Police confirmed...* Samhain put a hand to the ginger ball of fluff and found two kittens, separating in surprise. One curled around his fingers, while the other turned, and tried to struggle away on wheat-bending legs. 'My friend knew somebody who worked at an animal sanctuary. They'd take anything in. Cats, dogs – guinea pigs. They even had an owl once.'

Panzo had shown boy-Samhain around the shelter. Drowsy cats; thin, shivering terries. A pitbull with a head like an anvil. Jaws slavering, drool slopping all over the bars and floor. Panzo had said: 'Be careful of that one. It hasn't been socialised.'

An almost-starved greyhound was more bones than beast. There had been a cat with no tail, and skin hanging off him like wet canvas – a watchful, ungainly thing, with a mange patch the shape of Africa.

'They'd get these animals brought in,' he said, 'who were so scared. Some of them were half-dead. Nearly all of them were terrified. Some of the dogs were so scared of humans that you couldn't even look them in the eye. It'd make them go crazy. Some of the dogs had been beaten and starved – until they were hardly an animal at all. I don't know how anybody could treat an animal like that. A few of them couldn't even be rehomed after what they'd been through. They had to...'

He broke off. The dog with the bear-trap jaws had been put down. Panzo had explained that sometimes they had no choice, when the shelter was full. He had told him it was like going to sleep. Samhain had tried not to think about the dog climbing onto the vet's table, being spoken to gently by its handlers. Laying down for the injection that would end its life.

'So we need to find good homes for these little guys. I don't want them to end up in a shelter.'

'Ok. And by the way–' she got up, and went over to a box on the floor, filled with cat food sachets. Beside it were a heap of band t-shirts, bloody and ruined. 'I got you a few things. There's a litter tray here, and some kitty litter. Some food sachets – bowls – just set it all up – it's easy. Cat toys...' A toy mouse with curved felt ears. Mini tennis balls, all bright colours. Mama Cat's head jerked with interest; she slung one paw, grabbing, over the edge of the bed.

'What happened to our t-shirts?'

'Oh yeah. Sorry about that.' She picked one up, all stiff and stuck with brown-red blood. 'She gave birth on your merch box, and I didn't want to move her.'

'We were supposed to sell those on tour, Mart.'

'Blame the cat.' She shrugged. 'Anyway, I asked my friend who knows about animals. She said the kittens need lots of toys, and you need to play with them a lot – it helps develop their coordination and hunting skills. As well as that, you need to pick them up and talk to them all the time, so they get used to being around humans. I also made this.'

A cardboard box, with cat-sized holes cut in each side. 'It's a cat fort. For them to play in... and these...' Empty kitchen roll centres, which she lay on the floor, too: '...are toys too. It's like Urbex for kittens. They love shit like this, she said. You won't be able to get them away from it.' She paused. 'Just as soon as they can walk.'

'Mart, you should take them. You obviously know what you're doing.' He put his new friend, who had been biting the tip of his finger with a toothless mouth, on the ground beside one of the rolls. It meowed blindly, and fell over onto its back. 'You see?' he said, righting it. 'I haven't got a clue.'

'You'll be fine, Sam. They just need to be with their mother early on, that's all.' She lifted the animal back onto the duvet, placing it by its mother's belly. 'Until they're about nine weeks old, she said. And after that, you can start to think about giving them away.'

'Nine weeks?' Samhain paused, holding an encrusted shirt. This was the last XXL shirt, and the other two were the last two Mediums. All three were ruined with blood and goo. 'We're going on tour before that.' He showed her the shirts. 'Do you reckon this could come out, if I wash them enough?'

'Don't know. I'd throw them in the bin.'

'Christ.' Samhain leaned against the wall, closing his eyes. Toothpick claws on his jeans, and the soft mew of that one kitten, Ginger, trying to crawl up Samhain's leg towards him. 'Why does everything have to be such a fucking mess?'

She was quiet a moment. He still had his eyes shut, hoping that if he kept them that way long enough, when he opened them again she might be gone, leaving him to sort everything out on his own.

But that didn't shut out the splat of rain starting on the Velux window. The cracking, rumbling tumble of thunder. When he opened his eyes she was still there, sitting on the carpet, trying to force the empty kitchen roll ends into one another. 'So what are you going to do?' she asked softly. So quiet that, if he hadn't been watching her lips, he might have missed the question altogether.

'I suppose I'll bin them,' he said. 'Like you say. And then I could – I suppose I could get a book on cat care out of the library. It's a bummer, though. We needed to sell these for diesel money on tour. Then while we're away – I suppose I'll need to find somebody to look after this lot...'

'That's not really what I meant, Sam.'

Hammering drops, and a slammed door at the neighbouring house. 'It'll all need washing again.' David's voice, calling out. 'My slacks are done for, I'm afraid. And your blouse.' The rest disappeared beneath other thunder, and Samhain thought he heard metallic squeaking, which might have been Frankie coming back on the bike. He realised he was stroking the kitten again. His hand had gone there without his noticing it.

'I'm going to go to the CopWatch meeting,' he said. 'Like you suggested. Find out what they know. I tried the library, but I couldn't find anything out. There aren't any names published. And my Mum's still away, but even if she wasn't, I don't think she'd tell me anything. She hates talking about it.'

Mart was crumpling shirts into the wastebasket. 'But don't you think you have a right to know?'

'Look.' The neighbours' door slammed, and Sam spoke over it. 'You don't know my Mum like I do. She was in this weird depression for most of my childhood. Probably triggered by finding out her boyfriend – or the guy she thought was her boyfriend, anyway – was an undercover cop. You don't know, Mart – you should have seen her after she brought me back home to Bradford, after finding out. She wouldn't even talk about it. She hardly even talked to me for about six months.'

'When you were just a little kid?'

'It doesn't matter, Mart. It was a long time ago.'

'But Sam–'

'I can ask her, but I don't want to. I think it'll just set her off again, and I don't want that – not after she's spent all these years getting over it. I don't want to set her back.'

'If you say so, Sam. But I know if it was me–'

'It isn't you.' His voice came out with a roughness he didn't know he had. An unfamiliar savagery that shocked even him. He regretted it straight away. 'Sorry, Mart. I've got no right to – anyway. I know my mum doesn't like thinking about it. Whoever he was, he really did a number on her, and I don't really want to go dragging it all up again.'

'Up to you,' she said.

'Roxy doesn't know,' he said. 'Nobody does – not even Frankie. You're the only one who knows anything about all of this.'

'Yep.' Her hand was in amongst the cat food. She pulled a sachet out, and Mama Cat jumped off the bed. 'Poor thing, you must be starving. After all of your hard work.'

'Mart,' he said.

She pushed the cat food out into one of the saucers. 'Come on, Sam, I've already said I won't tell anyone.'

Mama Cat landed on the carpet with a pickpocket's elegance, and put her face in the food.

There was a rumble overhead: the sound of grand pianos being rolled over a temporary stage.

12.

'So.' Fox-Eyes looked exactly the same out of work as she did in it: sloppy beige jumper, loose jeans, battered old shoes. 'It's along here somewhere.'

'Up this hill,' he said. Then when he saw her looking, he added: 'I think.'

'Ah. Have you been before?'

Out on the cobbled street, passing an old closed department store with huge windows. Whitewashed insides, floors stretching blackly within.

'Yeah. I practise here with my band. In the basement.'

'I hope we'll be able to get a drink.'

'You will. The bar's pretty much always open.'

Steep steps, the familiar scent of old beer and cold walls. Unfinished walls painted gloss black; Samhain led Alice up the stairs. 'Bar's on the first floor,' he said. 'And then the library's a floor up from that.'

Coming with Alice had been a good ruse. It had been her idea – for them to turn up together, and say that he was there to help her. So many of his friends were regulars at the club. He didn't want any of them wandering into the meeting room, and finding out that he was a cop's son.

'The usual, Sam?' The barman was already bending down to the fridge. Rawlplug, grey-haired and practical, always with a spanner in his pocket, always seemed to be in the club. If Sam had ever known his real name, he'd already forgotten it. 'Didn't realise you were in for practice tonight.'

'I'm not,' Sam said. 'I'm here for the CopWatch meeting.'

'Huh!' Rawlplug glanced back at him for a moment; Sam wondered whether there was something growing on his face. 'New interest?' His eyes flickered between Sam and the girl.

'Cider, please,' she said.

At the meeting room door, a circle of eyes turned.

Rare for meetings at the club to start on time, and yet here they were.

Wooden chairs in a circle where the crowd watching a band would normally be: the space swept, and quiet, almost a dozen women in various shades of grey and black sitting together. He recognised at least three.

The air hardened.

'Evening,' he said. He was the only man there.

'Alice.' Endra stood up. She was wearing that eyeliner she liked, the one which looked like it had come out of a tattoo gun.

Endra, he knew. He'd known her a few times. At her house and at his. In his bed, in hers. In her boyfriend's bed. In quite a few different squats. He and Endra had known each other in lots of different beds. And then they'd stopped knowing each other when her boyfriend had found out.

Quite a few people had stopped speaking to him afterwards.

'Sam,' she said.

'Hi, Endra. Don't mind me. I won't interrupt...'

It was too late to leave now, not now they'd all seen him arrive, now they'd seen him walk all the way into the room like he meant to be there.

He found an empty seat, and dropped quickly into it. A stool dragged in from the bar, fabric-covered and tatty at the corners. He discovered, as he sat, that one of its legs was shorter than the others. 'Don't mind me,' he said again, because the silence was still there, thick and sharp.

'Hello, Sam.'

There was another woman beside him; he hadn't seen her as he'd sat down. Now he looked at her properly: soft face, grey eyes, chin the length of a trowel.

'Suzie,' he said.

Suzie. He should have known it. The smell of cooking fat on her should have given it away. She worked with Charley in the club cafe. In many ways, she was Charley's best friend. Most likely, this had been the woman who had got Charley through their break-up.

'How've you been – I haven't seen you in ages?'

'Three years.' She spoke as though she wanted to say the fewest words possible. 'To be exact.'

'Suzie,' he said, aware that his voice was tearing into the silence, 'will you ask Charley to get in touch with me? I've been trying to get a hold of her for ages.'

'You're unbelievable,' she said. 'Did you come to this meeting just to ask me that?'

'What's going on?' one of the other women asked; somebody he didn't know, somebody older. She looked to be in her fifties, her arm a sleeve of black skeletal tattoos. 'Is this CopWatch business?'

'Alice.' Endra was getting out of her chair. 'Can I have a word?'

'That was quick.' Rawlplug was sitting at the wrong side of the bar, reading a paperback of *Rogue States*. 'Fallen out already?'

'They chucked me out.' Samhain was glum, turning the beermats over and over.

'Really, why? Are you a cop?'

'Worse – a perpetrator of male violence towards women, apparently.' Sam drained the last of his beer, and set it down on the bar. 'You got any Jäger?'

'Jäger, Buckie – we've got every strong spirit known to man.' Rawlplug hopped down, and went back behind the bar. 'Brought some vegan mead back from the anarchist bookfair, you want some of that?'

'Why not.'

Small glasses appeared; two flagons, silver-polished, handled. 'Got to drink this sort of thing from the right jar,' Rawlplug said. 'Doesn't taste the same otherwise.'

The mead was the colour of unfinished whisky; it tasted of hazelnuts and twigs. 'That's disgusting,' Sam said.

Rawlplug tipped his cask backwards. 'I know. Been trying to foist this stuff off on other people for months. Nobody likes it.' He looked at his flagon with distaste. 'So come on. What do you have to do to get chucked out of CopWatch, exactly?'

'Right.' Sam was still drinking the mead – it seemed a shame for it to go to waste. 'You know me. I've never hit a woman in my life. Never would. That shit is disgusting. I'd never raise my hand to a woman, ever. Or anybody, for that matter.'

'Except for that time outside the CrustFest all-dayer.'

'That was different.'

'You punched two of Steve's front teeth out.'

'We'd been drinking since eleven that morning. He was as

drunk as I was.' Sam sank the last of the mead. It left a taste like a forest bed. 'Can I have a beer, please? Wash the taste of that stuff away.'

'There was blood all over the front step.' Rawlplug shook his head, bending down to the fridge. 'I've never had to ban anybody before.'

'Yeah, well – I've learned my lesson,' Samhain said. 'That was the first and only time I've punched anybody. And I'm grateful, don't get me wrong, that the ban was only temporary. But those girls are saying–'

'Which girls?'

'In CopWatch. In there. Suzie, Endra – that girl who runs it...'

'Titania?' Rawlplug fizzed the top off a bottle of beer. 'I wouldn't let her hear you calling her a "girl." She's got a PhD and two grandchildren.'

'They're saying that I'm a "perpetrator of male violence towards women." I don't know how they get that, when I've never hit a woman in my life.'

'Here.' Rawlplug left his beer on the mat, and settled back onto the bar stool. Anybody coming in would have thought he was a casual drinker, somebody who'd popped in to have a drink, the same as Samhain. He bent the book back, cracking the spine open, so the pages opened loose. 'As I understand it, CopWatch have a very broad definition of what counts as "violence."'

'Like what?'

'I don't know. Why don't you read their constitution? It's probably around here somewhere. Look in the library.'

'Can't go back up there. They'd probably... throw me out through one of the windows.' Samhain was glum. 'Do you know what? This is nothing to do with "male violence" at all, and everything to do with hurt feelings. I bet you that's what it is. Just because I've slept with one or two of them...'

Rawlplug laughed. 'One or two!'

'Listen, I wasn't going out of my way to hurt anybody, these things just happen. You know how it goes.'

'I don't.' Rawlplug had given up on his book, laying it print-side down on the bar. 'Why don't you tell me?'

Samhain let the beer drop, hard, bubbles fizzing down the side. 'If you had a life of your own mate, you wouldn't need to ask.'

'Alright, alright. Let's not get excited.'

'Sorry.' Samhain lifted his beer again. 'I'm just... they didn't even ask for my side of the story.'

'It's their group.' Rawlplug scratched a fuzzy jaw, making the sound of new sandpaper. 'They can do what they like.'

'And Suzie – I didn't even sleep with her. She's pissed off on behalf of someone else.'

'That's rough.' Rawlplug stared at the bar back, and spoke slowly. 'Thing is, though. Some of them have been pretty badly treated. Not by you. But by other men. Cops and that. So you can understand why they might be a bit sensitive.'

'I'm not a cop, though.'

'Mmm.' Rawlplug lifted his book. 'What about saying sorry?'

'They won't let me.'

'Oh. Well. That's that then. Not much more you can do.'

'That's what I said. They didn't listen. And I'm still banned from CopWatch.'

'Huh.' The barman frowned. 'Unlucky.'

'Yeah.' Samhain sighed. 'What about your book, any good?'

'Brilliant. You know how Bush is saying Hussein's a mass murderer – that he's got to be stopped, because of how many of his own people he's killed, or how many people he *might* kill? Get this. The biggest cause of death in Iraq isn't Hussein, it's the West. Millions of people have died because of our sanctions.

Five thousand children a month on average, it says here.'

'No way.'

'It's true.'

Rawlplug fell silent for a moment, fingers fidgeting over the book's worn edges. The cold of the unfinished brick started to press against Samhain. It made its way through his sleeves, prickling his arms; it always got like this, after a few minutes sitting still in the club.

He shivered.

'Fuck, though.' Perhaps it was the cold, making him want to do something: to jump up and down, to run back into the meeting room and demand they let him stay; anything to keep warm. 'How can you ban somebody from a radical meeting for having a sex life? That's oppression – that's what that is.'

'Well.' Rawlplug answered without looking up. 'I suppose it's the way you go about having a sex life, isn't it?'

'We're anarchists. One anarchist can't tell another anarchist what to do. Perpetrator of male violence, my arse,' Samhain grizzled. 'The – the – when I was going out with Charley, I used to clean the flat once a week, completely, the kitchen, the bathroom, everything. You tell me what's violent about that.'

'Sam.' Now, Rawlplug looked up. Lines of concern around his eyes. 'Calm down. It's only a meeting. There are plenty of other groups you can join.'

'But they're saying I hit women!'

Rawlplug tilted his head slightly, musing. 'Are they saying that, though? Doesn't their constitution say something about emotional carelessness counting as violence, too?'

'What the hell's "emotional carelessness" when it's at home?' Samhain jumped off the chair. His swinging arm made the empty bottle wobble and he only righted it, quickly, with a reflex quickened by anger. 'Can't believe I've been banned from CopWatch for hurting girls' feelings. Fucking... PC anarchists. You can't do anything.'

He swept his bag from under the chair, and ran out of the club and into the night.

13.

There was a drip, he had discovered. Sometimes he woke wet, with the crevice from the window pane trailing a damp necklace around his throat.

Flores,

I haven't got your address so I don't know if I will ever send this letter. Probably not. Maybe I'll just write all of this on a blog, and let you find out about it from one of your friends. Isn't that the way we do things in our family?

It turns out that you have known about PC Plod all along. Ever since I was a boy. I understand why you didn't say anything but that doesn't mean I have to like it. Mart thinks I should ask about it, I told her I wasn't so sure. The other thing I told her was that I didn't care about finding out more about my dad, which I think I meant at the time, but now I'm not so sure. Not because I want to know him (he's obviously a prick) but because maybe it would be good to know where I came from. See a picture. Find out his name. Or find out what his other family are like. I've got a girl myself now. Did you know that? She doesn't seem to know anything about me either. It must run in the family.

Fuck but it's embarrassing, having a cop for a dad. I can't even tell my best mate. And I don't even know who to be angry with about this. Him? You? The police generally?

If I could even talk to you about this it would help, but I can't. You've seen to that plenty over the years. Thanks a bunch, Flores.

A stirring. One of the darker kittens was awake, and climbing over the others to get to a teat. It straddled one of its calico siblings, kneading at his mother's chest with cent-sized paws.

Samhain put his hand in there to rearrange things, moving the splodgy kitten into a new space. It made a tiny squeak in protest, and lost its unsteady footing.

In a second it was back up again, and looking for milk.

Look when I think about it, I know why you didn't say anything. It must have been awful for you and I can understand that you didn't want to think about it. What the cops did to you is disgusting. But you let me find out about this from a friend. That's not right. That's not the way it should have been, Flores. You should have told me yourself – years ago. Give me a bit of time to get used to it.

Parents have got responsibilities, Flores. Don't you understand that?

The pen tore through the paper.

Samhain crumpled the letter, put it in his pocket, and went downstairs carrying one of the matchbooks. This was the sort of thing he couldn't leave lying around. Even if he put it in one of the bins, Roxy or Frankie were sure to see it.

It was going to be a fine day: he opened the front door,

and went out into a day that reminded him of Spain. Him and Frankie playing a gig somewhere up a mountain, where after the gig they had sat outside on the volcanic rock, drinking and talking. Drinking beer under the night sky, hardly noticing the time pass until the sun gathered strength again, and light came over them with the heat of an oven. When Samhain had stood, wobbling, little rocks had tumbled out of his shorts, and down the crevasse into a vast drop of perhaps 20,000 feet.

'Morning!' The neighbour, David, was out, circling a chamois leather over his car bonnet. 'Must be some party, eh?' He paused, and indicated at the bar window. 'Still going on, is it?'

Somehow, he hadn't got to all parts of the car. A clumsy slosh of water glittered on the tarmac, but there was still an angle-grind spark of dirt around the rear wheel arch. If David was washing the car, he wasn't doing a very good job of it.

'You've missed a bit.' Samhain pointed.

'So I have.' David saw to the dirty patch with a sponge. 'Tell you what. It does this place good – to have a few young folk around. Let me tell you, I certainly had some wild times during my years at Coventry – University, that is. I remember, one time Tommy Roberts said, David, let's get all the furniture out of the common room and put it in the Halls of Residence lift. Oh, it was such a grand prank. Stuffed everything in there, we did. Chairs – tables – the whole lot. We made it look like a living room in there. Tommy said to me, David, you'll never get the standard lamp in there. But I did! Oh, how we howled.'

He made the motions of squeezing an already-dry sponge. 'I expect it all seems very tame by your standards.' He rubbed away at the car roof, sponge squeaking. 'Though, saying that, I expect I don't even really want to know what you lot get up to.'

Samhain propped himself up against the picnic bench. He still had the letter in his hand, and the matches. It somehow seemed rude to think of setting them both on fire at this point.

'It's less exciting than you think. I'm just up early, that's all.'

David peered at him. 'On your way to work?'

'I'm between jobs at the moment.'

'Of course.' David wiped his hands on the chamois leather, and popped it in his pocket. 'Of course you are.' He looked at Samhain carefully. 'Having a comedown, are you?'

'A what?'

'A comedown. What happens to you when you've been on drugs the night before. I saw a programme about it on BBC2.'

'No. I told you. I just get up early sometimes, that's all.'

'Right. Jolly good.' David put the sponge in the bucket, picked it up by the handle, and made his way towards the front door. 'In that case, would you like some coffee?' He disappeared into the house, leaving the front door open.

Samhain leaned against their garden wall, struck a match, and lit the page at all four corners. It burned up in under a minute.

He scattered the ashes on David's lawn.

'Been meaning to invite you over for a while.' The house was smaller, more compact, than the Boundary Hotel. Clean and chintzy, with floral wallpaper in the hallway. 'Come on through.'

There was a large plate of assorted biscuits on the coffee table. Bourbons, custard creams; a couple of round biscuits in foil wrappers. David was intently plunging a cafetière into riverish coffee. 'Seems rude to have not had you round before,' he said. 'We are neighbours, after all.'

'This your family?' Samhain asked.

A smiling bride, with David's mouth and jaw, standing under a cherry-blossom tree. A husband, serious-smiling in a grey suit. Next to that was a picture of a little girl looking mildly terrified on a beach donkey. Then another picture, taken in a studio this time, of the same girl, smiling next to a baby propped up on a cushion.

'Oh, yes.' David smoothed his jumper, puffing his chest out. 'That's our daughter, Helen, and her husband, Jake. He's an IT manager – they met kayaking, which is what they used to be into, before they had the girls. Ever such a nice chap. They were married in Dunstan, which is where he used to live – where his parents still live. We couldn't have hoped for better for our Helen.'

David handed him the photograph, smiling, and Samhain took it, not knowing quite what to do. It looked the same close up as it had on the shelf. He couldn't take the oddness of this girl looking so much like David. She had his nose, his face shape, exactly. He couldn't quite take his eyes off it. 'Mmm,' he said.

'And *these* are our grand-daughters.'

The photograph was swiftly removed from his hand, and replaced with a picture of two little girls laughing on a sofa. The older one, he now saw, bore resemblance to Jake, the IT manager from Dunstan. There was something about the broader set of her brows, the wideness of her face. 'Now the younger one, Ivy, I always think, is very like Jake. But the older one, Eliza, she's got more the look of Helen about her, hasn't she?' David carefully placed them back on the mantelpiece. His movements were that of a man handling an actual baby. 'I think they're just about two of the best little girls out there.'

There was the sound of a door opening. 'That's Barbara up. We might get a bit of breakfast now,' David said, rubbing his hands together.

Breakfast. Samhain hadn't realised how hungry he was. He had already lain waste to a couple of the bourbons.

'Now then,' David went on, 'I met your girlfriend the other day. What do they call her – Martha?'

Samhain's mouth, clogged with crumbs and cream, was too full of biscuit to put him right. 'Mmmf,' he said.

'Seems like a nice girl. What is she – a nurse? Now that's a good profession. Very caring. Barbara was a nurse – when we first met. I was going around with this other girl at the time – this very glamorous type of girl, you know the type – Barbara doesn't like me talking about her. To tell you the truth, she wasn't the sort you'd settle down with. Not like Barbara. When I first met her, I said to myself, now *there's* the kind of girl I could get married to. I wasn't so bothered about the other one anymore. You know what I mean. Like you and your Martha, I expect.'

Now, he swallowed, making his mouth clear. 'She's not my girlfriend.'

'No?' David seemed perplexed. 'But she brought you that whole box of stuff over.'

'That was for the cats. She's nice, but we're not going out.'

'Shame,' David said, crunching on a golden oat biscuit, 'girl like that. You could certainly do a lot worse.' Glancing at the doorway, David brushed crumbs from his lap. 'Better not let Barb catch me doing this, or I'll be for the high jump.' Then he got up, reached for a dustpan and brush tucked away in the corner, and awkwardly folded himself towards the floor. 'Feet up,' he said. 'Thing is, with a lovely girl like that, you haven't to let 'em get away. If you leave 'em on their own, they soon start going out with somebody else. See, if this Martha got married to another chap, you wouldn't think much of that – would you?'

'She's already got a boyfriend,' Samhain said. 'And anyway, she won't get married. She doesn't believe in it. None of us do.'

'Oh ho,' David said, with a chuckle. 'That's what *you* think. There we are.' He shook crumbs out into the wastebasket. 'Now then. How about a bit of something to eat?'

'I don't want you to go to any trouble.'

'It's no trouble.' David went towards the doorway, and called out: 'Barbara!'

'What?'

David's wife, Barbara. A broad-set lady in faded blue.

'Samhain here's come around for a visit. He says Martha's not his girlfriend.'

'David,' she said, sharply. 'That's his business.'

'I only–'

She shushed him. 'Samhain, have you had breakfast yet?'

'Have we got any sausages?' David said. He turned to Samhain, winking. 'She'll never do them if it's just for me. But it we've got visitors–'

'I'm vegetarian,' Samhain said.

'Oh.' David looked as though he'd been given a paper hat instead of a crown. He called: 'Never mind about sausages. He won't eat them anyway.'

'How about fried mushrooms on toast?' Barbara came out of the kitchen with a steaming teapot. 'Mind you, look at the time. I suppose you'll be wanting to get to work.'

'He hasn't got a job,' David said. 'He's between places of employment.'

'Dear me.' She went out again. 'You should give him Peter's number.'

'Oh, *yes*!' David shuffled forward in his seat, all of a sudden sparky. 'I forgot all about that.' He turned to Sam. 'Haven't got a bad back, have you?'

'No.'

'David's friend,' Barbara explained, 'runs a removals business. Very successful. He's got his own warehouse, a whole fleet of vans. He's always on the lookout for help.'

The old man was up and hunting around the room for something. 'Peter's a very steady chap. I've known him for years.' He looked on top of the record player; underneath it, around the television, and on the shelf; he pulled out all of the drawers in the TV cabinet. 'Barbara, have you moved my address book?'

'It'll be wherever you left it.'

'I left it here.'

'By the television?' Barbara put the teapot down, and went into the kitchen. 'So you could phone people with the remote control?' Samhain heard a bread bag rustle, and a knife chopping on a wooden board.

'Ah, here we are, look, it's here.' David had a large burgundy book in hand. He settled back into his chair, with a scrap of paper and pen. 'Now look, you seem like the enterprising type – enthusiastic and so forth – you're not going to let him down, are you? Because Peter has all this trouble with some of the young lads he takes on. They come, and they work for a bit, a few days or what have you, then they don't come again – or else, some of them don't turn up when they're meant to, or they just stop coming to work altogether. He has a hard time finding reliable workers, he says. So I don't want to be putting you on to him if you're going to let him down.'

David had a face like a teacher playing good cop. Concerned, searching, and hard to say no to. 'I won't let him down, David.'

'Good.' David started turning pages. 'Now, don't you ring him yet. Let me phone him first, which I'll do today, and tell him you're going to phone him. Then you can call him in a couple of days. You can say that you know me – David Corby.' He handed the paper over. 'Don't show me up, will you?'

'I won't.'

'What would you like on your toast, Sam?' Barbara asked. 'We've got butter, margarine, marmalade...'

'Yes please!'

'Though you'll have to eat it in here, I'm afraid,' she said. 'The dining room table's in a bit of a mess.'

'Oh ho!' David rubbed his hands. 'Like camping!'

Plates came. On Samhain's, white toast was piled high with hot, fried mushrooms. He didn't know how Barbara had done it, but they tasted like something fresh from a truck stop griddle.

It was the best thing he'd eaten for days.

'So, David.' On the baby pictures, Samhain saw grinning girls, their milk teeth showing. In new clothes fresh from the hanger. The baby was in a romper suit, with a cartoon dinosaur on its front. These were children happy and round-bellied, children who were fussed and cooed over and scrubbed clean with a flannel, children who never wanted for anything. 'When you had your daughter–'

'It was me who had her.' Barbara had settled into the small leatherette bench by the telephone table. 'In the General Infirmary. Those were some fierce nurses, let me tell you.'

'Were you scared?'

'She was a marvel, Samhain. She was!' David's eyes swivelled around, shining. 'Let me tell you – you can't know what a woman's capable of, until she goes through something like childbirth. It gave me a whole new admiration for you, dear. Not that I didn't admire you before.'

'But you, David. Were you scared?'

'Er.' David chewed slowly, his eyes tracking the ceiling. 'Not so much scared, as – I just wanted to be sure that they would both be fine. Barbara and the baby. And knowing I couldn't do anything to help that either way – that was the worst bit.'

'I will say this,' Barbara said. 'You became very responsible all of a sudden – around that time. Taking on a lot of extra hours at work. Do you remember? Then when she was still quite small, you came home one day all excited, because they'd given you Arthur's old office.'

'I remember.' David's eyes glowed with pride.

'"They're giving me Arthur's old office!" you said.'

'That's right. They *did* give me Arthur's old office.' David started pouring tea. 'I was in there over thirty years. And do you know what they call it now?' His fingers hovered over the milk jug. 'They call it *David's* old office. They put two desks in there when I retired. Milk?'

'No thanks, I'll take it black.'

That face had put him onto something. The way David had softened talking about his grandchildren. He could be a soft old Grandpa himself one day. A grey-haired old fellow, who'd pull a ten pence piece out from behind your ear. A fellow who kept jelly babies hidden all around the house.

'I've got a little girl, too.'

'Well!' David's face went up like fairground lights. 'Isn't that something. Did you hear that, Barbs?'

'That's lovely, Sam. How old is she?'

Samhain looked down into the crumbs on his plate. 'Two and a half,' he said, which he thought was probably right. 'Or maybe three. I think.'

'You're not sure?'

The last time he'd seen Charley, she'd been crying. With tears spilling all down her face, running over her cheeks – red, as if she'd been out in the sun too long. He didn't know whether she'd been pregnant one month, or two months, or two weeks, then. She could have given birth to their daughter any time between June and November, for all he knew.

'Yeah. It's a bit complicated. The thing is, I didn't even know I had her, until last week. I've never even seen her.'

'David.' Barbara got up. She turned her wrist over. Her watch, a delicate thing with a thin gold strap, sparkled in the sunlight. 'I've just remembered. We've got to be at Helen's at eight thirty, to pick up the girls.'

'Today?' David turned, surprised. 'But it's Wednesday!'

'She had to swap her days.' Barbara got up, and started taking the plates in. They slotted into a stack with a clatter. 'Something to do with their budget meeting, I don't know.' She nodded at the clock. 'Look at the time. We'd better get a move on, or else she'll be late for work.'

'Just let me go and do my hair, then.' David stood, brushing his trousers.

The kitchen tap came on.

'Do you want any help washing up?' Samhain called.

'No, it's fine. Nice to see you, Samhain. You must pop in and see us again.'

The living room was a trick of compactness. In a moment, two steps, Samhain and David were standing in the hall by the front door, with the early light coming in over the carpet. David tapped Samhain briefly on the shoulder, and lowered his voice. 'Listen,' he said. 'You haven't to worry too much about the mess you've got yourself into. Just – try and put things right with your girlfriend... ex-girlfriend,' he said. 'You'll have to send her a bit of money. Say sorry – that sort of thing. Just, er...' he reached over Samhain for the door handle, and pulled it inwards. It made a quiet electronic chime as it opened. 'You will ring Peter, won't you? It's steady work. Probably just cash in hand at first. But that's not so bad, is it? Something to get you started – and then there's no messing about with tax and stamp, and all the rest of it.'

A foot over the step, into a morning where the sun was coming up fiercely, glaring into his eyes. 'Of course,' Samhain said. 'I'll see you.'

14.

Samhain spent hours looking for Charley on MySpace.

He went through all of his friends. Then through his friends' friends. He typed her name into the search box. Searched using her old email address. He trawled through everybody who had friended the social club, thousands of people. He had booked two computer sessions back to back, to do only this.

When his first search yielded no results, he moved on to looking at photos. Clicking through images of festivals and gigs that she might have gone to. Pictures from the past two D-Beat Festivals at Ypres.

Nothing. Nowhere. She wasn't in any of the photos. She wasn't friends with the club on MySpace, and she wasn't friends with Roxy, or Marta, or Rawlplug, or anyone on there. He couldn't find her picture anywhere and his eyes ached from looking. Hundreds of pictures had flashed in front of him: familiar, smiling faces, skin screwed up through sunburn or drugs, hands clutching shoulders, beer bottles, dog leads; arms around shoulders and grins at the camera, thousands of faces, but no Charley.

'Sir.' A librarian with white hair, and a whispering voice. 'I'm afraid you'll have to log out now. There are people waiting.' Twisting his hands, as though he wasn't sure it was his business to ask.

'Right.' Samhain reached over the desk to take his bag, his hoody, and the scrap of paper he'd been using, which was still blank. He had gone twenty minutes over time, and still had nothing. 'Sorry, I didn't realise I'd gone so far over.'

*

Fox-Eyes wasn't there. She had left him a note, given to him by a purse-lipped woman in a tight black cardigan, whose buttons met like steel armour. She looked at him as though she knew he had been in the back room, and didn't approve one bit.

Samhain,

I stayed a while at CopWatch after you'd left. Titania and Endra and the rest of them were all pretty mad at you. I don't know what you've done and I don't want to know especially, but I said I would help and so here is what I was able to find out.

CopWatch had possession of an inquiry report (don't know how they got that) and a bit of information about a few of the undercover cops working in the UK & Europe at that time. There's not much in the public domain about any of it because the police are trying to cover it up as best they can, but from what I was able to find out, I believe your father may have been one of two men.

Titania gave me some info about two possibilities who were undercover in D.G.R and Greenpeace in the late 70s and early 80s. The Met have denied all knowledge of either of them which she says is a good sign and probably means that they were undercover cops for sure. Apparently it is S.O.P. (standard operating procedure) for the Met to deny all knowledge.

Possibility 1:

Undercover alias Graham Porter (also used the nickname 'Fields' – this may be the name your mother knew him by), real name Graeme Stokes, d.o.b. 24.4.1953, Kilkenny, Ireland. This man was in the Greater Manchester Police in 1971-76 and the campaign group believe he then joined the SDS, an undercover police unit who specialised in infiltrating radical protest groups.

There is a birth and death certificate for Graham Porter (d.o.b. 09.09.1953 and d.o.d. 31.1.1958.) This is because SDS operatives used the identities of dead children to create their new, undercover identities. It appears that Graeme Stokes and 'Graham Porter' (a.k.a. 'Fields') are one and the same person. Graeme Stokes was married to a woman whose maiden name was Annie Crump and had two children called Gareth Stokes (b. 1980) and James Stokes (b. 1984). I can help you find marriage/birth certificates for all of these people if need be, but it is also likely that even if you are related, none of them even know you exist.

Possibility 2:

Undercover alias Jimbo Cobb, real name James Tibbs, d.o.b. 18.12.1958, Nottingham, England. Tibbs seems to have been an ordinary beat officer from 1979-81 until apparently 'disappearing' from the force (this is a hallmark of somebody going to join the SDS, Titania said.) I'm not sure the dates on this one completely match up but you or your mother would know more about this than me – I've been told 'Jimbo' travelled around northern Europe with various Deep Green Resistance Groups and was active in the Free Party Movement in the UK.

The campaign group think Tibbs married in the late 80s after *ending his deployment, but nobody seems completely sure; he seems to be a bit of a shadowy figure who may have fathered a child in the late 80s with one of his old activist friends (again, nobody seems sure about this) and there are rumours he had a breakdown, left the force and went back to his old life as an activist in his 50s. He may be living in Bristol.*

Again, if you think this may be the right one, I can help you find birth/marriage certificates, etc. to track him down.

Best thing for you to do next is probably to ask your mum which one it is. Now that you know their real names, it should make tracking him down a whole lot easier.

I'm sorry I wasn't able to get a photo of either of them for you. Titania was going to have a look through all of her stuff to see if she could find anything. I told her it was for somebody who had come into the library, not you.

It's probably best that I keep this link going. Titania seems to know a lot about all of these cases and she was able to get most of this information without even blinking an eye...

Samhain, sitting in a chair by the stacks, read the short article over and over again.

Graham Porter, also known as Fields. Jimbo Cobb. He couldn't remember Flores ever having mentioned either of these names.

He sat at the table by the window, turning the note over and over. She'd used good paper, ivory-toned, thick as parchment, and it clicked and rattled seriously in his hands.

One of these men was his father. Either a guy who'd had another little boy the same age as Sam, a boy growing up in a carpeted house who played the trumpet and went to judo, or a guy who'd stumbled from one life to another, and then had come back to anarchism, never fully been able to leave the life behind.

Samhain folded the note twice, slipped it between the pages of a fanzine, and got up to go.

*

Roxy was slicing a loaf vigorously in the hotel kitchen. 'Oh,' she said. 'It's you.' Her voice was colourless.

'I'm sorry,' he said, though he didn't know what for.

She hardly looked at him. 'Why?' She had made a mistake cutting the bread and it had torn. There were crumbs the size of asteroids all over the worktop.

'Don't leave that lying around. We've got mice.'

'I won't.' Roxy thumped together a breezeblock sandwich, and walked away, leaving the rest of the loaf on the side.

'Roxy. Can I ask you something?'

She threw herself down hard onto the banquette in the bar. Sighed, chewing hard. Perhaps she had already stopped listening. 'I can tell you're going to, whether I like it or not.'

'Do you know how I can get in touch with Charley? I can't find her anywhere on MySpace.'

Now, though eating, he saw her smile – on one side, the side that faced away. 'We wondered when this was going to come up.' She ate a bite the same way a snake might swallow a mouse, whole. 'Me and Charley.'

'What?' The last time he had seen Charley, she had used the words slut, whore, skank, slag, bitch – words she never used – but she had thrown them all out, and meant them all, every single one, about Roxy. 'Are you two *friends* now?'

Nodding, chewing, swallowing. 'She came to Fov's fanzine workshop at the Sheffield zine fair last year. And I was there as well – because I was helping him – carrying the boxes, the typewriter, the paper and glue, all of that. You remember?'

'But Charley hates you,' he said.

'Wrong, Sam.' More chewing, swallowing. 'Charley hates *you*.' She went on: 'She was thinking about writing a zine about being an anarchist single parent, and she wanted to come along and get some ideas. I don't think she ever did it, in the end. But we spent most of the workshop talking about it.' Roxy brushed her fingers clean. 'She's really nice though, isn't she, Charley? I never really realised how great she was before.'

'But that was last year.'

'Yeah, that's it.'

'So you mean to say, you've known about her all this time, and you never said a thing?'

'Well, she sort of...' Roxy looked around on the floor. 'She sort of made me promise not to say anything. Until she'd decided how she wanted to play it.'

'Are you fucking—' he was up; he wanted to flip a table over. 'Are you fucking kidding me?'

'Well, no. You always said you never wanted to be tied down.' She was up now, and shouting. Though Roxy was small, there was something terrifying about her. A hand grenade in a strappy vest top. 'So what the fuck else did you want? We gave you what you asked for.'

He grabbed the table edges, to keep his hands occupied. 'My *daughter*, you dick. How could you think I wouldn't want to know?'

'What I think, is that if you don't want to have babies, maybe you shouldn't go around fucking different girls all the time. You were bound to have one eventually, the way you put it about. You could have kept it in your pants, but you never bothered. Instead you've got babies and ex-girlfriends all over town, all over the world, probably, for all I know. But you can't keep it to yourself. Everybody knows that.'

Months.

He paced the floor.

Glasses behind the bar. All shelved and ready to smash. He could run an arm along the wood and break every last one.

He didn't.

Months.

Roxy had known about Astrid when they'd invited her to move in there. When he was out nights, early hours of the morning, looking for a new place to break.

When they'd been evicted from the squat before last, and walking the streets with bags over their arms and sleeping bags in a shopping trolley, looking for a place to stay. And Roxy had said, It's ok, you can move into my place, and then all sorts of people had started moving in, until it became an overcrowded slum. She had known then.

'When did you take those pictures? The ones you showed me.'

Roxy shrugged. 'Of Charley and Astrid? I don't know. About a month ago, maybe?'

'Is that her name?'

A month. Who knows what he had been doing when they had been taken. Messaging Marta at the library. Out scavenging in the restaurants suppliers' bins, looking for something to eat. Whilst Roxy was sitting round at Charley's place – wherever that was, laughing and joking, with a cup of tea on the table and his daughter on her knee. Having a good laugh with Charley about Samhain. Roxy had cuddled his daughter, played with her on the floor – maybe even taken her out for the day. She'd done things with Astrid that Samhain had never been able to do himself, because he hadn't even known she existed.

'Fuck me, Roxy. All this time you've known. Where do they live?'

She circled the table, eyeliner smudged, as though she'd been punched twice. 'I can't tell you anything, Sam. I promised.'

'I have a right to know.'

A mirthless laugh, sharp, like a tight snare. 'Listen to you, talking about rights. Are you going to be a responsible father now? You? The man who's never had a job in his life?'

'You never even gave me a chance.' If he had known, he would have done something about it. Taken a job working in a kitchen. Worked in a shop. Anything. 'Now that I know—'

'Samhain.' Tears dribbled down her face, bringing the black with them. She wiped it with the back of her hand, causing a smudge that made her look like a Vaudeville hooker. 'You can't even look after a cat. How would you manage with a child?'

'She's mine,' he said. 'And I can look after a cat. I've got the food for it, and everything. Mart brought it all over.'

'That's exactly it,' she said. '*Mart* brought the food around. And *Mart* brought the toys. And *Mart* taught you how to look after them. Can you see a pattern at all there, Sam? You've got the women in your life cleaning up and looking after you as though you're not much more than a kid yourself. And here you are, saying that you think looking after a cat is the same as looking after a child. See – this is exactly why Charley didn't want you to know.'

'You two-faced bitch.' All those nights when he'd said goodnight to Roxy at the door. When she had worn a sad, desperate look, wanting to come in, and he had sent her away. 'Don't do this, Roxy. Can't you tell Charley—'

'God, Sam. You think you can treat people any way you like.' Tears again. 'And people will just go, "Oh, that's Sam for you." As though you can go around doing whatever you want. But these things have consequences, Sam. Everything you do has an effect. The way you've treated Charley – the way you've treated me. You've shown us over and over again that you're not to be relied upon, that you can't be trusted.'

He hated when girls cried, and yet they were always doing it. 'Come here,' he said, reaching out for a hug. At least this way, he wouldn't have to look at her.

'No.' She pushed him away. 'You need to get your arse in gear, Sam. You can't just expect everything to work itself out.'

'I know that.' He felt into his pocket for the slip of paper David had given him. 'I'm getting a job soon. Then I'll have some money, and I can start sending some to Charley. That'll be the first thing.'

She laughed, shaking her head. 'You think it's all so simple.'

'Roxy, I'm not going to let her grow up without a dad.'

'Right.' There was the look, the defiance, the I Don't Care. As though she was looking down on everything being said from a stage four feet up. 'Do whatever you want.' He saw then that he had lost her. That this girl, standing in the bar, wasn't the same girl who'd been in his bed, begging him to love her. This was not the girl with the doe eyes, soft and forgiving, and all giggly afterwards. This Roxy was a new Roxy – one who thought he was an idiot.

No wonder, when she'd been taking him for a fool all these months, and he hadn't known a thing about it.

'Christ,' he said. 'Christ.'

'What now?'

He let go of the table, and picked his things up from the floor. 'I can't stand to be around you,' he said.

15.

11/8 Krusthaus Squat, Berlin
12/8 Rock Bar, Switzerland
13/8 Los Amenos Squat, Utrecht w/ Patrick Stewart The Band
14/8 ???? (try to get gig somewhere)
15/8 Boggy's Bar, Luxembourg (matinee show)
16/8 Frietag Hus, Koln
17/8 Solidarity Squat, Salzburg, w/ Patrick Stewart The Band
18/8 ???? (day off in Salzburg? Try to get gig)
19/8 HOME

t-shirts & records
Sleeping bag
PASSPORT

The kitties were havoc. They'd move around the room as he was counting them, so he wouldn't know whether he'd counted the one ginger kitten twice, or each ginger kitten once. He was trying to keep them all in one place, for now – his bedroom – until they'd had their jabs.

'Should let them out of here,' Frankie said. 'Get our mouse problem sorted.' Frankie carefully folded a lyric sheet down one side, then another, until the sheet folded neatly enough to fit inside the CD sleeve.

Frankie had spent a long time drawing the sheet until this would work. There was a way of folding it just so, so that the lyrics to *Estamos en Todas Partes* faced outwards, making the cover. The band had all agreed that *Estamos* was the song that should be on the front.

'No way.' Samhain's job was to slide the CD in afterwards, and add a sticker to each package.

In all 200 of them.

'Jesus, boy, you're wrinkling the covers. Come on. Look how bloody wonky you are all down that side, lad.'

'Looks alright to me.'

'You've got to get the edges straight. Like this, look. Won't fit in the sleeve if you don't fold them exactly right. Buck up.' He put his new one onto the high stack on the floor. The calico kitten pounced for his hand, and CD sleeves slid all over the floor. 'Christ,' Frankie said. 'Hope euro crust punks like cat hair, because there's going to be a free sample with every copy.'

'They're too young to go out.' Samhain had read, in a book from the library, that male kittens get into fights and get lost, and female kittens come home having made more kittens. If they so much as smelled the fresh air, he'd never get them back.

Animals this small could get through anything, or out for that matter. And when Frankie was home, the front or back door almost always seemed to be open. A young cat might pounce out of it while playing at something else, chasing a bit of dust or a buzzing insect or anything, and have the door closed after them by somebody who didn't notice they'd gone. At least up here, all the way up in Samhain's bedroom, they were a long way from being able to get out.

'They can't go out until they've been fixed,' he said. 'Otherwise they'll get themselves into trouble.'

'Oh really? That reminds me of somebody I know.' Frankie was down on the floor, pushing wayward sleeves back together. 'Dickhead.'

'We'll take you down the PDSA in your kitty box. Get you neutered. It's free for doleys on a Tuesday and Wednesday.' Frankie opened another spindle of CDs, and looked around for the stickers. 'What about when we're away – you done anything about that?'

'I don't know. I've had so much to think about.'

'Can't leave 'em home alone, boyo. Little tinkers like this. Starve to death. And your mate Roxy's not doing you any favours, is she?' The black splodged kitty had its chin stretched over Frankie's index finger, closing its eyes. Stretching its neck so far forward, it looked as though it might lose balance any moment.

'I might ask Mart.'

'Serious? Think Mart's going to want to come and live here – nice girl like that – sleeping in your stinking bed?' Frankie looked up, grinning. 'You're off your head, son.'

'Plenty of other rooms. She doesn't have to stay in this one.' Samhain reached for one of the CDs. 'Look smart, don't they?'

'Doesn't sound bad, either.'

They'd recorded it in their practice space, a black-walled, low ceilinged room in the social club basement, with a couple of microphones and the drummer's laptop. It had come out lo-fi and overdriven, buzzing with nasty digital distortion and mystery metallic clicking noises, the musicianship amateurish at best. Frankie had had his pedal turned up too high, so that in the loud parts, the tiny computer speakers rattled and buzzed painfully. There hadn't been time to record it over again.

It was live and furious and pretty shambolic – a completely fair representation of their actual show.

'Think about it,' Samhain said. 'We need somebody to look after the squat while we're away. And it can't be somebody who'll invite a load of twats over to get pissed up on old Kahlua. How many people do we know like that?'

'Just one.' Frankie reached into the t-shirt box, pulling out shirt after shirt. 'Are any of these ok for sale, or – Christ.' He pulled out the blood-hardened last men's medium, and dropped it onto the floor, shuddering. 'You could have warned me.'

'Sorry.'

'Look, if you want to ask her, just ask her. She can only say no, right?' Frankie pulled out the one remaining decent shirt, black, mostly clean but for a mane of cat fur around its collar. 'Oh great, men's XL. Nobody ever wants XL. We'll end up dragging this all the way around Europe and all the way home again.' He dropped it back in the box. 'But whatever you do, even if you ask Mart, you should check with Roxy first. She's the one who's going to have to live with her.'

'You talk to Roxy.' Samhain put a bend in the box without really meaning to: his hand came down harder than he intended. 'I'm never speaking to her again.'

Frankie was busy with the merchandise, occupied in putting things right. Shuffling and stacking CDs into a neat pile, and propping them down in place with the shirts. 'Come on. Don't be so hard on her. She was in a tough position.'

'Not nearly as tough as me. She should have said something.'

'Yes, but–' Frankie faced away, picking something up from the floor. 'Why do you think she'd do a thing like that?'

'Fuck knows, but it sounds like her and Charley have been having a good laugh about it all behind my back. Here, better use that other box instead. I've just put a big hole in the side of this one.'

'The one with the cat in it?' Frankie looked distracted: he was trying to get Mama Cat out of the old box, and into the new one, and she didn't want to go. She slid from his hands, and settled back into the box she liked. 'Nope,' he said. 'They'll never do what you want them to, will they? Here, you have a go.'

'She won't even talk to me,' Samhain said. 'Charley won't. I can't find her on MySpace anywhere. And god knows what Roxy's been saying to her, because from what she said, it sounds like they're *mates* now. She won't even give me her number. So you tell me – what am I supposed to do?'

'I don't know. Maybe get a lawyer?'

'What with?'

Two kittens stalked each other around the CD spindle. Ginger kitten pounced, making a prey of the calico kitten's tail. They rolled, wrestling, gummily biting each other's ears.

'You never know. Maybe she'll change her mind.' Frankie was struggling with wonky folds on some of the covers, and it seemed to be costing him some effort. Flattening, refolding carefully, pressing the new line down, over and over, to make it stick. 'You know how girls are. It's all one thing one day and something else the next. She'll come around.'

'You think?'

'I know so. Of course she will – Charley's not going to keep you away from your daughter forever. I mean, we both know she's mad. But she's not that mad.' Frankie was really engaged in the folding now, looking hard down at the crease. 'And you know that whatever happens – I'll always be right behind you.'

16.

The lady of the house looked on, holding a clean white Westie firmly under one arm.

'Careful around the doorway,' Samhain's new workmate, Kebby, called.

Samhain lunged, groaned, trying to move one end of the Welsh dresser around the front door without catching any corners. When they'd designed this house, they'd done it without thinking about furniture coming in and out. The stairs were not far from the side door, and the hallway was shallow and awkward. Everything came through this narrow crick of hallway around the front door.

The lady winced. '*Please* be careful. That piece came from my great-grandfather. It's been in the family years – totally irreplaceable...' she shielded the dog's eyes: 'I'm saving it for my granddaughter.'

'Perhaps you'd be more comfortable waiting in the

kitchen, madam?'

Samhain's workmate Kebby was more than a lad. A man really, father, and a grandfather. All tough hands and tight afro hair turning wiry grey and white. He had the sort of face that invited children to climb up on his knee. 'We haven't packed the kettle yet – you could make yourself a cup of tea.'

'You're right. And I'm being terribly rude.' She half-jumped, hand fluttering. 'I should have offered to make you all a drink hours ago. What would you like – tea? Coffee?'

And Kebby also had this way about him that could get the customers to do anything he asked, even though he was a paid hand, just like Samhain.

'Nothing, thanks,' Kebby said. 'We have a lot still do to. We won't hold everything up by stopping.'

These men had a long-standing system.

Always clear the upstairs first, to get the legwork out of the way. Then the same at the other end, as best you can. There were still boxes in the kitchen and living room, and three of them, on this job: Samhain and Kebby and another lad called Simon, who always went off to the gym as soon as they knocked off at night. Kebby ribbed him about it: 'I don't like to make Simon work too hard,' he said. 'That way he can save his energy, and get his money's worth from his gym membership.'

The money wasn't bad either, £60 per day, cash in hand. All there was to it was brute force, moving things from one place to another.

'Would you do something important?' Kebby asked. 'Could you go upstairs and do one last check?'

Empty rooms.

Samhain ran up the wooden stairs. He stood on the blank floors, around what had been the bedroom. Space, now, and sun glowed through the windows.

In here, a double bed and standard lamps and matching

bedside tables had all been pushed into the middle of the room, ready to go. Kebby had told him that it wasn't always like that. Lamps standing slightly away from the walls, with their electrical cords wrapped around them like tails. He didn't know the names of these clients, but they'd had all of their soft furnishings, including the duvet cover, in a soft, gauzy brown fabric. And now that, like all of it, was downstairs in the van.

There was nothing left. Just dust, visible in balls around the skirting. Grey mites and hair. Little scraps of paper, splashes of dropped coffee, single buttons. Signs that said, we were here.

'Sam.' Kebby's voice echoed up the stairs. 'When you've got a minute, maybe you could come back down here.'

Downstairs, boxes and boxes and boxes and boxes. Plates wrapped and folded and packed in newsprint. Others a rattling symphony of egg whisks and spatulas. 'Get a move on,' Kebby said. 'We can't hold these good people up from moving into their new place.'

The lady of the house perched in the bay window, feeding the dog treats, and Samhain picked up a box that was far heavier than it looked.

'Books,' she said. The dog barked and licked her fingers. 'I'm sorry, they must be terribly heavy. I'm afraid I couldn't bear to part with any of them. Here, let me get the door.'

'Not necessary,' Kebby said, but she hopped over to the far side of the room anyway, and placed her hand on the already open door.

'You see, it's only myself and my husband in the house now,' she said. 'No good us rattling around in a house this size.'

Her voice grew louder, more pointed, as Samhain took the box outside.

They were moving these two in one of the largest vans Peter had. Samhain shoved the box on the tailgate, and looked resentfully at the wardrobe from upstairs that had nearly done his back in; the dozen or so boxes of clothes and shoes that had come from the wardrobe, things with their smell of soap and dust and mothballs, things they must have been keeping around them for years, in drawers and cupboards which they probably never opened. The van was already three quarters full, and there was plenty more to come.

All this stuff, for two people and a dog.

'Come on, dreamboat,' Kebby said, pushing a box into the back with a grunt. 'You're not at a yard sale.'

They settled into the van. Kebby driving, and Samhain in the middle seat.

He had the map open on his lap. It was two page turns to the new house.

'This book,' Kebby said, jabbing a finger at the A-Z, 'will become your very best friend, if you want to stay a removals man.'

'Kebby ever tell you about the time we spent an hour driving around Hawes Industrial Estate looking for a four-bedroom detached house?' This was Simon, on Samhain's other side, texting.

'Simon ever tell you about the time he was looking for Sleaseby in an A-Z on the wrong bloody county?' The engine roared into life. 'Now wave bye-bye, everybody, the lady's waiting.'

And so she was. On the doorstep of her old home, dog in her arms, whipping its tail against her bosom.

'Turn right at the end,' Samhain said. It was his third day in the job, and muscles he didn't even know he had were troubling him. Forearms, upper arms, thighs, the small of his back, the large of his back; cricks in his wrists and fingers and small muscles in his chest and underarm – every time he moved, some new part of him hurt.

'Peter's just text me,' Simon says. 'About another job tomorrow. He says she's got a load of stuff.'

'I hope you're in this for the long haul,' Kebby said. 'Which exit now?'

'Rather a lot of stuff' was right. It was like moving a museum.

Up four flights of stairs to a cramped flat on the fifth floor, every inch of it crammed with costumes and feathers, metal that glinted.

Everywhere he looked, something caught a dim glowing light. The lady had not one, but two, large wire bird cages – both empty; a stuffed kestrel on a plinth, a mannequin in a tutu and leotard. He looked more closely at a canvas framed in textured gilt. It was a frightening old painting of a man with sharp eyes.

'Be careful, won't you?'

She was a highly-painted woman, pale-faced and with red lips. She moved slowly, like a large ship. If he'd had to guess her age, Samhain might have said the mischief in her eyes put her at about twenty-five. But then, how could she have collected all this if she was anything less than forty?

'It might look like a load of old junk, but to me, it's important.'

'We're always careful,' Kebby said.

In the bedroom was a rosewood sleigh bed, its covers thrown back and left unmade. A rose red, deep, pulled silk cover, and two wardrobes packed with full-skirted, highly boned clothes, like Victorian circus costumes.

Had Samhain been on his own, he wouldn't have even known where to start.

'Get the boxes,' Kebby said. 'Let's get on with this.'

Gathering things was pointless. Or that was how it had always seemed, to Samhain. It was no use accumulating things, bedding down, when he might have had to move again at a moment's notice. Every extra thing was a weight to carry from one place to the next. Things held you down, like muddy boots in a quagmire.

'Which road do I want?' Kebby barked. 'A58 or A660?'

'A58. Westbound,' Sam answered.

And now they were moving over the tarmac, the back of the van full to rattling with just one woman's things; things in the back knocked and made soft thumps when the van went over a pot hole. If there had been a piano on the tailgate, they might have heard the keys playing themselves.

She had said, 'Be careful – that was my mother's table.'

It was not the antique value of things that worried the woman, but the memories. A table that had come from her mother's house. A mirror bought in a flea-market. Dresses bought for student drama productions. It was those memories, not the wood or fabric themselves, that mattered.

Over the course of too many moves, Samhain had lost even the goggles a kind stranger had given to him in Genoa. He didn't even have a picture frame, never mind a picture.

He wondered how long it would be before he lost the bit of information he had about Graeme Stokes.

'I'll never understand why people end up with so much stuff,' he said.

'That's because you're a removals man now,' Kebby said. 'Every time your girlfriend wants to buy furniture, you'll look at it and think – I'm going to have to move that again. You'll never want to buy any furniture again, especially not if it's heavy.'

'Always the way,' Simon echoed.

'Always the way,' Kebby agreed.

'Time off!' Simon hooted. 'You hear that, Kebby? He's only been here three days, and already he's talking about time off.'

Past new build apartments. Low, two stories, with wood-slat

sides. They were down a dip, then up a side road, and along a long country lane with overhanging trees. All green, like the inside of a tent.

'Are you worn out already?' Kebby said. 'My God, and we thought you were a keeper. We were telling Peter all about how great you were. Now he's talking about abandoning us. Getting out! Making his excuses!' Out into the open: broad golden fields of rapeseed, yellow as hi-vis, a brightness to make your eyes ache. They passed sheep, then a trio of horses wearing jackets. 'Do you have good reason, Samhain?' His eyes were still fixed on the road: he spoke without turning.

'Going on tour with my band.'

'A tour!' Kebby's face opened into a huge, beaming smile. 'Well, that, you can't miss. It's a once-in-a-lifetime opportunity.'

'My brother-in-law plays in a band,' Simon said. 'They're great. They do Mustang Sally, Come on Eileen... what else... all the songs from The Commitments, actually. They played my mum's wedding reception.'

'I was in a band.' Kebby had gone all nostalgic; he was looking at the road as though it were an old photograph. 'We supported Janet Kay at the Irish Centre.'

'Who?'

'Oh, come on. Janet Kay. You know Janet Kay – Silly Games? Of course you know her songs. She was a huge star. Then another time, we played at the same festival as Thomas Mapfumo. The Thomas Mapfumo!'

'Never heard of him.'

'Thomas Mapfumo – you've never heard of Thomas Mapfumo? The biggest jit-jive star ever to come out of Zimbabwe – and you don't know who he is?' Kebby shook his head. 'Look it up!'

'I didn't know you were in a band,' Simon said.

'I played the drums.' Kebby thumped a paradiddle on the

wheel. 'I had a Tama kit with pink sparkle, and nobody could heat it up like me – nobody. "Kebby could get a dead man dancing," that was what people used to say.'

'Your drums were *pink*?'

'Yeah!' They were up on the hilltop now, and in the spread beneath them opened up a village of stone houses. 'Nobody else had pink drums. Mine was the coolest kit anybody had. Where do I turn?'

'After Aystalby Shelf.'

'Right. So you see, Mr Foss, you're not the only one with musical talents. I had my own band, and after that, I did a stint on the cruise ships. All the standards – These Foolish Things, Take Five, you know the kind of stuff. Every evening, whilst the posh ladies and their husbands were eating their dinner. Very well paid, good money, far more than I ever earned when I was playing in my own band. And you're stuck there on the boat, so you can't spend any of your earnings. Everything's paid for – room, board – you even got your meals for free.

'When I came back to dry land, I had hundreds in the bank. Thousands, actually. And Gloria said, we should use that money to put a deposit on a house, not just spend it on this and that, so that in a year we've got nothing again. That must have been in 1986.'

'And now look at him,' Simon said.

'Comfortable for almost twenty years now. Far better than throwing your money away on rent.'

'But don't you miss going on tour?' Samhain asked.

'Which part?' Kebby turned, eyes wide. 'Carrying a drum kit out of a stage door up two flights of slippery steps at two in the morning? Sleeping in the back of a van with all of the amps and guitars? Trying to catch the promoter to make him pay your fee? Waking up with a mouth tasting of old carpet?' Kebby shook his head. 'Anyway, we had Ayesha, and after she came along, I wasn't so keen on spending time away from home anymore.'

There was a church up ahead, a pale grey thing with a pretty gold clock. In front of it was a bench, with a laminated sheet strapped to its beams with clip ties. An old lady in a heather-coloured Barbour studied the village noticeboard.

'This must be the place,' Kebby said.

Simon waved his mobile around the cab. 'Awww, man. I could not live in a place like this.'

'No signal?'

'That, and only one pub, look.' Simon set his phone down on the dash. 'Here Sam, you should bring your band's CD in to work. We could listen to it in the van.'

'I don't know if you'd like it,' Samhain said.

'Of course we will.'

Down the village's only side street, and past the village Primary school. Sunflowers grew in stacked tyres behind a chain-link fence. It was a small building, not much bigger than a through-terrace. A little girl with blonde hair stared sombrely out of the window.

A moment later another of the children was up, a boy wearing the same dark-green jumper as the girl: greasy fingers sticking to the glass, as he jumped up and down.

'I really don't think you would.'

'Couldn't be any worse than some of Kebby's CDs.'

'Well, OK then. If you insist.' Samhain was still watching the classroom window as a teacher came and took the boy away from the window, while the girl still looked, holding her pencil tight.

17.

'Keep this door closed – they're so small, and one of them could easily sneak out. And they're too young to go out yet.'

'Right.' Marta was on the bed, sitting with the black one on her knee. Its hind legs were splayed over her tights, and it was guzzling her finger.

'There's two litter trays,' Samhain said. 'One here – and another one in here,' opening the wardrobe door, 'and I think I've got homes for two of them, but since they're not going to be rehomed until I get back from tour, there's no rush. They can't really be separated from their mother until they're nine weeks old, anyway.'

'You've got it all figured out.'

'Yeah, well.' Samhain looked around for the pound shop nappy bags. 'They're my responsibility, aren't they? I read up all about it in the library. They chose me. And now I've got to look after them. If the smell gets really bad – which it does sometimes, with there being so many of them – you can always open the top window. There's no way any of them can get out that way, it's too high up. I leave it open when I go out, sometimes. It's perfectly safe.'

'Sam.' Mart lifted the kitten off her knee, and set it pouncing all over the floor. 'Are you sure you should be doing this?'

'What?'

He was busy trying to get the one last good t-shirt out from under Mama Cat. She had chosen it for bedding, all curled up with her paws underneath, like a town hall lion. Slowly, slowly, he rocked it, and her with it, side to side.

She stuck a paw on the fabric, claws sharp, and stared at him with narrowed eyes.

'Going away on tour. I mean, maybe it's not the best timing. With Astrid, and everything.'

'Wouldn't make any difference if I didn't, would it? Charley still hasn't said I can see her, so I don't see why I should stick around. Might as well go.' He stopped work on the shirt, scratching Mama Cat behind the ears. 'Anyway, it's been booked for ages, and Frankie's so excited about going. I can't let him down, or Stick. It's not easy for Stick to book time off work.'

She was a beautiful cat alright. Deep, almost emerald eyes, with markings that looked like eyeliner. Mama Cat was a Cleopatra among strays.

'Well, do what you want,' she said. 'But I think you should stick around. Work a bit more – earn more money – try and get things sorted out.'

'It won't make any difference,' he said again. 'What am I supposed to do, when Charley won't even talk to me? She hasn't even got MySpace, or if she has, she's blocked me.' He watched the calico kitten tumble with both paws on the ball: it seemed to be trying to climb the string, as though it were a ladder. 'Has she even *got* MySpace?'

'Sam.' Carefully, slowly, she drew a toy mouse along the carpet, pulling it by the tail. Mart seemed to be choosing her words carefully. 'Look, like I said, it's up to you what you do. All I'm saying is, since Charley had Astrid, her life's different. It's not like when you knew her. She can't go out to gigs all the time, or run the cafe in the club every week, like she used to. When you've got a child – you can't do whatever you want, whenever you feel like it. Whatever Charley does, she always has to think about Astrid first, and how it'll affect her. I mean, she never complains, but it must have been a struggle, with money and everything. Doing everything on her own.'

'Yeah, well – that was her choice. I would have sent her money, if I'd known. She didn't have to do it all herself.'

Samhain was petulant, but what Mart had said about the club kitchen stuck.

He couldn't think of the club cafe without also thinking of Charley. She had always seemed to be there, behind the counter. The club was just a doorway in a wall, and behind that, up a tiny set of stairs, was a bar and a gig room, and upstairs from that, an occasional library made out of a donated bookcase and an old typewriter whose keys stuck. The kitchen was in an alcove on the second floor. Volunteers ran a cafe from four gas rings and a sink, especially Charley, always standing there with a spatula in her hand and a smile on her face.

She had always been trying something new. Grating cabbage for some new recipe she wanted to try. Their kitchen had always been full of herbs.

When bands played in the gig room downstairs, you could hear it all over the building, and Charley would take orders shouted over the noise. She had run that cafe every Tuesday night for years. And when she wasn't doing that, she was volunteering behind the bar, or joining in with some two-pence shout-your-opinion group, or organising a book fair, or getting involved with anything else. You couldn't have paid Charley to keep her hands still, even if she had been interested in money.

'Wait,' he said. 'So you're saying Charley doesn't cook anymore?'

'Hasn't done for a couple of years.'

'So that's why she never was in the club.'

Samhain had been in plenty, drinking. He went in to watch gigs, or drink in the bar after band practice. In the months following their break-up, he'd peeked in on a Tuesday night a few times, expecting she'd be there, working in the cafe. He had hoped for a talk – some kind of reconciliation. Forgiveness. But she had never been there, and he had started to think that heartbreak and anger kept her away from this place, the club she loved so much. His Sent Items folder told him, most mornings after, that he had texted. *I miss you* and *I wish we were still friends* and *Just text me back to say that you don't hate me, at least.* But Charley never messaged back. Samhain had thought, Boy, this girl has really got it in for me.

It had never occurred to him that there might have been any other reason.

'Christ.' He flicked fur shedding from Mama Cat's winter coat. 'But she always loved that place. And she stayed away, all that time. How…'

'How what?'

'Never mind.'

A secret kept, that big, was a conspiracy the size of everybody he knew. The things Samhain knew about people he'd barely even met. What they shouted when they came, their secret phobias of balloons or coat hangers – who slept with their feet inside the covers all night. He knew things about people he'd only ever seen once or twice. In their community, everybody knew everything about everybody, and a baby wasn't exactly a small thing.

Yet it was the kind of thing that could make a person disappear from the scene, the same way Flores had. Grabbing him out of the dirt and bringing him back across Europe in the bike trailer, on the cheap coach, without so much as a glance back. Their sudden vanishment must also have left a hole in the work rotas. Suddenly, the organising group would be missing somebody who always worked Tuesdays, or who always chaired the shouty opinion group. Somebody disappearing out of the rotas quickly was the kind of thing that made people talk.

Yet nobody had. Or at least, not to him.

'How does she manage it? I don't know, Sam, I really don't.' Mart paused. 'I think her mum helps quite a bit. And she's got this boyfriend – Tom, I think they call him.'

'That wasn't what I was going to ask,' he said.

Charley doing all that baby-raising alone, the same way Flores had with him. Being both mother and father. Work that had been so hard that at times it had sent Flores to bed, laying with the curtains drawn and the sheet drawn up over her, like a corpse under its winding sheet.

Men had kept on turning up. Holding carrier bags, looking hopeful, beers clinking inside. Flores told him to send them away. She used to put the chain on the door after them.

The sound of rattling links through the apse, that was the sound that said No More Questions, Samhain.

Panzo was the only one who came back and back and back and back. Panzo was the only one she would ever let in, though warily, never allowing him to stay overnight. He understood now, about Flores' mistrust.

The ginger kitten pounced after his hoodie strings. He tried to grab the little tom, but it twisted and wriggled and bit, trying to get away.

'I can't believe none of you told me. All this time, you've known. You and Roxy. Especially you. Don't you think I had a right to know?'

Mart sighed. She looked around. The black kitten was doing something scratchy against the divan. 'Well – yeah. I suppose you did. Believe me, I don't feel great about my part in this. But I also felt...' she picked the kitty up, and placed it beside its mother. 'I felt as though Charley had rights too. She made us promise. She needed a bit of time away from everything. A bit of time away from all of...'

She gestured around the room. At the t-shirt box on the floor with the cat in it; at Samhain's rucksack laying collapsed against the bed. At the spray of kitty litter thrown over the carpet like sea foam; at fanzines on the bedside table, stacked in a pile of bad origami. '...This.'

Samhain felt as though he were chewing on very sour fruit. 'I thought you were my friend.'

'I am. But I'm Charley's friend too. Sam, she just wanted a bit of time to get over it all, that's all. It took her a while to get her head back together. And then she found out she was pregnant – and she had to try and decide what to do about that. Try and understand, it was a really shitty few months for her.'

'Yes, but–'

'I know it all went on much longer than it probably should have. Maybe she should have told you sooner, but it didn't feel like it was my place to say anything, and Charley got used to having things a certain way. I mean, it wasn't easy, when she was first born – they were both in hospital for a while, because Charley was ill, and then Astrid was ill, and everything in those first few months was chaos. Then once things improved and settled down a bit, she managed to get Astrid into a bit of a routine, and I guess... well... maybe she didn't want any disruptions.'

'Disruptions!' Samhain tossed a pair of fighting kittens off his knee. 'I'm her father, Mart. You know me – I'm an easy-going guy. I could have fitted right in.'

He turned his attention to his bag. Sleeping bag and spare shirt were already packed, and he was wondering whether or not to take a towel.

'I wouldn't have caused any bother.'

Samhain was in the wardrobe bottom. He was looking for a clear plastic wallet, which had in it notes and coins from the last time they'd been to Europe. Enough money to keep him going a few days, until they got paid from the first few gigs. 'She could easily have called me.'

Not that there was much in the wardrobe bottom to hide anything. He pulled out the litter tray, and a pair of old canvas shoes; he put them on the floor, then sat beside them on the carpet, thinking.

'Where the hell is it?' he asked.

'Where's what?'

'My Euro-wallet. It had some money in it for the tour.'

'Where did you last have it?'

'I don't know. A while ago.' Samhain thought. 'In the slum, probably.' He'd had a whole stash of stuff in Roxy's bedside cabinet. Two books, three DVDs – Muriel's Wedding, Pretty in Pink, and Night of the Living Dead, all of which he'd found in a skip in high summer, when the students were moving house – one stripy jumper, and a wallet of notes and coins. 'I'm sure I brought them with me. I wouldn't have thrown them away.'

He rummaged in the wardrobe bottom. Nothing. Had he even put them in there when they came to this place?

Samhain lifted the trainers, sighing. Head starting to hurt, as though it was being rolled flat by a baker.

'Are you really going to go away now?' Marta asked. 'Do you really, really think it's a good idea – at this point?'

'What difference does it make?' Now, thinking back, he realised he couldn't remember having emptied that bedside drawer. The books, the DVDs, the wallet – all left behind, and now belonging to whoever slept in that bed. He and Frankie had been in such a rush to get out, he had only come carrying one bag. That had been all. A single bag slumping against his right shoulder. Tools. Address book. One hoodie. Hardly anything else. 'Shit,' he said.

'So you're sitting there, and you're telling me how much you want to see Astrid, and that you can't believe none of us told you about her, but at the same time you're packing to go off on this stupid squat tour around Belgium, or wherever it is you're going...'

So many people in that place. Always people came and went, needing a place to sleep for one night, maybe two, and then gone. If he had left it there months ago, it certainly would have gone by now. Like the bedroom, occupied by whoever needed a place to sleep, the others would have started rooting through the drawers the moment he and Frankie had come to break this place, to see whether there was anything worth having. Money! That would have slid right into somebody's pockets.

'It's – Jesus, Mart, this has all come as such a shock. First off I find out my dad was an undercover cop, somebody I never knew and now I know why, I can't get in touch with Flores to ask her about it... I never knew my dad, Mart, and now this. I know my little girl's out there somewhere, and she's not going to know her dad either, because Charley won't let me anywhere near her. What am I supposed to do? You can't blame me for wanting to get away for a while.' The trainers stank: not even the kittens would go anywhere near them. He shoved them back in the wardrobe bottom. 'I can't believe it. Of all the stupid, irresponsible–'

'Look, I don't want to be a Polly Piss on Your Chips.' This was a different Mart, a stern Mart, using a voice that could get fifty children sitting, without them even realising they were being told. 'You know I've got a lot of time for you, Sam. You're a great guy. Or at least, you can be, when you want to.'

'I know, Mart,' he said. 'And–'

'Shut up. I'm talking now. You know I don't mind looking after the cats. I've said I don't. I know this has been a rough few weeks for you, right? It's been hard on you and I can't even imagine how some of it must feel. But to be honest with you, I'm starting to see a bit more of what Charley means when she talks about Irresponsible Samhain. Do you think she could run away off to the continent when she was having a baby? You think she could just stop and close her eyes and pretend none of it was happening?'

'But I've already said that she didn't have to–'

'Samhain, quiet. You must see that some of this is your own fault. You treated Charley like shit. You moved into her flat, and only paid rent part of the time. Then you started seeing another girl behind her back, and then you got her pregnant and ran off. Now you're complaining that she's angry and doesn't want to talk to you.'

'I didn't know she was–'

'Shut up, Sam, and listen. You acted like an irresponsible prat, so that's why she treated you like one. And here's the other thing. Then, when it all came out, all you can talk about is how hurt and betrayed *you* feel, and how you can't *believe* nobody told you about Astrid, but instead of trying to get your arse in gear and get yourself sorted out, and trying to make things right with Charley – who has been managing with a baby on her own for two years, don't forget – you're in here, in this dump, looking around for an old Euro-wallet full of coins and notes so you can go away on tour with your band for a fortnight.'

'It doesn't make any difference what I–'

'It does, Sam. It *does*. It bloody well *does* make a difference. All of it makes a difference and all of it matters, and this is exactly why Charley's angry with you – for this sort of thing – can't you see that?' She sighed, and threw the ball of string on the floor. 'Look, Sam, you're my friend. I'm your friend, and I always will be. And that's why I know you'll take this the way it's meant, which is with love, by the way, when I tell you – that you can be a complete fucking idiot sometimes.'

GET IN
THE
VAN

GET IN

THE

VAN

I.

It was a place with pale pink walls and a screen at the front of the room. Eyes half-open and he could feel the light streaming in, really bright, golden, light that said: it is the middle of summer, July, August, and you're here, in the middle of the holidays, here with your head on the school desk while everybody else is in their own bed, sleeping.

He recognised it as being his old primary. One he'd joined mid-term, a few weeks before Easter. Standing at the playground's edge watching while other boys chased, pulling one another to the ground. They already knew each other and he feared it might next be him, lying there in the dirt with grit in his face. Unfamiliar, rough games. He felt it all, laying there in this empty room with his face on the desk, and a slight breeze at his back from the open side door.

Miss Firth, his English teacher in Secondary School, was a woman of odd clothing and very fixed, black hair. The girls called her Panda because of the amount of eyeliner she wore. She was outside the open door, talking to a man who sounded very sure of himself. Samhain couldn't turn his head, but he knew the man's pockets were full of money, and the desk held him down and he was close to closing his eyes against this glinting, beautiful August light.

They both came in, the man bringing with him a smell like an old, tattered piece of cloth. The man trailed her slightly, hand hovering lecherously a couple of inches behind Miss Firth's backside. But he hadn't touched her yet, and Miss Firth seemed not to realise what he was doing.

Sam's throat ached, a soreness that stopped him from saying a word, and they walked around him as though he wasn't even there.

Miss Firth said, 'What are you talking about, Die Hard 2? Look at the number of letters, you idiot!'

It took a moment for Samhain to pull it all together.

Stick was in the seat opposite, head newly shaven, beautiful blue eyes glistening with early tour madness. He was holding up a sheet of paper, slashed through with lines and curves in magic marker. A part-finished demarcation of a splitter van, crudely drawn, was underneath the gaps.

Newly on the road, almost two days into the driving, and they hadn't yet got truly bored.

'Guess again, fucktard,' Stick said.

Samhain looked out onto the road, rubbing his eyes. A six-lane road, concrete and tarmac, neat white lines dividing almost black, completely equal, lanes. 'Where are we?'

'Eh up, sleeping beauty.' Frankie turned his head. 'Finished cleaning the windows, have you?'

'What have I missed?'

Stick gestured at the van floor. Between their feet lay twenty or so finished games of Van Man, their touring version of the game Hang Man. They had first played this game two years ago, on the long drive from Salzburg to Munich, and Frankie liked to say that he had invented it. Though, because Frankie also said that he didn't believe in copyright or bullshit protection of ownership of ideas, other touring bands were welcome to use it without making him any sort of royalty payment. He was generous that way.

'You've missed me nearly reaching my maximum tolerance level for Frankie's shocking level of illiteracy.'

Samhain followed the sheet as Stick moved it around. 'Mean Girls 2,' he said.

'Yes.' Stick pointed the Sharpie at him, triumphantly, and filled in the rest of the letters. 'Die Hard 2, my arse. It's not even the same number of letters.'

'You know I'm dyslexic,' Frankie whined.

They had been up since before five, all of them, spending more than a day on the road already, and all that without yet playing a gig.

'Dyslexic enough to only draw eight spaces for Terminator.' Even with the early start, Stick's skin was new as a petal. The boy was a genetic wonder. Twenty-six, but looking like a lad in his last day at sixth form.

'Anybody want to make a stop?' Lemmers, the driver, threw this over his shoulder. 'I know a little village about half an hour away, with this mom-and-pop bakery that does these great pretzels. All vegan.' Lemmers filled the seat solidly, all bulk and shoulders, in a CND t-shirt that he'd been wearing ever since the Cold War.

'Lemmers,' Frankie shouted. 'The human guidebook! Knows every corner of Europe.'

'I bloody love touring with Lemmers!' Stick called.

'Lemmers!' they chanted. 'Lemmers! Lemmers! Lemmers!'

Romey, the fourth person in the back, who was sitting behind Samhain and had been silent until this point, joined in with the voice of a damp chainsaw starting. 'Lemmers! Lemmers! Lemmers!'

This last, was tour deadweight. Not in the band and unable to drive, Romey was along for the tour, not for any other useful reason. They had brought him along for the sake of their endless affection for him, and pity. Officially, they'd told him he was there to mind and sell the merchandise, because they knew Romey wouldn't come if he'd known they all felt sorry for him. Poor Romey, who lived on his own, had nobody to go away with, and never went anywhere.

'Is that a yes for the stop, then? Because if we don't, it's about another four hours to the squat.'

Their driver was a man who seemed to know every road in Europe without needing to look at a map. Fifteen years of hands on the wheel, driving DIY and punk bands all over the continent, had taught him every place to stop in front of hunger or thirst, each spot with a hidden vegan option, and each place with a clean toilet and sink. You were always safe with Lemmers, the human AA Roadmap.

'Yes, stop,' Samhain said. 'I could do to get a bite.'

After the pretzels, silence.

Stick and Frankie leaned back in their seats, becoming propped-up scarecrows; Stick was further forward than he had been on the earlier leg. Every time they hit a bump in the road, his knees touched Samhain's.

Lemmers had this music on with a girl and a harp. It sounded as though it had been recorded in a barn, and she'd just happened to be singing whilst milking a cow, and the cow was just out of reach of the microphone. You could almost hear it moving its cloven hoof in the straw.

He fell back to sleep, head resting against the window.

Out front of the squat, and four hours later, a rangy man in a falling-apart vest strung rope lights amongst the branches in a large and overgrown garden. He looked as though he might have been stretched on a rack.

'Ah,' he said. 'You must be one of the bands, right? Go in.' Night was starting to fall.

There were two dogs, whip-tailed and dark, with fur that looked like something from a shoe brush. In the kitchen, half a dozen people were occupied in something. A man stirring a steaming stew-pot. A woman stapling fanzines on the table. 'Hello,' they said.

The band passed through, carrying their guitars. Into the hall, past an open doorway with four mattresses on the floor, and they hadn't even got to the gig room, which was down two steps at the end of the corridor, before Lemmers ran into somebody he knew.

'Lemmers!' A man in black jeans and a leather vest, with a bountiful maritime beard, threw ham-hock arms around their driver. 'You old tour dog, you!'

They stood with their arms around each other, slapping backs as though trying to beat the air out of line-caught fish.

'Tonight,' the man said effortfully, with a thick accent, 'tonight, we drink!' He produced a bottle of Buckfast, smiling. 'I want all of you to feel at home,' he went on. 'Because any friend of Lemmers, is a friend of mine. Glasses!' he roared. 'Welcome to my restaurant!'

Off he went, wobbling towards the kitchen.

Somewhere between locking the van and arriving at the bottom of the stairs, Lemmers' bushy hair seemed to have sprung up like a lion's. 'Lukas,' he said, by way of explanation. 'Old friend.'

'Now, then.' The friend reappeared. Shot glass, wine glass, highball, mug, mug, tumbler, shot. Lukas carried a tray of mismatched and still good-enough glasses, each brimming with maroon liquid. 'Fine service, for fine people.' He gave each willing hand a drink. 'Cheers!'

Frankie was wearing a louche grin, like a man just freed from jail. 'Well, Lemmers, all I'll say is this. If we keep on bumping into your friends on this tour, we are all going to have a very, very, very, very...' he paused, to knock the Buckie back from the shot glass, and winced: 'A *very* good time.'

'Friends of yours brought this.' The friend leaned over, to refill the glasses. 'You know the boys from Patrick Stewart The Band? Came through here, two days ago. No job too big, they said, if it is going to help our friend the legendary Lemmers.'

'Lemmers! Lemmers! Lemmers! Lemmers!' Romey began chanting. 'Lemmers! Lemmers! Lemmers! Lemmers!'

This, Samhain said to himself as he raised his glass and then sank it, this is touring. He watched a grin spread, warm as marmalade on toast, over Romey's worried, tense little face. Smiles equally spreading over Frankie and Stick's faces, as though out here and among friends, their worries had all melted away, like sugar in tea. This, he told himself, this is what true happiness is. 'Lemmers! Lemmers! Lemmers! Lemmers!' he shouted.

The dogs yapped and barked, chasing their tails.

That night was the clearest sound they'd ever had.

He didn't know how she'd done it, the girl. Kick drum thumping through the speakers; his and Frankie's guitars separate, and distinguishable. He could hear his own voice coming back to him through a monitor by his feet.

Frankie's too, more thick and raspy than ever, by the speaker just next to him, and Samhain started to think, funny that it should sound so close, when Frankie is all the way over there –

by the windows.

The crowd were all right up in it, tattooed black sleeves and dancing. A woman with grey dreadlocks had a can in her hand and her arm in the air; face all mushed up, and smiling.

A man – fat, bald and shiny – stood aside from the throng, singing every single word. They were all doing it, the whole crowd. A young lad with a dog on a big of string danced with one foot almost touching Frankie's, while his dog, a large blondish thing, quivered by the speaker stack. Voices so loud they might carry the whole song, if the band were to suddenly stop.

But Stick never would. Face slippery with sweat, wearing that joyful-sex look that he wore when he was drumming. Eyes closed, smiling, slowly shaking his head.

Stick, always there. Forever smiling, no matter how many days you spent on the road. And Frankie, over there with the bass touching his belt buckle. Frankie, good, solid, dependable Frankie, who you could rely on no matter what. These two best boys were the finest you could ever find anywhere. You could not find better bandmates. Samhain knew that for a fact. He took a step towards the mic.

'Keep on moving faster...'

He'd sung these words so many times that if you wrote them out, they'd fill a phone book.

Silence. The old man stared, jaw hanging slack. A clatter of drum stick on the kit. Samhain's voice shouted out into the nothing. The end of the song had caught him by surprise, somehow.

'Oh Christ,' he said. 'Sorry.'

Laughter: the crowd clapping, cheering. 'Est-a-mos!' they shouted. 'Est-a-mos! Estamos! Estamos!'

All the way around the room, the chant went up. A clap on every syllable. 'Estamos! Estamos! Estamos! Estamos!'

Samhain felt a hand on his shoulder. The grey-haired woman

leaned forward, grabbing his upper arm with bony fingers. 'You guys are the *best*,' she said.

2.

Without even being fully awake, Samhain knew he was not home.

Bed. Floor. Mattress. Sleeping bag. He wriggled his toes.

He opened his eyes, and looked at the other bodies sleeping nearby. Frankie was closest, snoring, as usual. The smallest dog, a black-haired wiry terrier, lay curled between Romey and Stick.

Somebody was making coffee. The smell of it got him up, and the dog followed.

'Boxy,' she said. 'Boxy, here.' It was Hanna, the sound engineer from last night, snub-nosed and manga-eyed. 'This dog is such a slut for attention. Always wants to make friends with the touring bands. You want coffee?'

'Please.'

Sun came into the room from two sides: a large window at the front, and through the side door. The dogs ran in and out, bringing with them the scent of jasmine.

'Pretty sweet squat you've got here,' he said.

Hanna had the type of face you don't see too often. Appealing and broad, clear-skinned. It was the kind of face that said, Go on, Tell me things. 'We're lucky. There used to be another one, not too far from here, in an area marked for "regeneration," or gentrification, if you want to call it that, that was evicted two weeks ago. Fifteen people were living there – cops in riot gear went in and hauled them all out. They attacked them with tear gas, and everything. Can you believe it?'

The coffee tasted of hot tar, and dried out the inside of his mouth like a bush fire. 'I can. Bunch of fuckers.' He coughed, and added sugar.

'That's why we are so crowded here now. Four of them came to live here, and they brought their dogs. So, that's also why we have so many dogs.'

Samhain added water from the kettle, but his coffee still looked blacker than an oil well. 'What about you?' he said.

'For now, we're safe. Nobody wants to build luxury flats here, yet. But maybe, one day, once prices have gone up over there, and the developers see that there is more money to be made, here. Eventually, they'll clear us out, too. But not yet.'

'We've got a squat in an old hotel – me and Frankie,' Samhain said.

'Yeah?' Hanna climbed into a chair, bare legs folding over the wood like a cricket's. 'Do you have, like – chocolates on the pillows, and stuff?' She was turned right towards him with this eager, fascinated face, that said, Tell me, Tell me, and she smelled gently of coconut oil. 'How many of you are there?'

'Just three. I noticed it first – found it. The place is hidden away, behind all of these hedges. It's not even on a main road.'

'Wow.'

'Yeah. And when we moved in, we found a load of stuff. All the hotel towels, with the name embroidered in the corner. All their matchbooks, guest soaps, tea trays, all that sort of stuff. It was almost kind of spooky, the way they'd left it. Like they meant to come back later. But then... everything was covered in dust. They must have been gone years.'

Hanna had a splashing tap laugh. 'You're so lucky! Only three of you, in a big place like that. Sometimes I wish we had more space here.' One of the dogs jumped, slobbering its big stupid tongue all over her face. 'So, where do you go next, on your tour?'

'I don't know. Romey's the one with the tour schedule.' Written on a sheet of foolscap, folded up into eight and deep in Romey's back trouser pocket, was the list of dates. With addresses, and all of the promoters' phone numbers and email addresses written on the back. He and Frankie had given Romey this bit of paper, and started calling him the Tour Manager. It gave him something to do. 'I do know that we're playing at an all-dayer in Belgium, with our friends from Nottingham–'

'Yes.' She poked the table with a dollish finger, sending a surprising aftershock through the wood. 'I know about this gig. My friend is putting it on. It's a benefit for the Deep Green Resistance women – the ones who had children by undercover cops, in the eighties. It's a really good cause. Did you know about it?'

A feeling started, rising through him as long-journey car nausea. It began in his legs, and left him with a shivery feeling, as though he'd passed through a gastric fever. 'I didn't know it was a benefit.'

'Yeah, of course. In the eighties, the police were infiltrating groups all over Europe. There were undercover cops in groups all over Europe, in Britain, in Switzerland, everywhere. They went into the groups and then fed information back to their bosses, to police in their home countries, everywhere. Some of them were in the groups for years – they were supposedly there to gain information only, and maybe to disrupt the activities. They weren't supposed to get into relationships with the activists. But a lot of them went way over the line of duty, *way* over. I have heard of four, maybe five women, who had *children* by these animals, not even knowing they were cops. Can you imagine?' She rolled a cigarette, flicking bits of tobacco off her fingers. 'Not only is it bad enough that your group is infiltrated by undercover cops, but to have your body taken too. It's like being raped by the state.' She lit up: every word breathed smoke. 'Wouldn't you know, the cops have fought just as hard as they can, to keep everything secret. To keep the women in the dark, just like they always have. My friend is trying to raise money, so that there's enough for a legal fund. She will do it. I know how strong these women are.'

He watched her, poised over the glass ashtray, spitting these things out as though her vehemence could make a difference, any difference at all, as though knowing it was wrong and putting it all right were one and the same thing. As though one led automatically to the other, instead of being a long, exhausting and bitter struggle, where the unarmed and dispossessed used as their weapons photocopied flyers and banners made out of bedsheets, fighting an enemy that had money, and uniforms, and enough resources to keep the war going forever. An enemy that was as well-organised, and more powerful than any government.

Samhain felt dishcloth-wrung, as though he had been used for cleaning pans. 'Good luck to her,' he said, finally.

'More coffee?'

Noises overhead. She looked up, and started pouring before he could tell her another cup wouldn't make any difference. The tiredness was marrow-deep; it lay in his veins, moving sluggishly along. It lay over him and in him like a second epidermis, a reptile that would never shed its skin, only ever lay heavier, shrink tighter, and hang its weight upon him always.

'That's Lukas.' Hanna blew smoke towards the ceiling. 'He'll be down in a minute to make you all something to eat.'

She was not his counsellor, he saw that now. In the coal black tattoos and the way her mouth contorted to blow smoke away; she was a punk, the same as him, and she had her loyalties. She lifted the coffee pot and he saw a tattoo of a city in flames, and knew that anything he said to her would go straight to Lukas, and from Lukas to Lemmers, and from Lemmers to home. In one mistaken step, he could have told everybody a secret that whizzed around inside him like a stuck firework.

'You alright?' she said. 'For a minute, you looked miles away.'

Upstairs, the gurgling of piss in a bowl. The gush; a horse of a man. He pulled a smile up onto his face with a winch and some clockwork. 'Tired. Bit of tour madness, that's all.'

'On your second day?' She shook her head. 'Don't worry. One of Lukas' breakfasts will put you right.'

The table was well hidden, in a sunny dell overhung by roses, and Lukas kept coming with more plates. Chewy pink strips, hot and crackling like bacon, but not bacon. Beans in a rich sauce, with the taste of tomatoes and molasses. Thick rye bread and olive oil.

They drank coffee, with the long grass tickling their legs, from a jumble sale of chipped mugs and jam jars. 'I know how you British like your coffee,' Lukas said. 'Like dishwater. For you, I make it the British way.' The sun was all over them like the first morning of a holiday.

Romey shovelled food into his mouth with his fingers, as though he hadn't eaten in weeks. 'Why do you never get food like this in England?' he said.

Lemmers was looking in his pockets for the van key. 'I blame Tony Blair,' he said. 'Better do an idiot check before we go, boys. Nearly time to get back on the road.'

3.

Neither Romey, nor Frankie, not Stick, or Samhain, could get the van doors closed.

'Come on, Sam,' Frankie said. 'Don't you do this for a living?'

Lemmers was the only one who knew how to load it, and he had wandered off somewhere. He'd been gone ages, and none of them knew where he was.

Nothing was straight in the back, guitars and amps shoved in like clutter into a cupboard, with sleeping bags yawning everywhere. These things, once in carry-bags the size of Coke bags, had become things the expanse of a double-king sized bedspread. Stick was the only one out of all of them who'd managed to get his sleeping bag back into its case.

'This is no good,' Samhain said. 'We need to have it all out and start again.'

'Fuck this,' Romey groaned. He wombled away to the passenger seat, slamming the door behind him.

'One down, three to go,' Frankie said.

'Come on, lads,' Samhain said. 'Sooner we start, sooner it's done.'

They had it all out onto the pavement.

Stick stood with one foot in the gutter, pushing things – the holdall containing all of the leads, Samhain's nylon guitar bag – back onto the pavement. He was yawning, tired. They all were.

'We need to start with the big stuff,' Samhain said. 'Then we can pack all the little stuff like the leads and the bags in the gaps.'

'Whoa, everyone.' There was a grizzle of grey around Frankie's chin. The long drives had got into him, as they had to them all, and he was starting to look old. Yet in his eye, mischief still twinkled. 'Professional at work. Everybody stand back.'

Behind him, a shop owner rattled shutters open and opened a door, and disappeared inside. All the way along the street, shops were opening.

'Make yourself useful, dickhead, and get those sleeping bags small as you can.'

'Tetchy.' Frankie reached for Romey's bag, a blue and white diagonal striped thing that looked as though it had done fifteen round-world trips. 'Where'd you want this, boss?'

They'd spent a long night on a hard floor. The gig had not been one of their best – a cramped stage in a basement bar, watched by a small group of teenagers with lip rings and sharp-straightened black hair over their eyes. They had started with an audience of ten, and ended up with two.

Afterwards, they'd come back here, to the promoter's flat, a stamp-sized place over a takeaway with a dirty kitchen floor and nowhere else to sleep. Space had been so limited, Samhain had as good as slept in Frankie's arms, with his feet wedged up against the cupboards. At six, they'd been woken by the dual beep of two digital alarm clocks: the promoter's, and his roommate's. He had almost been glad of the excuse to get up and off the lino.

'Drums in first,' Samhain said.

Things fit together better this second time. Starting with cymbal cases, a drum, the amp heads. Samhain got one door closed, then stood holding the other still open, looking at the tightly packed other half.

'Where the hell is Lemmers? Romey!' he shouted. 'Romey!'

A bad-tempered grunt in response.

There had been no coffee that morning. Last night's promoter, Aleks, had gone off to work in a crumpled white shirt and a black tie, apologising that he didn't have time to make breakfast, but that there was a place to get it somewhere down the street. Romey had taken this news the worst of all. He had gone to try and find the cafe Aleks had mentioned, only to come up against a locked door. The place didn't open until 11.

'Bloody tour ruiner,' Frankie grumbled. More loudly, he roared: 'Come on, lad, you're the tour manager, for Pete's sake. Go and find out where Lemmers has got to.'

The passenger side door opened. 'I don't know where the hell he could go at this time in the morning,' Romey grumbled, 'when everything in this shithole is *closed.*'

'Hang on.' Samhain counted the Swiss-roll ends of the sleeping bags they'd managed to get in. One, Romey's zig-zag thing. Two, Stick's professional level camping sleeper from Millet's. Three, Frankie's old grey war horse. Four, Lemmers' trusty navy blue nylon thing, a sleeping bag which, he never tired of telling them, had history: it had been all over Europe, all over Scandinavia and the United States and South America; this was the sleeping bag that had been under his arm when he'd met Henry Rollins. This was the sleeping bag that had been on tour with the band Crass.

It surprised them all that he wasn't a bit more careful with it.

'Where's my sleeping bag?' Samhain said.

Romey passed, grumbling on his way to the corner: 'Nothing's ever simple, is it?'

'Open the other door again,' Frankie suggested. 'I think it went in under my bass.'

But no, it wasn't there either, and nor was it under or behind anything else, once they'd unpacked everything back out onto the pavement again, to check. Samhain stood amongst the pile of bags and guitars, with Stick's cymbals leaning up against his leg, and with the holdall containing all of the leads and pedals on his foot; he looked up at Aleks' apartment window, and said: 'It's in Aleks' flat. I left my sleeping bag in Aleks' bloody flat.'

Just then, Romey reappeared. Grinning, with Lemmers a few steps behind him, carrying four takeaway coffees in a cardboard to-go tray.

As they came, Lemmers looked up from his coffee at the mess of guitars and drums and amps, all standing crazily out on the pavement, and said: 'Haven't you loaded that bloody van yet?'

'We won't take your bullshit! Uniformed bodies and uniformed thoughts! We say "no" to the lies of yours!'

Coffee cups, empty now, rolled around the van floor as the boys in the bus sang along to a band from the first night. Nursery rhyme melodies sung by aggrieved men with sandpaper voices. Samhain's ears hurt; he was staring out of the window at the rain. They'd been listening to this CD for days now. Nobody ever said, Put something else on.

They didn't make fanzines about Samhain's situation. 'What to do when you find out your father was an undercover cop, #1 – the first issue in an irregular series.' Nobody had started a self-help group, because no anarchist was ever about to admit to having a shiny-buttoned father.

If only it stuck out obviously, in a hard polyp on your neck, rather than being written in a sequence of letters in your DNA, in every single cell of your self. Samhain would have cut that part of himself out with the sharpest scalpel he could find.

'We're stopping in the next town,' Lemmers shouted. 'It's worth it. You'll all enjoy it – I promise.'

The place was a small stone village. It was still raining, a cold soft grey, heather-coloured clouds throwing spit onto cobbles. An old lady walked up the hill carrying a wicker basket. Samhain jumped out of the van, feeling as though he had stepped into a postcard.

'Just up that hill,' announced Lemmers, 'is the country's largest folk and agricultural museum.'

'Here?'

'Yes, and it's lucky we were out early,' Lemmers said, 'because it closes at midday on a Tuesday.'

He went up the hill, Romey and Stick following.

Someone nearby was baking bread. The wonderful smell of it, roasted almonds and cooked apple, wafted gently on the air.

Frankie rolled a cigarette, leaning up against the van. 'Alright, kiddo?'

'Yeah.' These streets: they took Samhain back to childhood. Low doorways and curving lintels, bowed windows and leading. He thought he might have been to this place before, or somewhere like it, as a boy. Perhaps to buy supplies for camp. 'I could live here,' he said. 'Place like this – pretty – quiet. I could stay here, and never go back to Bradford.'

Frankie's arm around his shoulders, most of the weight towards Frankie's body, as though he didn't want to hold on too tight. 'That's tour madness talking, if ever I heard it.'

'It's not.'

'It is, jizzlip. Come on. We all have that moment when we're away, when we think – yes, I could live here. My life would be so much better.'

'It would, though.'

'Is this about being banned from CopWatch?'

'They tried to make out I was some kind of domestic abuser, Frankie.'

'I don't know why you're even interested in those old witches.' Frankie's cigarette burned down to a tingle of amber. 'Are you into librarians now? What's wrong – have you run out of punk girls to shag?'

'It's not just that. It's everything else. I feel like everybody's talking about me. They think they know me, and they don't. I just want to get away from all the bullshit...'

'Bullshit like what? Like all of your friends? Like that massive house you live in?'

'Squats never last Frankie, you know that. Look how many places we've been in over the past few years. Christ, I can't even keep my guitar at home, in case we have to move. It's impossible to settle. We never know when we'll have to move again. For all we know, that squat might be over by the time we get back off this tour. I'm so sick of it, Frankie, just so sick of it. That and finding out that everybody knows my business before I do, and they're all talking behind my back.'

A net curtain moved in one of the houses. A woman stared from an upstairs window.

'See, if I lived somewhere like this, I'd be away from all that. Away from the people who said they were my friends but, all along, were the ones who knew about Astrid before I did, and didn't say a word. People who were smiling and acting friendly but it was another story behind my back. Even Marta. Those aren't friends, are they? They can't be. Otherwise they would have said something to me.' Samhain said: 'I just think I'm better away from all that.'

Frankie forced a toe between cobbles. 'This is delayed shock, mate.'

Samhain moaned. 'You have no idea what it's like.'

Graeme Stokes was another story that would be too good for anybody to keep quiet. A thing that couldn't be told to a single other person, not even Frankie, lest he should tell one more, and they tell one more, until the whole thing bloomed and spread like mould setting spore under a large wet log. He'd come here to get away from it, and it had followed him. It was in the faces of the lads in the van and in the places they stayed, in the music they listened to and in the gigs they played. It popped up in every squat and house and basement gig and there was no getting away from it no matter where he went.

'Well, there's me,' Frankie said.

'Do you ever wish,' Samhain went on, 'that you could just push a button, and reset everything in your whole life, and get a new start? Go some place where nobody knows you, and start all over again?' He crouched down, feeling suddenly safer closer to the cobbles than he had at full height.

'Listen, you're making a big deal out of this,' Frankie said. 'I honestly don't think that many people knew. Maybe they might have seen Charley with a baby. But that's not to say that everybody thought it was yours.'

'People talk, that's the trouble.'

'Are you going to sit there all day?' Frankie said, grabbing his arm. 'We've got an agricultural museum to visit.'

Entry was €4, money taken by a bun-fed old lady whose hands were full with knitting. She gave them a long explanation in Flemish, and pointed to a room full of horse tack and softly gleaming metal, and then to another, a room with glass cases whose edges caught the dim light. Romey and Lemmers were nowhere to be seen.

Everything had the darkness of a provincial museum trying to preserve, and all things were lit with a low, amberish light. A large case by the door in the first room was all lace. This was draped on shelves, and knitted into the fabric were images of farming boys and machinery. A perfect miniature boy in white lace overalls had a hole dotted in his chest; in the same doily, a girl pointed a rifle from behind a crocheted wall.

The next case was all clothes, baby things, crushed velvet and smocked cotton, all with collars and ruffs of the same type of handmade lace. On the shelf sat a baby, a realistic looking doll, in a brown crushed velvet frock. It had pale cheeks, and looked glassily surprised.

'Where the hell has Lemmers brought us?' Samhain whispered.

On the back wall, another case seemed to contain what looked like a dead silk farm. Ancient, brittle cocoons, blackening now, all laying together like eggs, in a box the size of a lizard tank. A butterfly, turning sepia with time, had been stuck with clear glue, by its abdomen, to the glass.

Grinning, Frankie pulled a disposable camera out of his pocket. 'This is way too good to miss. Say cheese!'

The red light came on for the flash; a second later, the bleach of it whitened Samhain's vision. The woman called through from the next room, in heavily accented English: 'No photographs, please!'

'Sorry.' Frankie shoved the camera into his jacket pocket. 'God, I hope that one comes out. You should have seen your face.'

The back room was all furniture. Tapestry-cushioned chairs along one wall, and on an elevated dais at the end, four slightly different wooden chairs. There was a cabinet painted with men riding horses into war, and a tiny rocking chair with a highly carved wooden back.

'Now then, you're the furniture expert. You should be able to identify some of these. What's that?' Frankie pointed at a plastic chair, the type found in most primary school classrooms.

'That,' Sam said, 'is a modern-day milking stool. Found in most modern farms and outhouses. It's where the farmer sits to milk his dairy cows. Please note, the cow doesn't get to sit down. Where is Daisy's comfortable chair? Where is the comfortable chair for Flossie?'

'Nowhere!' Frankie was laughing, and reaching for the camera again. 'Right then, get sat down – let's get your picture again.'

'This is easily the creepiest museum I've ever been to.' Samhain sat in the chair, and waited again for the flash. 'Not sure I'd come here again.'

Stick appeared in the doorway, and glanced at them both. 'There you are. Shall we get a move on? Lemmers is saying we need to get back on the road.'

4.

Three hours in the van.

Legs cramped and each other's faces imprinted into memory. There was nowhere to look except for into the face of whoever was sitting opposite, which in Samhain's case had been Frankie.

They arrived at the next squat to grey skies and warm air: Samhain jumped down from the van with a feeling of being in the wrong place. The night air rested against his skin the same way a cooling oven exudes heat.

He grabbed his guitar, sleeping bag, and one of the bags, and went inside.

The place was a large, old house, with narrow corridors and not much in the way of lights. There were people everywhere. In one of the downstairs rooms, six dreadlocked punks were drinking beer, and kicking a football around.

Noise trickled down the stairs – guitars and drums, and something that sounded electronic. It seemed to be coming from the top of the house. Samhain stopped on the first floor, when he found the bar. An ingenious thing, punk-built. It looked as though it had been nailed together from a set of table legs and a broken-up chipboard bookcase. The girl behind it had a pint in her hand, and a glow on her face that said she wouldn't make it to the end of the night.

They were pouring beer direct from the barrel. It smelled good – fresh hops, and it was a wonderful honeyed colour. Samhain tasted the brewer's care when his first gulp hit the back of his throat, and he was already friendly by the time he started looking for the gig room.

It was up two more flights of stairs and, by the time he'd found it, everything else had already been brought in, even the amp heads.

A band were playing. Four women scratching away at guitars and cellos, dancing around the stage in torn vests. The stage times stuck to the door table told him that they were the fifth band on, and that the gig was already running late by an hour.

Never mind. Samhain stood at the back, watching them play, sipping his beer. It was a good gig room. A low stage, lit by strings of fairy lights dipping from the ceiling. Back and forth, a dozen lines of them, crossing one another in a sparkling, dewy web. And under them the crowd, numbering maybe fifty. It would be a great night: he could tell that already.

'Samhain?'

A familiar voice – he knew it straight away. Gruff and Northampton-tinged, with the sound of his name ending in a lean. Samhain listened to that voice a lot. He'd got two records full of it back at the Boundary Hotel.

'Ned!' he shouted.

'Please tell me you haven't played already.' Ned grabbed him in a manly embrace; it was a hug that semaphored three days without washing. The face was two years older, mostly covered with wiry hair, and the smile turned grey eyes into twinkling boat lakes. 'I've missed you guys.'

'Me too, and not yet.' Samhain raised his glass. 'Reckon I might be in a bit of state by the time we get up there, though. I can't stop drinking this beer. It's the best thing we've had all tour.'

'Tell me about it.' Ned raised a glass of the same. 'How great is this – playing together again?'

'It's great – high point of the tour, for me.' He said, 'Frankie sort of talked me down earlier.'

'From what?'

'Long story. Tell you later.'

'Right you are. Cheers.' They clinked glasses.

He'd known Ned five years, ever since his band had played the Ambland Road squat. In those days, Patrick Stewart The Band had only just started out. They were still working out how to play, and sounded like a bargain basement Devo. It hadn't mattered to Samhain: he'd still danced his way through the soles of his shoes, and bought a t-shirt, and a record. Afterwards, he'd buttonholed Ned and spent hours talking to him in the kitchen.

There was no corner, no nook of science fiction or occult literature that Ned didn't know. Throughout the conversation Ned had kept on nodding, and starting sentences with the words: 'Have you heard of...' or, 'Have you ever read...' The man was a sort of dermal-layered encyclopaedia, and there was no major, or minor, work of science fiction, horror, fantasy, or speculative fiction, or young adult fiction before it had been called young adult fiction, or original horrors upon which classic films like *The Woman in Black* or *Dr Jekyll and Mr Hyde* were based, or novelisations of derivative version of films like *Legend of the Seven Golden Vampires* or *The Bride of Frankenstein*, which Ned hadn't read.

Yet despite this interest in all things macabre, Ned had a

musical theatre disposition. He was all smiles and enthusiasm: he always seemed just a few seconds away from opening up an umbrella and starting a dance number.

'It's good to see you, man,' Samhain said. 'Good to see a friendly face.'

There was the clang and squeal of a crap guitar being plugged in onstage. Ned nodded towards it, and said a load of things that Samhain couldn't hear for the noise. The gist of it seemed to be, this band are worth watching – let's stick around.

Samhain had almost forgotten how brilliant Patrick Stewart The Band were. Sharp, percussive guitars, drums that snapped and stopped, yet never ceased moving. Their music was all diagonal and hard-sided, in a way that got you on your feet and kept you there, and they'd got much better at playing it in the two years since he'd last seen them.

He had this bottle of whisky that he'd got at the bar, and after Patrick Stewart The Band came off stage, the whole inside of the squat started to take on the look of a ship's innards. There was a party, and it was happening all over all four floors. He and Ned settled onto a sofa in a dark corner, in a room that seemed more and more like a galley slave cabin – a small wooden thing, oppressive and dark, taken to on one of the long sailing nights. They might have been inside the Arctic Circle: Samhain felt the deck shift and lurch.

It was a night like a memory. He and Ned had had so many nights in squats like this one, and nights after playing gigs in cricket clubs and empty bars in places like Stoke and Grimsby. There had been one night – Samhain remembered sitting on a ripped kitchen chair in Ambland Road, talking to Ned when everybody else had gone to bed. Watching in the morning as soft light glimmered over the red-brick wall in the backyard, and shyed its way through the net curtains.

'Here,' Samhain said. 'D'you remember that kid – Mike?'

'Yeah!' Ned poured more whisky into his glass. They were both on the hard stuff now, but Ned was more civilised, drinking from a jam jar. He claimed to be trying to keep an eye on how much he was drinking, but more than half of the bottle had already gone. 'Puts on gigs in Grimsby? He put us on a couple of months back. Great guy.'

'You know,' Samhain said, 'it's great hearing about kids keeping it up. Nothing better. You know, when somebody grows up but they don't give up.' The whisky tasted like an action movie explosion. 'That's the dream.'

'I'll drink to that.' Ned raised his jar.

'Never change, Ned,' Samhain said. 'Always stay exactly like you are.' It felt good, to be sitting here beside him. That was the same smile, the same boyish face. All points around the world could change, and yet Ned – he would always be a sticking post.

The night had started to take on a dishonourable, slanting hue. The bands over, and there was a disco somewhere, in one of the other rooms – people kept getting up and disappearing upstairs – he could hear the sound of S Club 7 pouring through the corridors. But Ned, Ned would always be there, and always be what he was. A glinting, smiling anchor in an old green t-shirt.

'You're a great guy, Ned. One of the best.'

'Shucks.' Ned grinned.

'No, I mean it,' Samhain said. 'I really, really, mean it. This isn't just the drink talking.'

'What about Frankie?'

'Yes.' A broke-dam spill of Grouse poured down Samhain's chin. He didn't know how it had happened, and he wiped it with the back of his sleeve. 'Frankie is also a great guy, and one of the best. You know, there aren't many people in life that you meet, that you can just totally rely on. People you can trust completely. And Frankie is...' he waved the bottle around; his thoughts changed and metamorphosed as he tried to get a hold of them: 'Well, he is really great. I tell him everything.' Then a thought lit a dull flame in his mind, and he added: 'Well, not everything. But most things.'

'You know, Frankie once...' Ned reached for the bottle. 'Once drove a box of our records all the way over from Leeds to Bradford in his bike trailer. We had to get them over there, for some reason, and we couldn't do it ourselves. He went, "Don't worry lads, you leave it to me. I won't drop them in the canal." And Frankie – Frankie said—'

'I know. I know.' Samhain was nodding. He knew this aspect of his best friend well – the side that would do anything for anybody. 'I bet he said, "It's no trouble," didn't he? I bet he went, "Don't even think about it. Don't even thank me."'

Ned was grinning, shrugging, and said words that, in a jumble of conversation, Samhain couldn't make out. There was a new knot of people around them – people perched on the chair arm and sitting cross-legged on the floor – and they were talking this loud, foreign language, a language which seemed to be all consonants and voiced plosives. With the ringing of the gig still in his ears, Samhain was struggling to hear anything but the rattling gun of the conversation going on all the way around them.

Then Ned took a phone out of his pocket, and started fiddling with the buttons. Samhain was amazed by this phone. He had never seen one like it: it flipped open, and the screen was inside the lid. It was so bright, it turned Ned's fingers a ghoulish, ambulance-light blue. He stared, closing one eye.

Ned was smiling, holding the camera-phone towards him. Out grinned a pretty girl with a sharp cut blonde bob, with dark eyes, and a broad, fifties star of stage-and-screen face. 'That's my girl,' he lipread. 'Dolly.' He also thought he saw

Ned say, We're getting married.

He said, 'What?'

Ned took the phone back, and cradled it gently in his palm as he gazed at the screen. 'You know, when I met her...'

Again, his words disappeared into the chatter-storm. Samhain shouted, 'What?' but Ned didn't hear, and went on talking. He looked happy, in a way Samhain hadn't seen before. His whole manner so calm, and his face had this dreamy look. 'I feel like I've known her all my life. You know?'

There was a bump on the sofa cushion behind, and Samhain felt a strong arm encircle his chest and shoulder. 'Now then.' Frankie, eyes circular as Saturn, lips loose with endearments. His eyes closed slowly, and he looked at Sam and Ned as if they were a pair of sugared doughnuts. 'You two,' he began, 'you look – you are, a pair, of very beautiful people.' He reached over, and started stroking Ned's beard. 'So soft. Samhain, you should touch Ned's hair.'

Ned turned, and half-winked. He leaned forward, letting Frankie run his fingers over his head.

'I don't want to,' Samhain said. He looked over. Ned was giggling. Frankie had got both hands deep into his hair, right on top of his scalp. 'Honestly, Frankie, I can't take you anywhere.'

'Touch it, go on. It's like baby hair. Just touch it.'

He let Frankie lift his arm, and pop his hand on Ned's crown, and found to his surprise that Ned's hair was as soft as kittens' ears. 'Hey, you're right. He does have very soft hair.'

'You see? Mmmm.' Frankie plopped back into the chair, a satisfied smile on his face. 'You can always trust me. You should always listen to old Frankie. Old Frankie knows what he's on about.' His words dwindled away into a soft, barely coherent mumble.

Frankie was very good at finding drugs when drunk, at making new friends and getting them to take things from their pockets and put them into his, into sharing their stash with a garrulous new friend who wouldn't even know their names in the morning.

Samhain sucked at the bottle, twisting to look at his smiling, blissed best friend. There wasn't anybody else in the world, nobody at all, who would have said, Sure, let's go and break into an old hotel and squat it, no problem. Or, there wasn't anybody else who would have said, Sam, you and me and Stick, let's get in a van and go all the way around Europe, and forget about all this crap with Charley and Astrid, just for a few weeks. It was only Frankie, Frankie who knew what he needed at a time when Mart was saying, No Samhain, you shouldn't go. Forget about having fun and being in a band and doing all the things you love. Get a job where you have to spend all day, every day, moving furniture. Lose weeks and days and hours of your life to dusty sideboards and rattling, fragile boxes. Get paid to shift the detritus of other people's lives from one place to another, so they can move from a smaller house to a bigger house, and work more hours, giving up the joy in their own lives to do it. That was what Marta wanted. But not Frankie. Frankie would never tell him to do a thing like that. Frankie was the kind of guy who'd give you his right arm, and then as he was ripping it off, nearly passing out from the pain, ask you whether you needed the left one as well.

How dim Samhain had been, to think that he couldn't tell Frankie about Graeme Stokes. Frankie was there, he was always there, to be trusted. He wouldn't pass it around as a bit of gossip – wouldn't think any the worse of Samhain for it. This was the kind of guy you could trust with your life.

He was just reaching over to shake Frankie's shoulder, when he felt a soft touch on his leg.

'Hey.' He turned to see Ned, glass empty, looking contrite. 'I didn't realise you and Charley had split up.'

Samhain tipped the last few drops into Ned's jar. 'Yeah. Ages ago. It was...' Time swirled and dissipated before him, like coloured solution into water; he found that he couldn't see any of it well enough to call out the colours. 'Ages ago.'

'Shame,' Ned said. 'Still – it's probably best to split up when she's still a baby. That way, she'll hardly even remember it.'

Samhain was swinging the empty bottle in his hands, too loosely as it turned out. It dropped, smashing at his feet. 'What did you say?'

Ned had the sort of eyes that were given to looking taken aback very easily. 'Sorry, I must have... maybe I got it wrong. I thought Frankie said... you'd got a little girl. When he was moving our records that time.' He looked like he might be backing away. 'Sounds like I got the wrong end of the stick, though. I'm sorry if I said the wrong thing.'

Charley had always used to say, you knew when it was closing time because of the amount of broken glass on the floor. Samhain looked at the shards around his feet, and turned around to Frankie.

He was smiling absently, rubbing his fingers together as though feeling the fur of some white, fluffy bunnies.

'You knew.' Samhain punched him on the arm, hard.

'Ow.' It took Frankie a moment to react. He drew the arm away slowly, and managed to make his eyes focus, eventually. 'What the hell, man?'

'You knew, you fucking prick.'

Samhain had never hit before, but he was hitting now. Fists to shoulders and chest and stomach, anywhere he could get a punch in, and Frankie wasn't quick enough out of the way. It took him some time to struggle to his feet.

'Jesus, boy.' Frankie staggered backwards, finally coming to rest against a nearby wall. 'What'd I do?'

Ned was up. A tall lad when he was at his full height, and

he stood between them, with his hands on Samhain's shoulders. 'Calm down, Sam.' He spoke calmly. 'Whatever it is, it's not worth it.'

A swimming fury. Samhain had a feeling of wanting to hit until his knuckles were raw. Punch walls, snap hard until brains started bleeding from ears – this was how he wanted to hurt Frankie. 'You stay out of this, Ned.'

But Ned wouldn't go. Wherever Sam's feet went, his went too, matching him step for step. 'Frankie's your friend.' His voice had taken on the tone of a kindly teacher. Those hands on his shoulders, reassuring and firm. 'Come on, Sam, listen to me. Don't do anything you can't take back.'

Frankie, by the back wall, squirming now, the same way he had when he'd been caught leaving dishes for other people to wash up at the club cafe. 'I didn't know how to tell you, Sam,' he called. 'She made me promise not to tell you.'

'Get out of the way, Ned.'

'No.' Ned's grip tightened. 'Think about what you're doing. Is it really worth it?'

Arms kept him at length. Ned was sober as a dancer, and could step anywhere even before Sam had thought of it himself. He was more than evenly matched, and miles further away from Frankie than he wanted to be.

'She said she was going to tell you herself,' Frankie continued. 'You know – soon. And then I sort of forgot about it, until...'

There was only one way to get at him.

Samhain took a breath, and stepped back.

'...until you and Roxy had that argument... and by then I realised, it was too late to say anything.'

Breathing too, Ned slackened his stance. 'That was the right choice, Sam,' he said, giving him a greengrocer's squeeze on the bicep.

'It was Charley's fault, really,' Frankie said. 'If you think about it. I mean, she was the one who made us all promise to keep it quiet.'

His old friend waved his hands around carelessly. Then his attention was caught by his hands, his thumbs, and he stopped, staring at them as though they were new chicks coming out of a shell. 'Life is a wonderful thing,' he said. 'Wouldn't you say, boyo? And we'll always be friends, won't we? No matter what happens.'

'That's right.' Ned, though relaxed now, still blocked the way. 'Violence is never the answer, Sam. You know that. And you would have always regretted–'

Sam said, 'I'm sorry, Ned.' He punched Ned in the guts, hard.

Then leapt over Ned's folded body, all fists and teeth. He felt flat walls, warm surfaces. Grabbed and pulled, tearing at fabric with his hands. Frankie gave no resistance: he was crying for mercy.

Samhain hardly knew what he was hitting, or where. He felt knuckles and ribs. Teeth and hair. He tried to get a hold of Frankie, so he could get a better aim, but Frankie moved sideways, his shirt ripping, tearing himself loose.

Shouts broke up around them. People were calling at him to stop, trying to pull him away, and he kicked back. Still clawing to reach Frankie. Ignoring the voices, the sound of Ned coughing. Metal on Frankie's zipper tore the webbing between finger and thumb – Samhain felt his flesh tear open, and he was all blood, screaming, aiming for Frankie's face, but instead getting the wall.

'Samhain, come on,' Frankie shouted. Deep back into the corner, exactly where Samhain wanted him. 'It's me.'

Breath a beer-smell, warm and soft. Talking by the bar late nights. Samhain was half hoping to have the air knocked out of him, only Frankie wasn't punching back. Fists hit shoulder, moving arm, wall. Knuckles crunched and cracked and bleeding.

'Sam?' Lemmers' voice. 'Come on Sam, stop it.'

Frankie was back against the wall, with his hands up, shouting: 'I'm sorry! I'm sorry!' and trying to slide away.

It wasn't enough to stop him. Samhain kept going, neck tense as an underpass. He caught a punch against Frankie's eye. Felt the bone resist against his fingers. It felt good, hard as cooking pots. He tried again, and bust Frankie's lip. He kept going, hitting, one two three, the left and then the right, one two three, finding spaces and looking for soft parts, somewhere to hurt, anywhere at all. Blood burst, dribbling out of both nostrils. It was redder, brighter, than he'd expected. Hadn't thought there would be so much of it. On Frankie's face and his hands too, slick, warm, gooey. Could have been coming from the lip or the nose or his eye, or all three. More striking, four five six, left, right, four five six, landing on fabric, on Frankie's torso.

He kept going, reaching, thumping, and then his punches were landing on nothing at all, hitting the open air. Samhain was being pulled away. Two sets of hands, one under his left armpit, the other under his right.

'No fighting allowed,' said a strong, heavily accented voice. 'We do not have it here. And now you must go.'

Lifted bodily away from Frankie, from Ned, from the sofa. The arms held him as though he were in a full body case, and he couldn't even get a hand free to stem his own tears.

'Just let me–' he said.

'No,' the man repeated. Samhain couldn't even see his face. 'That's enough, now. We do not allow that in here.'

Ned was getting to his feet. An abattoir of cuts bled freely down his arm.

'I'm sorry,' Samhain called. 'I'm sorry. I'm so sorry.'

'It is too late for apologies now,' the voice said. 'You must go.'

Down the stairs, the rush of cold early morning air. It blew through the open doorway, up the steps, and then, closer, closer, right into Samhain's face, as they put him out at the door.

'My bag,' he said. 'Please don't throw me out without my bag.'

5.

Steel seats, bus station doorway.

Turning. Rivets punching his back and sides. The cold.

Another dream: Frankie rolling t-shirts, sticking them into a soft cylinder with a rip of masking tape, three inches long. 'See how it's done? You can always rely on me.'

Half-awake, eyes a little open. The digital clock inside the station said it was still too early for buses. He tried to sleep some more, crossing arms across his bag.

His friend on a bike, ringing the bell and pulling the trailer, full of records and CDs. Up a ladder, round the back of the stairs, with screwdriver and tool belt, working away at the fuse box: Frankie, who could make any light come on, who could trick any call-centre worker from British Gas or N-Power, into sending out an engineer to hook up a squat to the grid. 'People will do anything if they believe it's legit,' he always said. 'They have the best intentions. They want to help you. You're appealing to their better nature. And – bang!'

Lights, warmth. For a moment, he felt it. Arms scraping him from the cold bench, under his back, shoulder, dragging him up. Away from the cold. Briefly, another body's warmth. Hands strong at his back, a shoulder in his torso, carrying him safely away. The same fireman's lift that had got him home a dozen or more times. 'Can't have you staying here all night. Come on, let's get you back where you belong.'

'Thankyou,' he murmured.

The sound of his own voice made him stir.

Eyes flicked open. Woke to a cold light: Samhain blinked, and looked at the dirty grey walls, starting to brighten in the day.

Somebody was trying to move his legs.

He woke in a panic, quickly, grabbing his bag closer.

It was all there. He checked. Zips still closed, front pouch intact. Nobody had slashed the front open. Sometimes thieves did that. But not him, not today. He had been lucky.

'Darf ich mich setzen?' A scarf-covered old lady gestured at his feet, still awkwardly, unfairly, taking up more than half of the bench. She was wearing a black coat and carrying a large paper bag.

'Umm, yeah, sure. Sorry.' Samhain sat, rubbing his face. Dried blood flicked off onto his palms, gritty as sand.

She sat as far away as she possibly could, on the far end of the bench.

He must look a real state, he realised. Better get a wash before getting the coach.

Romey was a careful man. Tucked away in the front pocket of Samhain's bag was a roll of twenty, ten, five euro notes, where the tour manager had put it. Throughout the tour, Romey had been dividing up the money, and stashing each bit into one of their bags. This way, he said, was safer. It meant that if one of the bags was stolen, they wouldn't lose all of the money in one go.

Lucky for Samhain that there was enough of it in his bag to buy a coach ticket along to the next place.

*

Samhain washed in cold water. Every bit of dried blood came free, running down the sink. He was his usual self, without a scratch on him. Just bruises, and knuckles swollen as a broken leg; a mark from broken glass slashing the width of his palm.

The bus ride was long. Scrunching gravel roads underwheel and endless, white-grey skies. He held on, trying to still a mouse-fast heart.

When he closed his eyes he saw Ned. Ned's face, Ned's arm. Those cuts probably needed stitches. Would he be able to play guitar with his arm like that? Samhain thought probably not.

Fighting was something Samhain hadn't done since the infants. He didn't solve things that way, or at least he hadn't thought he did.

He looked through his reflection in the window and out into a yawning black scar of earth, and felt sick.

Somewhere around the Dutch-Belgian border, the old lady offered him a sandwich. It was in something like a French stick, and had ham hanging out of the side. She was very generous with it – she had two of them, and he didn't know how to say no.

'You want?' she said. 'Take, take.'

There were only two of them on the bus by then, and her whole face transformed when she smiled. Black eyes opal rather than oily; she had a pointed little spaniel nose. 'Take, take,' she said, almost forcing it into his hand.

'Thank you,' he said, and then when she wasn't looking, slid the ham out.

*

In Bruges, he sent Marta a text. *In Belgium. Had a scrap with Frankie and left the tour. Hitching to Calais.* He added: *Bruges is pretty.*

He picked up a ride on the outskirts of town.

A black Mercedes, driven by an immaculately dressed blonde woman, pulled up at the kerb. She opened the passenger side door and told him, in perfect English, that he reminded her of her husband.

'Not now,' she laughed. 'But fifteen, twenty years ago. That's why I stopped.'

Samhain stared at her, sliding into the car. For an older lady, she looked good. A cobweb of crows' feet wrinkled out from around her eyes, and she had smile lines all the way into the corners of her nose, but she wasn't smiling now.

'Do you know,' she said, 'that I used to be a little bit of a punk rocker myself?'

'Were you?' he said.

'I was in Greenpeace,' she said. 'Close the door.'

'Huh,' he said.

'Yes, and look at me now – driving a car! This I would never have done, not when I was your age. Definitely not, no.'

'Well, I'm glad you do,' he said. 'Thanks for the lift.'

'You would have had to hitch a bunch of different rides to get to where you were going, otherwise,' she said. 'Believe me, I know. I did it enough times when I was younger.'

'Thank you,' he said, again.

'I didn't want to leave you there, waiting for ages.'

It was such comfort, after the van. Soft seats, cushioned and adjustable. Air conditioning. He breathed in, and took in the synthetic smell of pine cones.

There was a slight dip of wear in the passenger side door; perhaps the point where her husband, or her son, put his hand every day when pulling it closed. A scuff of sand in the footwell could only have come from a day out by the sea.

'Nice car,' he said.

'Thanks, it was just cleaned,' she said. 'It's not like this normally. Not with the kids. Sometimes, when I'm working, I take it to the valet place to get it cleaned out, on the company's ticket. My little treat.' She said, 'That's what counts for excitement, when you get to my age.'

Now she said it, he saw the signs. A scuffed patch in the backseat upholstery, where a child must have dragged a toy over the seat, a trench small enough for a toy soldier. The valet had polished the mark as clean as he could get it, but you could still see the scar.

It wasn't a car brand new and bright, but old, with pocks and marks, a thing with history. Like the furniture he moved at work, each scratch and ding adding sentimental value. One day eventually, there would start to be a judder and bump every time the brakes were applied, and after that was put right with new pads and discs, there'd be a mysterious knocking noise every time the car went over sixty; and that would be the point when she would go to her boss and say, 'I think it's time you gave me a new car.'

A car clearance. Sand hoovered out of footwells, toys pulled from door pockets and seat pockets, empty sweet wrappers swept out of the glove box, hands shuffling around under the seats in search of old pens and coins, and anything else that might have fallen there. Until you hold the bits and detritus of a life lived when the children were young, in a bag smaller than something you'd use for shopping, up to a teenage face who no longer wants to be seen with you in this car or any other.

He gave a start, realising that she had been talking the whole time. She might even have asked him a question.

Four days on the road with those reprobates had turned him into an animal. He said, 'Sorry, I think I fell asleep for a minute.'

'I was asking, what brings you to Belgium?' She glanced at him sideways, with deep, marbled green eyes. 'I mean, don't feel that you have to answer if you don't want to. But bear in mind that I'm not your mother, and I won't mind if you've been doing something, er...' she shrugged. 'Well. I might mind if you were one of my kids. But you're not. So indulge a middle-aged lady with some of your adventures.'

'I was on tour.'

'With your band!' Her face lit up like sun on a mirror. 'I knew you were a musician. You look like you play an instrument. But wait.' She frowned, pulling smoothly around a truck. This wasn't the same as being in the van, where you felt every single loose piece of tarmac under the wheels, where a flat road could judder the suspension like a dirt path. 'What happened to the rest of them? I mean, there must be others, right?'

He didn't answer right away.

'It's a long story,' he eventually said.

'Well.' She stared at the road. 'I would say that we have about another two hours together, anyway. So even if it's long, you might as well tell it.' Perhaps it was the way she spoke, as though she wasn't going to stand for a disagreement – but something about her reminded him of Marta. 'And you and I are never going to see one another again. I don't know any of your friends, or your bandmates, or anybody you know. So. It doesn't matter if you tell me something bad, because nobody will ever find out.'

'Christ,' he said. 'I wouldn't even know where to begin.'

6.

He started talking about a childhood locked to diggers, and somewhere in that found himself talking about Graeme Stokes, a man gone before he could even remember it. A man who had left them to go back to a four-bedroomed detached house where a wife and two boys, only a year or two older than him, already lived. Lads who had everything Samhain could never even hope for, like karate classes and music lessons and places in a good school, half-brothers who didn't even know he existed, a man that Flores wanted to pretend didn't exist.

Elsa drove carefully. She let him talk.

'All this happened a long time ago,' Samhain said. 'My mum was...' he struggled to find the right word. 'She was raped by a police officer.'

'Recently?'

'No. Years ago. Before I was born. He was my father. She didn't know he was in the police – she thought he was an activist, like her. And I'm the result of it.'

She nodded, and glanced into the rearview mirror, before changing lanes. 'And have you always known? Or only now found out?'

'My friend told me. My friend who's looking after my cats while I'm away. My mum – Flores – doesn't even know that I know.'

'I see.' Over and around a slow-moving Fiat. 'So, your friend told you – and how does she know? Are you sure she's right?' Back, softly, into the slow lane. 'For all you know, if you don't talk to your mother, you may never know. You could be adding two and two and making five.'

'There was another man in Europe at the same time. Jimbo something. But it couldn't be him. Or at least, I don't think so. The dates don't seem quite right. So when I get back, I'm going to try and find him – Graeme Stokes. I've thought about it. Everything about it makes sense.'

Samhain had turned it over in his mind until the pictures had sharpened to hyper-reality. He remembered going into the small house on the estate for the first time, and how he had been thrown by the smallness of it – how closed-in the rooms were. Flores had shut the front door, and they'd gone into the hallway, which was the colour of a dust-storm, with its single light hanging over the stairs. She'd said: 'This is where we live now. No more camps.'

'We moved back to the UK,' he said. 'When I was quite young. Somebody in one of the camps had told her something – something had happened, some argument or fight, and she packed us both up and brought us away, that same day. I'd never understood what it was, until now. But it makes perfect sense. Leaving the camps like that, when normally she would have just hidden out in the tent for a few days. She completely cut herself off from her old activist friends, from everybody we'd ever known. Apart from one or two of them. And after we came back, she was always different.

Like somebody had let all the air out of her. She just didn't seem to enjoy things anymore. Not like she used to in the camps, when she'd always been laughing, always busy, always involved in some thing or other. When she – when we came back to the UK, she wasn't like that anymore. She used to spend days in bed, sometimes. Weeks. I never knew what was wrong with her – but I got used to it, after a while. I thought it was what everybody's mum did.' He said, 'She gave me a front door key to play with. You know, because we'd never had one before.' He had turned the toothy, round-headed thing over and over in his hands, staring at it in wonder.

'It all makes so much more sense now,' he said. 'Lots of things. Things from when I was a kid.'

'Yes.' Elsa nodded. 'How horrible. What an awful thing for you to find out. And how horrible for your mother.'

Samhain felt a curious sense of relief. As though a water balloon between his ribs, once tied, was now pricked and gushing loose, leaving him free at last to breathe. 'Oh God, it feels like such a relief to finally be able to tell somebody.'

'You haven't told anybody else? For how long?'

'A few weeks.'

She slowed, pulling the car up a slip road. Services: petrol pumps and a square, concrete building. 'What a burden. And I'm sorry, but I have to fill the car.' She stopped by the pump. 'I'll get us both something to eat.'

A text came through from Marta.

U ok? Nt like u 2 abandn tour 1/2way thru. Wt hppned?x

Elsa heading back from the shop, two blotchy paper bags in hand.

Fnd out Frankie's knwn ab Astrid 4 ages. Pnchd hm & gt thrwn out f sqt. Also pnchd Ned. Prbly stupidst thng Iv evr dn. A moment later, he sent a second text: *How r the cats?*

'Here!' Elsa got in. 'Apple or cinnamon. You can have first choice – being my guest.'

His stomach growled. 'Either.'

'Then, here.' She passed him a bag. 'Bon appetit!'

Long stretches of flat land. Sky pale as a Turner.

Samhain wondered what the rest of them would be doing. Round about now, they might only just be waking up: Romey pacing the floor, fretting about maybe having to cancel the rest of the gigs – not that anybody would hold him responsible. Maybe, with Ned all torn up the way he was, Patrick Stewart The Band might be in the same position. They'd both be going all over the rest of Europe, explaining what had happened. Now, whatever people thought about Samhain Estamos, these would be the legends that stuck, the man so unstable he fights members of his own band mid-tour, so badly they have to join up with another band, whose guitarist he also maimed, to make a single band out of the torn halves of two. You know: the guy who went nuts at the squat in Utrecht and got thrown out in the street at two in the morning, leaving his band without a guitarist, right in the middle of a tour. No, we don't know how he got back, either. Perhaps he bought a ferry ticket using the money he stole from the rest of the band.

He groaned.

'What's wrong?' Elsa asked.

'Another long story,' he said.

She looked again at her watch. 'I think you have time to tell it,' she said.

This new story was about how he had not just lost a daughter he had never known, but a best friend too, as well as four other good friends, and how, as soon as he got back to England, he'd have to find a new place to live – and that was if his boss was

willing to give him any work, after he'd pissed off on tour two
weeks after starting his job.

'Everything's a mess,' he said. 'My life is always such a
fucking mess.'

Elsa spoke carefully, as though negotiating with an armed
man. 'Do you know, I think that you can put all of this right.'

It occurred to him for a moment to say, What the hell do
you know, lady.

'No, I don't think so.' He screwed up his paper bag, and
sprayed crumbs all over the footwell. 'It's far worse than it
sounds. My best option is probably to move to a new city and
start all over again.' From what he'd heard, Charley and Astrid
were doing just fine without him. They probably didn't need
some loser coming around and screwing things up the whole
time.

Starting again would be easy enough. After all, it wasn't as
though he had a lot of furniture to take.

'You want to run away.'

'That's not running away.'

'That's exactly what it is. Going to a new place, maybe
making all of the same mistakes again. In four years' time, you'll
be saying: I need to move to a new city, and start all over again.'
She said: 'Can't you see that you're throwing everything away
before you've even had a go at sorting it out? You can get a job
you like – find a good place to live, where you can have your
daughter on weekends. Lots of people do it. You're talking about
it as though you think somebody is going to force you to work
in a bank, or something.'

'I don't want to have to work all week. Only having two days
a week off...'

'You know, you talk like this, and I can see your ex-girlfriend's
point. She says you're immature, and you prove it. Lots of
people do it. I do it. My husband does it. You can't always have

absolutely everything you want. That's not what life is. Look at me, in this car. I was like you, once – young, and idealistic. Never thought I would live a life like mine – with a husband and two kids and an apartment in the suburbs. And your "two days off a week," only with children, you don't even get that. You never have a day off, once you have kids. When I was your age, I thought I would be out there fighting the good fight, forever, out there on the ocean. I didn't want to stop going out on the actions. But then I got old, and tired, and I wanted to give my children a better life.

'Pert – that's my husband – said, we have to try and make the world a better place, for our kids. So we discussed it, and we agreed, Pert will keep going on these protests, for all of us. Only the short ones, for a day, or three days at a time. I could never go, because I had really bad sickness, both pregnancies, actually. At times I was just spending whole days at home, and after I had them, the same, too. At home all day. I said to him, you can go on any protest you like, for all of us, but try not to get arrested. Because I could hardly even make myself a sandwich, let alone get to the police station to pick him up.

'So he started to do things that were less radical – where he didn't have to do anything that was against the law. Once, he went to an oil spill on the north coast, where all the birds had been caught in the oil, and it was killing them – glueing their wings to their bodies. He and many others were picking up the birds and washing them, getting them clean enough to be able to fly again, and then keep them there so they didn't fly right back into the oil spill again – because nobody was cleaning it up. And these volunteers kept turning up from everywhere all the way around the world, and they were picking the birds up the wrong way, either being too rough with them or not cleaning them enough – or letting them go right back into the sea, where the oil was. And these birds were all over the beach. You can imagine it – gulls and puffins and moorhens – all covered in oil – so sticky they can't get up and catch anything to eat – and there is nothing to eat anyway, since all of the life in the sand and in the sea has been suffocated by the oil. All these birds croaking and crying, and Pert said, there were all these bodies – the birds – and you couldn't tell which were alive or dead, since none of them could flap their wings, and you could just see their eyes, black and terrified, and often there was oil in their eyes too. He said, the whole beach was full of them. And there was all this oil covering the sand – and as the volunteers and activists trod on it, they trod it further in – and he said that he felt like every step he took, it meant even more and more that the oil would never wash out of the beach.' She was quiet for a moment. 'It really broke his heart.'

'And after that,' she said, 'we decided – instead of protesting, we will work hard with our kids, and teach them awareness of these issues, and try to live sustainably, and so on. So that there are always at least two voices in the next generation who understand what slow living is, and who know how to do things in a way that is green and ecological. You know?'

For the first time, they passed a sign saying *Calais: 60Km.*

'It's not quite the same as my situation,' he said.

'I know. But what I'm saying is, you reach a point in life where you have to face up to things. You can't go along running away from it forever, pretending these things don't exist. It's not ideal, but what in life is? You're not a child anymore. You're a father.'

'If she'll let me be.'

'Listen, really, if you want my advice – and I know you didn't ask for it, but here it is – you should be thinking about what you can do to sort out all of this mess, not thinking of moving to another city and pretending none of it ever happened. There are lots of ways where you can be there for your daughter, and help her, without compromising your principles. Your priority now should be her, not yourself. That's what being a parent is. Setting an example – working out ways to do better next time. And don't you want to get to know her?'

'Yeah, of course.' That was, if he could ever get to Charley. If she'd ever let him contact her. Any way at all – a phone call, an email. He started to close his eyes, and heard his phone chirp. 'You know, you remind me of my friend Mart.' He twisted around, and started to unzip the front pocket.

'Mart?' Elsa smiled. 'I like the sound of this Mart. He sounds like somebody you should be spending more time with.'

'She,' he said.

It was a text from Stick.

R u ok? Nbdy angry. Frankie wants u 2 no he is sry. Txt bk plz.

Stick. Frankie. Long days in the bus. Closed windows and games of Van Man. Throats sore from laughter and shouting. Driving all over Europe, sardined in the back of a van, with one more body's worth of space, now.

He texted back. *Am ok. On way bk to UK now. Will hv mved out f sqt by time u all gt bk.*

Where was he going to go?

He pressed send.

7.

He walked by a high table in the hotel, and saw mouse corpses, six of them. Hind legs curled up towards their heads, front legs curled as though they had fallen asleep in the act of bringing a crumb to their mouths.

A bed in the corner was his old bed, with his childhood blue-striped duvet cover. Flores had made him keep it on the bed for years. Now it lay on the bed, somehow downstairs in the Boundary Hotel, with somebody lying under it.

This was a place of dust and shelves, like the inside of the linen cupboard, and the floor was dotted with cardboard boxes. His writing on the side said kitchen, living room, bedroom. They were the same brown moving boxes they used at work.

The figure beneath the bedspread began to move, stretching legs, moving arms. 'When are you coming back to bed?' she said.

'In a minute.'

He hadn't packed his records. They were stacked together

on the carpet, in a long row. At the front was his copy of Fresh Fruit for Rotting Vegetables, the one with the bent corner. He thought he'd lost it years ago. Left it in Charley's flat. Yet here it was.

He lifted it up, sliding the inner sleeve out, and felt the floor lurch with the suddenness of a ship.

A kid was staring at him. Grey eyes magnified by huge, round glasses.

Samhain blinked hard, and wiped dribble off his face.

His cheek stuck to the seat as he forced himself up. Shouldn't have fallen asleep there: God only knew who'd had their arse on it last. He yawned. The place smelled of terrible coffee and cheap chips.

The English Channel lay in a metallic grey strip outside the window.

'What time is it?' he asked.

The boy turned and ran away.

On the other side he hitched a ride on a goods lorry, with a driver with china-blue tattoos who said he was glad of the company.

It was evening by the time he got back to Bradford. The sky glowed with a blush like a new bride. Scaffolding outside the old mill flapped with bin liners, like a bat's broken wing. They were turning the lights out in the library as he passed. Samhain's bag felt heavier than it ever had.

He sent Marta a text: *Nearly home x*

HOME

SJ Bradley

HOME

Guest

I.

Marta sailed into the Boundary Hotel car park on her bike, swinging one leg out. She didn't see him at first: she was still in her work clothes, and her face said she'd been told bad news. She pushed the bike towards the front door as though she might run it forward hard enough to break a hole in the wood.

Then she saw him, and everything changed. 'Oh, hi!' A broad smile. 'What are you doing here?' For a second she had her arms around him. 'Haven't you got your keys?'

'Only just got here. Didn't you get my text?'

'Been riding home.'

Inside, she leaned the bike at the side of the stairs. She turned to face him, hands on hips, expectant. 'So.'

Why did women do that do him? Charley, Roxy – even Flores, a couple of times – and now Marta. 'So' wasn't even a question, but still could have all kinds of dire consequences if you got the answer wrong.

He stalled. 'So,' he answered.

'Where are the others?'

'Still in Europe. Stick messaged me yesterday. Yesterday? Maybe the day before. No, yesterday.'

Quickly, she grabbed his bad hand. The one with the bruises and glass-gash. 'Samhain...' There was this new look on her face, as though she'd seen him strap a firework to an animal. 'What happened?'

He turned the hand painfully around the wrist, wincing. 'Yeah. I'm not very proud of that.'

'You shouldn't be.' She almost pushed it back at him, then mounted the stairs. 'Come on. I've got something to show you.'

Acridity stronger than boiled vinegar, sharp enough to water your eyes. There were three craps in the litter tray, and the cats were all over. Prowling the bedspread, black and golden, miniature tigers and leopards, so much bigger now than when he had left them.

'I haven't been sleeping in here,' she said. Mart was on her knees by the tray, shuffling the poop out with a small plastic spade. 'You can't possibly keep it clean enough, with all these in here. It stinks. But they're nearly old enough to go – eight weeks – so I've been asking around, and I've found homes for pretty much all of them – except...'

Samhain held the ginger tabby, all fur and bones. There was nothing to it – it weighed about the same as a box of matches. It writhed in his hand, leaning, stretching, meowing: its voice was the sound of a tiny, very distant cat.

'...You two have already found each other, I see. Well, I didn't want to give him away. Since the two of you are such good friends.'

Warm, too. The kitten had a purr like a toy truck. 'Did you give him a name?'

'That one,' she said, 'is called Frazzles.'

It kneaded its claws into his sleeve. 'Hello, Frazzles.' He sank down onto the bed. Moving slowly, so as not to disturb the cat. 'Oh, who am I kidding? I can't keep this cat. Not when I'm going to be moving again.'

'What do you mean?'

'Mart, this whole tour has been a complete disaster. Everything went wrong. We played a benefit for women who've had children by undercover cops...'

'You played a benefit for yourself?!'

He shrugged. 'Not on purpose. I left my sleeping bag in some guy's flat – then we went to this awesome squat, and played an awesome gig, and it was all ok until we got wasted and Ned told me that Frankie has known about Astrid for ages... because he thought I already knew... and I ended up punching them both.'

'You punched Ned?'

'Yeah, well.' The back of his hand resembled recently butchered steak. 'I wasn't trying to hurt him. I was trying to get him out of the way, so I could fight Frankie.'

'That sounds like a great idea. Did it work?'

He showed her his fist. 'What do you think?'

'Good one, Sam.'

She went quiet. Continued collecting all of the shit in nappy bags, tying knots in their handles, then putting all of those bags into another, bigger bag; she tied its handle together, then put it outside the door. He could tell that she had plenty to say, but that she wasn't saying any of it.

'Mart, what's up? You might as well tell me.'

'Well. While you were away – me and Jeff split up.'

'No!' Mart and Jeff were the longest two he knew. They'd been together forever. He couldn't remember a time when they'd ever not been a couple.

Calm, dependable Mart, and smiling, nerdy Jeff, who knew about computers. Jeff was the guy to ask if you wanted something building that didn't run Windows. Jeff, who started stories with the words: 'Look, I'm not going to bore you with details about operating systems,' before launching into a dense, almost fractal level of detail about Ubuntu; Jeff, who never hit on women or seemed to watch bands, merely stood around the edge of the room, holding his pint, and looking mildly up at the ceiling. 'But you've been together ages. What happened?'

'Yeah, well.' She shrugged. 'I don't know. It wasn't anything in particular. We were both a bit bored, I think. Jeff's a great guy.' He saw then that she was crying, and trying not to. 'I don't know whether I'll meet somebody like him ever again.'

He could get up. He should get up. Put his arm around her, make her feel better.

But she might not like it. And he'd probably make a mess of it, anyway. His horrible, hairy arm around Marta's elegant shoulders. And there was the cat to think about. Sleeping, settled on his belly.

Probably best that he didn't.

Samhain said: 'You're right. Jeff *is* a great guy.'

Long, silent tears. Her hair fell in drapes around her face.

'But Marta, you're great too. You'll meet somebody else. Somebody just as nice as Jeff – better still, even.'

'Yes, but if I can't make things work with Jeff – who's a great guy, the kind of guy you'd be mad to break up with – maybe I'm not cut out for relationships at all.'

'Don't say that.' Her voice was all hiccups, whines. She was sitting there like a grieving widow, with mascara running all down her face. He couldn't believe it was Mart sitting there crying like this, Mart who had steered things so steadily over the past few weeks, Mart who never seemed to be fazed by anything. He hated to think of her feeling like this, when she had been so kind to him, again and again, even though she knew what a loser he was.

'Mart, it's not your fault. Sometimes these things happen. To everybody. You can't beat yourself up for it – thinking you messed up like this, or like that. Maybe you and Jeff weren't right for each other.' He wasn't really sure about this bit, but it seemed like the sort of thing he ought to say. 'People break up sometimes. You'll be happier for it one day – and so will he. You've got to find a way to move on.'

'Covered in cat hair,' she muttered, picking it off her shirt and leggings with precise, pinching movements.

'You'll be alright, Mart,' he said. 'In a few weeks' time, you'll look back on this and laugh. It'll all be for the best – you'll see.' He thought for a minute, and added: 'There isn't anybody else like you, Mart. You're always so...'

How to describe it?

Mart's ability to take things in her stride, to always seem to know what to expect. The whole world could be destroyed in a series of nuclear blasts, and the first one to get back on her feet would probably be Mart, probably with a whole pallet of bottled drinking water that she'd got from somewhere, and a bunch of tarpaulins the survivors could use to build shelter. In that situation, Mart would be the one standing on the remains of whatever was left in a hi-vis jacket, waving her arms around and shouting: 'Hey everybody, come over here, I know how we can survive this.'

'...Resilient,' he said, not knowing quite how the word had arrived in his mouth.

'Yeah.' She paused. 'I just miss him, you know? I miss the ordinary things. Like at work today, one of the kids said, I wish I was a robot, not a boy or man, because if I was a robot I could do a sum in under one second, and my name would be ArithmoBot. I thought, I'll tell Jeff that when I get home – he'll love it. And then I realised, no, I won't tell Jeff that, because I don't tell Jeff things anymore.' She looked up at him, through dewy lashes. 'Do you know what I mean?'

Frazzles stretched, and jumped off Samhain's arm, leaving a thin red streak where his forepaws had gripped a moment. 'Of course I do,' he said. He got up, and went and sat on the carpet beside her.

Putting his arm around Mart was a new thing. She was a wiry thing, and she'd got a dried leaf caught in her hair. 'When I first broke up with Charley, I missed loads of things about her. Just having her there – around the house.'

It had been her efficiency he'd missed. The million things he hadn't realised she'd been doing, until they stopped. That there had always been soup in the pot, waiting to be heated – that was Charley. Bunches of fliers on the table for gigs he wouldn't want to miss – also Charley. There had always been toilet roll and washing up liquid. Charley, Charley, all of those things Charley.

Then they'd broken up and he'd moved in with Frankie, and started living the type of existence where sometimes he'd wake up and see somebody else wearing his trousers. In the slum, he'd started going to sleep wearing his clothes, because it was the only way he could be sure they'd still be there in the morning.

'But you get over it, you know? I mean – I wouldn't want to go back to living with Charley now. Not for anything. After a while, I got to see that I was better off without her.'

He had spent weeks longing for somebody to come home with leftovers from the social club cafe. Two unwanted burgers, a bit of misshapen cake. For somebody to come home and surprise him with a DVD they'd found in a charity shop, even if it was something stupid and cheesy like Mission Impossible: 2.

'When I split up with Charley, I used to miss how nice she was.'

Mart laughed suddenly. At last, a smile.

'You know, because she's a very kind person, Charley, but

she also doesn't take any shit, and that was one of the things I really liked about her. She was absolutely right to throw me out when she did. Any other girl might have given me a second chance, when I didn't really deserve it.' He drew his arm away, and stroked Mama Cat along her long, sleek back. 'If she'd taken me back, I would have lost respect for her, and it wouldn't have been the same.

'What I'm saying is, things will start to look better after a while. You'll see why you did the things you did, and they'll make more sense. You can't stay with somebody out of habit – because of the few things you do like about them. Sometimes, two people aren't meant to be together.'

She was crying again, quietly this time.

'Let me get you a tissue,' he said.

The bedroom door was only open a moment, and Mama Cat clipped out. Racing as though chasing a fly, and she reached the laundry cupboard before him, looking up at the door handle with her tail swishing. Unnerving green eyes: that was a hunting face.

'Alright, alright,' he said.

She went in through the open door, and crouched under one of the lower shelves.

Samhain picked up a toilet roll. Something had been at the tissue, tearing strips free with tiny, nibbling teeth. Not quite stripped bare, but ribboned enough to be of limited use to humans.

Mama Cat looked narrow and lean enough that you might take her for a young huntress, not a mother who'd given birth only a few weeks ago.

He found a whole toilet roll further along the shelf, and left her inside, propping the door open with one of the beaten-up rolls.

2.

'Your computer session starts at half past.' Today's librarian was broad, bearded, smelling ever so slightly of sandalwood. 'Oh – and one of the librarians upstairs left this for you.'

An envelope, with Fox-Eyes' writing on the front.

There was a note inside, on the same creamy paper she'd used before.

Samhain,

I did a bit more digging and found this. It's a clipping from the local paper in Manchester. I couldn't find anything on James Cobb, but I did find this of Graeme Stokes. It might help you track your brothers down at least, if this is the right guy.

Anyway, have a look and if you think it is him, I'm sorry Sam, I really am.

She had copied the article and folded it into the envelope

for him.

A grainy photograph accompanied the story. Graeme's wife, a pixelated woman with a fixed smile, kneeled beside a child's wheelchair, with balloons tied to its frame.

Two younger men stood awkwardly behind two other wheelchairs. Their faces were younger than the inset picture of Graeme Stokes – tall, big-set, with rounded and jowly faces – and yet, in them, he could see his own eyes, his nose. Graeme's other sons. His half-brothers.

...the Head of Beechside Special School, Jennifer Black, praised Graeme Stokes for his generosity and kindness towards others. 'Without Graeme's tireless fundraising, we could never have afforded our new sensory room. It was typical of him to embark on a project and stick at it until he'd done what he'd set out to do. With his help, we were able to kit out a fabulous resource for all of our children to enjoy. He was a truly altruistic man: rarely do you meet anybody who gives their time and energy so gladly, to those less advantaged than themselves, than Graeme did.'

The inset photo showed a man, middle aged and smiling and bald. It was the face of a man who ate chips, who watched soaps with his wife, who cleaned the car on Sundays. It was the face of a man who took his family to Spain for a week every Summer, and to the in-laws' every Boxing Day. This was a man who chanced a single pint in the pub when he was driving, a man who wouldn't buy lighters in the market because he'd heard the money supported terrorism. He was the man who dreamed of the day when he could move full-time into his garden shed, to get ten minutes' peace from the wife. Ordinary. Blokeish. The kind of man you wouldn't even notice in the street. He was this man or that man. He was every man and no man. He was Samhain's father.

Samhain studied the photograph again. He couldn't believe Flores would ever have liked somebody like that.

If you decide you want to make contact with his widow, or anybody else, just pop up and see me on the third floor. Apparently his older son followed him into the police force, so they should be pretty easy to find.

Samhain folded the note and the article, and put them back in the envelope. Almost every computer was occupied. Office chairs with zip tops and hoodies slung over their backs; rows of people, backs hunched, clicking and scrolling through bright white mailboxes, other people's MySpace profiles.

Only one, in the corner, was not taken: his.

He sat down, and got started.

There was an email from Frankie:

Hey man I'm in Utrecht. Writing you this messgae from a cafe a few streets awa yfrom the squat.

Look Sam, I'm sorry. Ive been going over it and over it in my mind and I know I did wrong. Not that its an excuse but I found out by accident and when I got in touch with Charley she made me swear to keep it a secret. She said she was going to tell you herself and I kept on thinking she would but I never saw her to ask. Girl seems to have disappeared from the secne totally man. I thought it wasn't really my place to say anything. She said she would tell you herself. I feel such a dick about it now. You should have known earlier and Im sorry.

We\re best friends, aren't we? I want to make it up to you, anyway I can. What do you want me to do? Whatever it is, I'll do it. I miss you already Sam. Can't stand the thought of us falling out for good over this.

We've canselled the rest of our gigs and are playing Patrick Stewart

Guest

The Band's dates instead, with us hopping on their bill. Ned;s arm is pretty beat up so I'm playing guitar for them and their bassist is doing their best to play guitar for us, not that the guitar parts are that hard anyway haha. The only thing is, we haven't got contact information for the promoter in Cologne. Romey can't find it anywhere on the sheet. Can you sort it out please?

Frankie

That explained the second email:

Hi Samhain, it is Freidrich from Freitag Hus in Koln. We are concerned that your band did not make it here last night. Did you have trouble finding it? Please get in touch to let us know you are all O.K.

F.

Then, from Flores.

My little bug,

What a break we've had! Sorry I've been a long time out of contact. Badger and I went to a hippy music festival somewhere in Bedford, then onto the retreat in Wales.

The retreat has the most amazing garden. Huge roses and bushes, and raspberry canes and strawberries everywhere. It has the most heavenly smell. We went out into the garden every day to pick fresh berries for breakfast. You can't imagine how great it tastes to eat something only a moment after picking it fresh from the plant. It made me want to take up gardening again!

All the rest of the cooking was done by this one woman, Rosetta, who made the tastiest vegan food EVER. The first night she did this mushroom risotto and honestly, Sam, I thought I was in heaven. I've never tasted anything like it before and I don't think I will again. Another night she made these broccoli and beetroot burgers - I didn't even know you could make burgers with broccoli, did you?!

Anyway, she was amazing, better than any professional, and everybody there was so LOVELY. We met this amazing woman who spends six months of every year running radio projects in West Africa to help villagers learn how to set up and run their own radio stations, so they can communicate with one another across the Savannah. Isn't that amazing? Anyway I took her email address so we're going to stay in contact afterwards. The world is really full of amazing people. Sometimes you forget, or I do anyway.

So, what's this big news you were talking about? I can't believe you'd say 'I've got news' and not tell me what it is. That's just cruel, little bug!

We're travelling around a bit more this week, me and Badger, and I'm not sure when I'll be home exactly. So, you can try to ring, but I can't be sure when I'll be back.

Kisses
Flores

Flores would be pleased to find out Graeme Stokes was dead, he thought. The man she'd worked so hard to keep out of their lives – not that the old dickhead had ever made any attempt to see them. He'd done his business then gone, leaving the two of them to struggle their way through life.

Graeme Stokes' other family, who didn't even know Flores or Samhain existed, had no doubt lived a mortgage-free life in a huge detached house, with a garden, and karate lessons. They'd got off to a good start – they'd lived a life like the Tomlinsons. That was how he imagined their lives, against a template of Emmy Tomlinson's family, a girl at his primary school who, for some reason he'd never understood, had invited him to her seventh birthday. The sort of family who smiled a lot, who never forgot to return library books, who never forgot when it was

Guest

Comic Relief day or Sports Day. Emmy Tomlinson's mother kept a stash of blank birthday cards in a drawer, just in case, and her father lived with them all the time, and always came home when he said he would. Emmy always had on neat, pretty clothes, and always said please and thank you; they were a marmalade on toast, pass the butter, would you like one sugar or two kind of family. Only Emmy Tomlinson's father wasn't the type of person who would have a second secret family that he never saw.

It was time they faced up to the useless old baboon, and flicked two fingers to his grave.

Mum,

Just back off tour! It didn't go well. Ended up coming home early (long story) because I've got a lot of shit to sort out. There is a lot of news to be honest, not all of it good, or not all things that you'll like, anyway.

My friend Marta sent me a news story about undercover cops infiltrating eco-activist groups in the UK and Europe in the 70s & 80s. Did you ever know a man called Graham Porter ('Fields')?

I know this is not easy for you but I have always wondered about my dad and all I want, is to know. He is dead now so it's not like I can see him, this guy's real name was Graeme Stokes and I think he might have been my dad. Please can you get in touch and tell me what you remember. This guy had another wife and kids who probably never even knew we existed.

Just typing it turned his whole self to ice. Hands, arms, the back of his neck, all felt as though they were being pressed against a sheet of snow.

Mum I don't blame you, for not telling me, or for the way you dealt with it when I was a kid. He was a bastard and it wasn't your fault.

Anyway the old fucker

He paused for a minute: typed, deleted.

Somebody in the library helped me find out a bit about him, and I've got a newspaper clipping about him that I can show you if you want. It's got a picture of him but you can see the likeness. Between him and me I mean, and his two other sons. I am going to try to meet them if I can. I can't stand the idea of not knowing.

Also the other thing is that I've just found out I've got a little girl, with Charley. I had no idea that she even existed until about a month ago. She's about two years old and her name's Astrid. It's all a bit complicated but I'm going to try and find a place of my own so that I can have her to come and stay with me sometimes.

I did want to tell you all of this face to face but it's a bit hard with you being away all the time. Message me back when you get this.

Congratulations, Flores! You're a grandmother.

Grandmother. He wasn't sure whether she'd like that.

Samhain spent a while staring at the screen, until the letters began to wobble. He stared, eyes fixed, until he perceived a woody smell somewhere behind the chair: the faint scent of a farmer's field and new, wet lambswool.

'I'm afraid there are others waiting.' A gentle touch on his shoulder. 'You'll have to finish what you're doing and log out.'

All this, and he hadn't even had time to post a bulletin on MySpace asking about flats to rent.

'Right,' Samhain said.

3.

'This is what we call the house of a burrowing man. Your first one.' Kebby's grin showed sparkling incisors, sharp as a cat's. 'This will be a baptism of fire.'

Simon moaned, leaning against the van window. 'If you ask me, Peter should leave these jobs to the council,' he said. 'Let environmental health deal with it.'

'They won't do it, that's the trouble.' Kebby peered out of the window at the house. Window frames rotten and splintering. Guttering and pipes hung loose like straws in a drink. 'Too many of them in the union.'

'The smell inside some of these places,' Simon went on. 'If you imagine a sad old man who's lived by himself for twenty years – never throwing anything away – not even taking the rubbish out half the time... and if he's had a dog – or cats – which crap *inside* the house...'

'In a minute, he won't *have* to imagine it.' Kebby put on a horror-movie narration voice. 'The removal men never suspected, for a second, what they were about to find behind the doorway of...' he squinted at the number: '38 Woodville Place.'

'The pets won't still be in there,' Samhain said, 'will they?'

He imagined piteous poor things, loose skin, drought bones.

'Oh no, don't worry,' Kebby said. 'The council will have already been for those.'

'Good.'

Back home, Mama Cat had brought her young a live mouse to play with: he had found them all gathering like a crowd at the gallows. Each took a slicing claw to it, taunting the poor thing, batting it around the circle, until at last the black kitten pounced and did for it by biting its neck in two. Samhain hadn't been able to get the mouse away.

After its death, each kitten tore a strip loose. They all gnawed and tore at its greasy skin, its red quivering innards, until there was nothing left. Mama Cat had watched them do it with her glittering, agate eyes, a mother cat with the look of an Egyptian Goddess.

'The man from the council will be here any minute,' Kebby said. 'To let us in – and that's as much as he'll do. After that, it's up to us.'

Their boss had a subcontract for places like these, the houses of burrowing men. Places where lonely, hoarding old men had lived alone, slowly closing themselves in behind a rising mountain of daily newspapers, takeaway cartons, cut hair, and blunt razors, like an animal building itself a nest. There never was any family to clear it.

'How do you think you get like that?' Simon asked. 'How do you get to the stage where you think: I won't bother throwing away all these old papers, I'll hold onto 'em. How come they never think, hold on, I don't really need the football results from six months back – maybe I should have a clear out?'

'What would happen if you started keeping newspapers like that?' Kebby asked.

'You're joking, aren't you? My mum would kill me. She doesn't even let me wear my work boots in the house. She makes me take 'em off in the front porch.'

'Exactly. A woman keeps you in line.' Kebby leaned forward.

A small council van was entering the street. It was being driven by a bloke who looked like he'd rather be somewhere else.

'Let's get to work, men,' Kebby said.

Samhain reached for his gloves.

The dead man – whose post gave his name as Joe – had left a narrow path from the door to a rotting red sofa, and another from there to the kitchen at the back of the house.

In this path they all stood, looking at the stacks of things.

'Well.' The man from the council leaned in from the front doorway, his feet remaining firmly where they were, on the step outside. 'Good luck.' He left the keys on a hook by the door. A minute later, they heard his van engine start.

'Sooner we get started, the sooner it's done.' Kebby produced rolls of bin liners, and gave them one each. 'Bag everything up. These are extra strength, but they're not invincible.' He waved a roll threateningly in Samhain's direction. 'So you be careful. I don't want to be driving a van around with bin juice rolling around in the back. Don't overfill the bags. You understand?' Samhain nodded. 'Now, go and see whether there's anything worth eating in the fridge.'

Simon laughed, gurglingly. 'Oh, snap!'

Samhain took the hint: he was lucky to have been taken on for this job, lucky to have been given any work at all. Kebby was testing him out, to see whether he'd disappear again.

The kitchen smelled of sour milk. On the cooker top,

milk blue with spores settled between the rings in a textured map. Here was a lake, it seemed to say; and *here* are all of its tributaries. 'How clean do we have to leave it?' he called through to the living room, where Kebby was throwing old takeaway cartons into bags.

'Not very,' his workmate replied. 'Just tidy – tidy. We have to bin up all the crap so the cleaners can get in. We don't have to clean it ourselves.'

'Good,' Samhain muttered.

The sink was filmed with stagnant water, its surface textured by a junkyard of forks and knives.

'And by the way, you can take whatever you want,' Kebby called. 'It's not as if he's going to want it. Only all going to go to the dump otherwise.'

'I know.' Peter said.'

A dead man's things.

Peter had also said there was enough work to keep him busy all week. This today, then house moves on Wednesday and Thursday; then on Friday, Simon was going on holiday, and there was a piano to move.

Samhain ran the tap, and the water came rusty and cold, splashing everything with a fine brown grit.

He would need forks. He started to lift them free of the greasy water.

There was usually a will, Peter had said, when there was something worth sharing out. What Joe Belling had left behind was a kingdom of nothing. Cheap cutlery, chipped mugs, wobbly-handed pans, bent baking trays. It would all be thrown away, Peter said, unless they wanted any of it. 'Perk of the job,' he'd said.

Still, Samhain felt strange about putting cutlery aside to take for his new place.

'Christ.' Simon shouted from upstairs. 'You guys want to come and have a look at this.'

Kebby had already mostly cleared the living room. Samhain raced through it; there was floor space, and it seemed twice the size.

Upstairs to a narrow hallway, with an open doorway off to its side.

'Look.'

Samhain couldn't see Simon at first. He was hidden behind a wall of magazines, floor to ceiling, the floor curving under their weight.

'This is...' Kebby said. 'I've never seen so much...'

'Porn?' Simon gestured at the mattress on the floor, the VCR in the corner. 'Old man liked big tits. Just look at this.' He flipped through one of the magazines.

A rat's nest of hardened socks on the carpet. Everything smelled of sweaty cheese and stale piss.

'I wouldn't touch that if I were you,' Samhain said.

Simon dropped the magazine. It fell, leaves flying, to his feet, and landed open on a picture of a blonde woman with a breast in each hand. 'Christ,' he said, making a noise like he was going to throw up. 'Where's the bathroom?'

They had to take the mattress out to the van, and because there was no hot water in the house, none of them could scrub themselves clean enough afterwards to want to eat their sandwiches.

'Never mind,' Kebby said. 'I know a cafe around the corner. They know me there. They'll let us wash up in their sink.'

Dust, years of it, when you moved somebody still living, was a clean kind of dirt. But this, grease sticking and trapped, had the weight of death on it, the shame of a life poorly lived. It made for a sombre atmosphere in the van.

'Now there,' Kebby said, 'was a man who had nobody in life. You young lads, take that as a warning from history. Don't you become a burrowing man, living on takeaway chips and wanking yourself dry.' He pulled the van up to the kerb. 'Now! Who's ready for a bellybuster?'

'So,' Kebby said. 'Did you take anything from Joe's house?'

'Nothing.' Samhain had found a good pan in the back of one of the cupboards, that had looked wedding-present new. But it had felt too strange to take it. He had thrown it away, along with the plates, all mismatched and dirty, and crusted with mould. He wouldn't want to eat from any of these, no matter how hot they could be washed. He had thrown everything away, as well as the mug Joe Belling had drunk from. 'Well – just a couple of spoons and forks.'

'That's gross.' Simon shuddered. 'He might have been eating off one of those forks when he died.'

Kebby was covered in ketchup. 'Simon, when you move out of your mother's house, then you can talk.' He licked sauce out of the corner of his mouth.

'I need stuff for my house.' Samhain was eating a plate of fried mushrooms on toast. There wasn't much choice for vegetarians here, and even these tasted slightly of bacon. 'I can't buy everything new. It's too expensive.'

'Do you need plates and dishes?' Kebby chewed heavily. 'Because I think we've got an old set in our garage. Ayesha took our old set when she first moved out, and then when she got married, she brought it back again. She said, "Dad, I don't need this old stuff anymore." Because they'd got Debenhams vouchers to buy all new stuff when they got married, you know. And I said, "This house isn't just a dumping ground for stuff you don't need, Missy." But my good lady wife said that I wasn't to argue and to let her put her things wherever she liked. So now it's in our garage. You want it?'

'Anything to get me started.'

'Yes, that's the way.' Kebby twisted his napkin into a boulder, and threw it onto the plate. 'You know, you should ask Peter about this. He's got a whole warehouse of furniture somewhere, full of all sorts of things. I bet he could get you a few bits and pieces.' He stood up, and wiped his mouth with the back of his hand. 'Well don't just sit there, boys, we've got work to do.'

4.

When Samhain came home, the band's t-shirt box was on the reception desk beside a scattered pile of fanzines and records, and the back door was open, sending a breeze blowing through the house. The wind brought with it a gust of dried leaves: Mama Cat came trotting in through the back door, paws and legs all lean with the hunt.

Only Frankie could be careless enough to leave the door open like that, knowing there were kittens in the house. Kittens too young and tumbling and too un-neutered to go out yet.

He started towards the stairs, then heard a noise outside the back door: the wheeze and squeeze of a bike pump. That would be Frankie, trying to get some terrible bike on the road, some bike more rust than frame, a bike he'd probably pulled out of a hedge on the way home. He'd have made Lemmers and Romey stop for it, when all they wanted to do was get home and sleep.

On the first floor, the end room's door was wedged open.

Roxy had shoved the bedside table in there and pulled all the drawers out, showing they were empty. There was a note written on hotel paper on its top: *Gone to live with Morris.*

This thoughtlessness was Frankie all over. Leaving doors open and curtains flapping. All the kittens might already be out by now, prowling hedges and bushes, chasing butterflies, following their noses out into a world full of fascinating new scents – other animals and cats. Scents they might follow over walls, and through gaps; prowling through open doorways, scampering over roads, until they found their way into some new place with different floors and lights, and new people. Somewhere where a hand would come down and a voice might say: 'Look, a kitten! Do you think it's a stray?'

A place where, if luck would have it, there would be kind people with good hearts, not cruel ones who drowned kittens in sacks in rivers. A place where the doors would close, in a room the kittens didn't know, and didn't know how to get out of, because they'd followed their interests so far that they hardly knew which turns and corners they'd taken, and had arrived somewhere from which making the journey home was impossible.

The smell of the open was too much for an animal to bear. You couldn't expect them to be able to smell it, and not want to go out in it. Frankie should have known that, but he didn't, because it never occurred to Frankie that some things mattered. That details were important. That it *didn't* matter whether you meant to hurt somebody or not, what mattered was what you'd done.

Frankie always thought he could make things right by smiling and saying sorry. It never occurred to Frankie, who, at the age of forty, still could never hold onto a girlfriend for more than a year at a time, that what counted were the things you did, not the things you said.

Samhain opened the door to five much larger cats.

A tawny beast with cockleshell eyes and a mane like a Junior School lion came rushing at him, saying meow in what it probably thought was a terrifying roar.

Four siblings followed, prowling with the slinking grace of panthers, blinking at the sudden expanse of space. A whole new world out on the landing: the pure black kitten came with its nose tracing a line along the floor, and had got down the first two steps before Samhain was quick enough to react. He scooped Bat Cat up by the ribs, and put him firmly back on the landing floor.

He made a gate of two bedside cabinets at the top of the stairs, to stop them getting away, and made a play area from upsided drawers, bedsheets, and cardboard boxes.

They loved it: the calico settled into one of the drawers, becoming a furred loaf, eyes closed and purring.

Frankie was still up to something down there. Making another kind of noise now, light hammering, as though he were striking a Christmas bell with a toffee hammer.

A minute later the back door slammed, and the whole house shook. 'Samhain?' Frankie's voice came up the stairs. 'You there?'

Samhain expected to see a man with long shadows across his face. That was how Frankie usually looked coming back off tour, either almost dead, or recently exhumed. But his ex-friend must have scrubbed the grime clear from his face, because his skin was a clean pink, and his eyes bright and enquiring.

'Look, you.' Frankie nodded down at the cats. 'Can't believe they're so big, now. How old did you say they were?'

'About nine weeks. I think.' Frazzles climbed into his lap, mewing, padding his sharp claws about him as he settled into a doughnut curve on Samhain's thigh. 'I can't talk to you, Frankie. I've got nothing to say.'

'No. I know. I know.' Frankie's voice had taken on a familiar tone, contrite and high-pitched. It was the voice he used when he was apologising to girls. 'Just let me say one thing, though.'

In the duvet cover tent between upturned drawers, the fabric billowed and tussled, making shadow puppets of the cats beneath.

'Frankie, did you ever think about how much longer you've known about Astrid than I have? About how much I would have loved to have known? You know, I can't stop thinking about – how you knew about it all that time – when we broke this squat, when we lived here – together, and before this, in the slum – you've known for months, all that time, pretending to be my friend, and you never said a word?'

'Of course I do, of course I think about it. And I feel terrible Sam, really I do. I know I did wrong. All those months, I've felt bad about it. Some days I've thought about nothing else.' Frankie sighed. 'Honestly mate, do you mind if I sit down?'

He climbed over the furniture at the top of the stairs, and sat cross-legged on the carpet by the balustrade. 'You might not believe this, but I found out by accident myself, boyo. Saw Charley on her way to the clinic with Astrid, once. She was on her way to have her weighed, or whatever they do, and I knew straight away she was yours. Looked so much like you, there was no question. So she was on her way down there to take her to see the nurse, and she looked knackered, so tired like, and I felt a bit sorry for her, you know? Because the Charley I know, she doesn't look tired. Or at least, she never used to. Anyway she clocked me too and she said, Just keep it quiet, Frankie, please. She begged me to, and because she looked so bad, I said I would. Felt sorry for her, didn't I? She said she was going to get in touch with you herself, right? You know how straight up Charley is. She's a woman of her word. Didn't think anymore of it, not at the time, anyway. I thought, she'll get in touch with Samhain soon, any day. Kept on thinking that for months. Knew one day you'd come and say, Hey Frankie, guess who's just phoned me, and guess what? Only that day never came, did it? That was when I started thinking, Jesus, lad, maybe I should say something. Only I didn't want you to be more angry with me than you were with Charley. A whole shoot-the-messenger type thing. Anyway it all went on so long, months, until there was no way I could say anything myself. You would have been mad then anyway if I had.

'You see? What would you have done, if you'd been me?'

From here, the day being clouded over as it was, his old friend looked exactly that – old. Face bloated from two weeks' drinking, with his scar – a pale, diagonal metal-mark down one cheek – that he'd got from falling over into a drum kit once – shining.

'Look, I couldn't bear it if we fell out, lad. You're my best friend in the whole world. Only one I've got, I think, sometimes. At least can you say you understand why I did it?'

'Frankie...'

'Didn't mean to hurt you, that's the thing. None of it was done on purpose. You know I would never do that.'

'I don't know.' Samhain sighed. 'Look, my main thing now is to think about how I'm going to get to see her, when Charley won't even talk to me.'

'That's it! I'll help!' Frankie yelped. 'I'll talk to her for you. You've got a job now, right? You're steady. I'll tell her that – how hard you're working – that you're going to start sending her money.'

Mama Cat reappeared, jumping elegantly over the chests of drawers. She found the kitten in the drawer, and settled down beside it.

'No. You just stay out of it, Frankie. I mean – I know you're trying to help. But stay out of it.'

A soft thump and tumble of paws, and the black cat was in

with its mother and sibling. Trying to force its way under the ginger cat's legs, to get its own back and neck groomed.

'I'm going to ask Marta,' Samhain said. 'She'll know what to do.'

5.

Red brick and curved handrails, a wooden desk that looked like a Post Office counter. A poster on the wall said, *See it, report it!* He almost had to stop himself from tearing it down; that was what he would have done if it had been anywhere else.

'Can I help you?'

This from a boy about Samhain's own age behind the counter, a boy in policeman's navy, a shirt new and white.

First time Samhain had ever entered a police station voluntarily. Now he was here, it seemed less of a smart idea than it had that morning.

Cameras pointed. Two behind his back, over his shoulder, and two in the office corner, pointed at his face. Even if his brother never met him, he still might be watching him. Somewhere in a back office, face lit by screens.

'I'm hoping to see Gareth Stokes.'

'Gareth.' The boy glanced at him, picking up the phone on

the desk. 'No problem. I think he's around somewhere. What's it about?'

'It's kind of... kind of a long story.'

The boy listened to the phone for a moment, and stared. There didn't appear to be any answer on the other end; he reached for a biro. 'What's your name, sir?'

'Samhain.'

Scribbling. Scraps of paper from the desk. 'Samhain what?'

'Samhain Foss.'

'What's it regarding?'

Samhain tapped the desk. This place, so calm and clean, meant to reassure the public. You would never guess that this was the same force that drove protestors back into concrete buildings with police horses; a force that pressed you bodily against others, crushed your ribs, left you unable to breathe. A force that took your photograph as you tried to leave Trafalgar Square after a war protest. 'It's personal,' he said.

'Right.' The desk sergeant sighed. 'Well, at least try to help me out a bit. You got a crime number?'

'No.' Samhain answered.

'Have you committed a crime?'

'No.'

'Warrant out for your arrest?'

'No.'

'Here to sign bail?'

'No.'

'Will *he* know what it's about?'

'Look, I told you, it's personal. Private. It's a bit of a delicate situation.'

'I'll see whether he's busy.' The desk sergeant grabbed the paper, and went to a back door which was half toughened glass. 'Wait there.'

A small room, grey, windowless. Desk, two steel chairs. Mirror. A place the same as any other police interview room, only this time, he was free to go.

'Well.'

He was ushered in. Gareth, six inches taller, had a belly starting to overhang trousers. 'Sit down.'

He had the same nose and same eyes. Strange to see himself like this, across the table, with a wobbling extra chin, a wrinkled uniform. Gareth didn't wear his things quite so neatly as did the boy on the front desk.

'Dad warned us you'd come one day.'

It was not a friendly comment. Gareth, double-chinned and jowly, looking at him the same way as any policeman did: as though he was a piece of gum stuck to his shoe.

Had he thought it would be like this? Airless, atmosphereless, two men in a closed-up room. 'Did he?'

'Yeah.'

This man, almost his exact age, related to him, paunch-bound and uniform-striped. He sat by a desk most of the week and ate donuts; at night, he went home and watched soaps. This was a man who supermarket shopped at the weekend, with a girlfriend with identikit blonde hair, who tossed Ronan Keating CDs into the shopping trolley. He probably had a mortgage and Type 2 diabetes.

Samhain rested his elbows on the desk, and noticed that Gareth was already doing the same thing. One hand folded over his left forearm, exact way Samhain did it.

Gareth reached idly for the clippings and notes on the table. The newspaper story, the letters from Fox-Eyes. He turned them over, glancing at them as though they were somebody else's till receipts. 'What are these?'

Notes from Samhain's first time in the library. His writing, the names of groups Flores had been in. Deep Green Resistance,

Earth Fight!, Women at Menwith Hill, plus the countries he thought she'd been in, before he'd been born.

'The names of protest groups my Mum was in. When she knew your father. Our father.'

'Who art in heaven,' Gareth said. It wasn't a joke; he shuffled the bits of paper together, and pushed them back across the desk. 'The thing is, like I said, I don't know what you've been told, or what you think you know. But you've got no business being here.'

Gareth spoke these words as though they were facts from an encyclopaedia. As though he was saying there were nine planets in the solar system, each with its own system of gravity.

'You knew about me?'

'My father warned me, yes.'

'So you knew. You've known – for how long?'

'I don't know.' Fat shoulders shrugging. 'When we were young lads. Teenagers. We'd always known about Dad's half-brother. Uncle Phil. Your father. Dad didn't like to talk about him. They didn't get on... and then Mum was ill for a while. It looked like she might pass on, and Dad sat us both down, and said – you've got a cousin – because your Uncle Phil's got at least one son that we know of...'

'Hang on, hang on.' Samhain started drumming on the desk. 'Your father – Graeme Stokes – told you we were *cousins*?'

'That's right.'

'Jesus.'

Gareth breathed out with the energy of a sleeping bear. 'Like I said,' he continued. 'I don't know what you've been told, or who's told you it, but you've been misled.' He started to get up, extending his hand for a shake. 'I'm sorry you've had a tough time. There's not a lot more that I can do to help. Let's say that that's the last of it, shall we? All the best.'

This took Sam right back to the time in Genoa, when the

police had been determined to get something out of him, for something he supposedly knew. They'd been sure enough of it to break two of his ribs. Their truth had no bearing on the actual truth; it didn't matter that what they believed was wrong. They'd kept on at it for three days, and let him out without admitting they'd been mistaken.

When the police believed something, they really believed it. It didn't seem to matter that the evidence said something totally different.

'Now, wait a minute.' Sam got up too, chair scraping backwards. 'I think you're the one who's been misled.'

Gareth had his hand already on the desk, templed. 'Sam, you've been led a merry dance. I don't know what your mother's told you – she's always been a troubled soul. Probably wants you to have a father, any father, so long as it's not Uncle Bill. But she's told you the wrong thing.'

'Your dad was an undercover cop in Europe in the eighties. He was in activist camps with my Mum in Switzerland and Belgium around the time I was conceived.' He pointed to the back of the room. 'You and me, stand side by side in that mirror. Turn around and look. You'll see it for yourself.'

'Sam.' Gareth seemed hypervigilant and weary, both at the same time. His back was showing in the glass: broad, the size of a wall. 'You've been told a lot of things that aren't true. It isn't your fault.' He was between Samhain and the door, the way all police sat in an interview; there was no getting past him. 'He did warn us you'd turn up some day.'

He looked at Samhain with something approaching pity. 'Never knew your father, did you?'

'No. He left my mum when she found out who he really was – an undercover cop. Ran out on her, leaving her on her own, in one of the protest camps, when I was still young.'

Gareth was shaking his head. 'No,' he said. 'I'm really sorry you've been told that Sam, but that's not the way it happened.'

They really would tell you anything, the police. That was how they got people to stop and give them their names and addresses; the uniform gave them the seeming power to get it. They made it seem as though you had to do it. Let them stop you; let them pull your scarf down, and take a photo of your face. Sam had been told no end of lies by the police. They'd say anything to get you to do what they wanted.

The difference here was that Gareth really did seem to believe what he was saying.

'I remember coming back across Europe as a small boy,' Samhain said. 'The buses – the ferry ride. Coming to live in a house...'

'Don't remember your dad though, do you?'

He was up, standing, the way they did when the interview was over. No more 'no comment', no more 'I want to see a lawyer.' Getting up was usually the last thing they did before they put you in a cell for the night.

Samhain shook his head. 'No. But–'

'Uncle Phil,' Gareth said, 'was trouble. Always here, always there, going from woman to woman. He told them all kinds of lies, all sorts of things. Sometimes he'd have two or three of them on the go at once; he used to tell them he was in the SAS, on a secret mission, all kinds of stuff. Anything so they didn't put two and two together, and realise they weren't his only girlfriend. My dad didn't have much to do with him. Mum wouldn't even have him in the house. You knew when he turned up it meant trouble. If it wasn't women, it was money.'

'This is bullshit,' Samhain said.

'Look,' said Gareth. 'I'm sorry you're hearing this from me. It should be coming from your mum, but... I don't know, maybe she's blocked it all out.'

'You're making out that my mum's loopy. She's been lied to

by the police.'

'I'm sorry.' The way Gareth said it was final. Made it clear their conversation was almost over. 'My father was a straight-up man, honest almost to a fault. He dedicated his life to Queen and Country – gave his whole life to the force. Hundreds admired him for it, for the work he did. You wouldn't understand. When he passed away, they couldn't even all get into the church. There were people crowding outside. Grown men weeping – half the Greater Manchester Police force were there. He wasn't an undercover cop or a spy or anything else. There's no way he would have done... what you're saying he did.'

'He was there. In Europe. You would have been too young to realise, and some of it was before you were born. But he was there alright, and he got away with it, because most of it's been covered up.'

'That's enough.' Gareth was at the door. 'I've given you too much of my time already. Now look – I'm sorry for what you've been through, but don't try and drag my family into it.'

'Our family, you mean.'

Samhain saw a moment's flicker, a second's hesitation before Gareth opened the door.

Then he turned, quickly. Faster than a man of his size ought to have been able to. It brought Samhain up short, his nose close, breath, the smell of coffee in his face.

'Now you look here,' he said. 'Don't you bring my family into it. If I find out you've been anywhere near my mum – *especially* my mum – I'll be down on you so hard for harassment, you'll wish you'd never been born. Right?'

A quick pinch, hard as a hypodermic needle, somewhere in Samhain's ribs. It winded him; he tried to pull away, tears spiking at his eyes.

'We can get away with a lot in here,' Gareth said. 'How much would surprise you.'

Samhain didn't answer. He couldn't. The pain caused blotches, like splashes of engine oil on tarmac, blurring his vision.

'You understand, son?'

Ears hurt. Pinching inside, roaring, like the agony of cold air. Samhain nodded.

'Good.'

Release. The skin loosened, and Samhain felt a bruise forming; he gasped for air.

'Just so long as we're clear.'

Gareth was friendly again now, a professional with a busy diary. He opened the door, and ushered Samhain out. A woman rushed by in the same uniform, hatless and haring.

'Good to see you,' Gareth chirped. 'All the best.'

The woman ran around the corner. Gareth muttered: 'Don't contact me again, you understand? When I come back down here this afternoon, you'd better be gone.'

It was the first time Samhain had ever gone out of a police station without a bail sheet or notice of caution in hand.

He came out into a day so weakly fine it seemed to have been diluted. Standing out there on the busy Manchester street, hearing the distant ding of the trams, trying to figure out the quickest way back to the train station.

There was a buzz and whistle from his pocket. Sam took it out of his pocket, and looked at the name flashing on screen: Flores.

6.

This time it was animals. A stable and all its tack, and a few boxes of things from inside the house. The one thing they didn't have to move was the horse itself.

'Little girls,' Kebby remarked, 'all want a pony.'

It was early, the morning dewy. Simon was still on holiday, and the pony stood out in the paddock, sunlight on its dappled haunches. These people were friends of Peter's, and he'd promised them a bonus if they did the job well.

'That so?' Samhain said. 'I hope my little girl doesn't. I don't know where we'd keep it.' A saddle, which looked much too large for the animal in the field, hung over a wooden beam in the centre of the room. It looked heavy as machinery.

'Morning, chaps.' A ruddy faced man appeared, clapping his hands together. 'Peter said you'd be early, but I didn't know he meant this early. Very impressive, I must say. At this rate, you'll be all done by lunchtime.'

Guest

Samhain noticed Kebby turn a smirk into a smile, flashing those great strong teeth. He wanted the bonus just as much as he did. 'We'll do our best, Mr Midden,' he said.

The place they were going to was not in the same village.

Their journey to it took them over hilltops; through pretty villages with stone walls and low cottages, around a small red-bricked industrial town sitting deeply in a valley, past highly polished car dealerships, by a car wash (closed), twin concrete tower blocks, then back out into open, rough moorland. Pheasants hopped, their heads just showing, while sheep tore at the grass. They were woolly, shaggy things, black-horned and sprayed with a blue insignia of ownership.

'When Ayesha was about five or six,' Kebby said, 'she was obsessed with this series of books called The Pony Club, and she had My Little Pony. You know My Little Pony?'

'Horses?'

'Plastic horses, with love hearts and clover and rainbows and so on, all on their rear ends. She had about twenty of these and all she ever read were these pony books. I couldn't wait for her to grow out of *that* phase. At least twice a day, she used to say, Daddy, I want a real pony. I don't know where she thought we were going to keep it, living in a terraced house.'

Mr Midden was following them with the horse box: Kebby drove carefully, keeping him in sight.

'I've got all this to come,' Samhain said.

'You'll be fine.' Kebby took a gentle pace, slowly avoiding pot holes. He was making a smooth journey for Mr Midden, and his horse, to keep Mr Midden happy. 'It will surprise you what you can deal with, when you need to.'

Samhain already knew what he was going to do with his bonus, if they got one. He would put it in an envelope, every bit of it, and give it to Marta to give to Charley. 'Do you think he'll give us a bit extra today?'

Kebby nodded. 'Yes – if we do well. Peter is very reliable, on the subject of bonuses. He's not one of these ones who will say he'll give us a bit extra, then change his mind later. Lots of bosses would say it and then move the goalposts, and say, Oh, but you forgot to fill in the mileage on the van, some tiny, petty excuse, about something you were "supposed" to do, and you didn't, that means you now can't have the bonus you were promised. Believe me, I've had bosses like that. But Peter isn't one of them.'

'Good.'

Flores had brought Samhain up not to mind about material things: Boy-Samhain had never been in clothes that hadn't been worn by somebody else first. And he had been fairly happy, never having known anything different. Only now, thinking about Graeme Stokes' other family, his half-brothers the same age, who had lived in a huge, insulated house with central heating and all new carpets, did he feel anger. As a boy, he'd spent hours riding his bike aimlessly around that tiny, suffocating estate, watching the sun set, trying to make fun from nothing, while Gareth and James Stokes, wherever they'd lived, had played on their Gameboys, or Megadrives, or whatever else they'd had, in a large warm house full of snacks.

He didn't want Astrid to go without, not the way he had.

'Peter going to give you a reference – to get a place?'

'Said he would.'

'Then he will.' Kebby brought the van around a low stone wall, beyond which was a deep green valley, in which they saw the brick-built, high-chimneyed town from another angle. 'You see, he's a good man, Peter. Did I ever tell you about my old boss – from the cruise ship?' He drew them into a car port in front of a stone-coloured, new build house, and stopped the engine. 'He was a bad man, a real bad man. A control freak. You wouldn't have liked to work under him – nobody did. We weren't allowed to bring our own ideas into the set. If we had just changed the order of the numbers around, it would have given the set more shape, more variety, you know? Instead of playing Get On Up at the very end, after all of the ballads, when the customers were already worn out from dancing, we could have built back up to it, or put it in the middle, to spice things up a bit. But my old boss had a certain way he wanted things doing, I don't know why. Everything had to be played at the exact speed he'd set, which he'd memorised from this electronic metronome he carried around in his pocket – and those things were very expensive at the time, it must have cost him a fortune, and he carried it around with him everywhere, even though he didn't need it. We had to play it all exactly at that speed, the songs in exactly the same order, his order, night after night after night after night.

'He never read the crowd, this one, never, no sir. Another band leader would have seen the customers really going for it in the groovy songs and said, They like this, let's throw in everything we've got that's got a bit of groove to it. Not Charles. Everything at the same pace and in the same order, every single night. And if you put a beat out of line...' he blew his cheeks out, and whistled, shaking his head: 'He'd dock you an hour's pay.'

'Is that even legal?'

'Maritime law.' Kebby pointed at the cottage. Wide blonde stone, broad windows. 'The captain makes his own rules, once you're a certain distance from land. It wasn't like this. I tell you, it was a relief when I came to work for Peter. I couldn't get used to it at first. I kept on turning up for work fifteen minutes early, and asking for permission to do every single tiny thing. I couldn't even move a box without asking the customer, Are you sure you want this one in the van? And then at the other end, I had to ask them again exactly where to put it, and I wouldn't put it down until I was sure I had precisely the right spot. Here? I would say.

Here? Are you sure you want it here? Just here?

'Peter used to work on the van sometimes too, in those days. He said to me, Kebby, you've got to loosen up a bit, you look like a frightened rabbit. He said, You're making the customers nervous. Try to get a bit of banter going. So I did.'

Mr Midden hopped down from his van, and waved over at them in the cab. They waved back.

'Nowadays, as you may have noticed, I don't really bother,' Kebby said, through his faked grin. 'Not unless there's £50 in it for me.' He unclipped his seatbelt. 'Well? Shall we make nice and move all these bits of horse paraphernalia?'

A woman in riding jodhpurs opened the door. She looked like Mr Midden, only thirty years younger, and gave them both a look as though she were deciding whether or not to let them in.

'These are the removals men, Tibby,' Mr Midden said.

'Well then, hurry up,' she said. She stood aside, hair swishing like a horse's tail. 'They can put the boxes anywhere.'

'You heard the lady,' Kebby said. When her back was turned, he turned to Sam, and tugged an imaginary forelock. 'Boxes anywhere, and quickly.'

It wasn't a big place, not the way Samhain had expected. He had thought of large rooms, and plenty of them. But this place had only two bedrooms, and a terrible draught: there was a wind blowing through it like the North Sea on a clifftop. You could have flown a kite in the upstairs bathroom.

He heard Mr Midden's voice all over the house. Odd words came up the stairs. Combi-boiler, electric cooker. Convenient, manageable. He seemed like a nice chap, the way he was taking her all around the house, showing her everything.

Tremendous views. Samhain put a box down in the second bedroom and looked out to the East. From here, you could see the village down in the dip. A single car ran along one of the rural roads. All this took up less than the bottom half of the sash, and everything above it was sky.

He heard a light, frightened scurrying, and looked down to see a brown mouse running along the skirting. Thinning itself finger-width, it vanished into a hole the size of a pencil.

Kebby came to the top of the stairs with another box. 'When you are quite ready,' he said.

7.

He was in his home, but not his home. The same colour walls as his boyhood bedroom. Pale green and yet the floor reaching between them was larger, much larger. There was no bed. He walked a vast expanse of pine on barefoot.

This was warm wood. It felt real to him – something like a floor of forest – he could feel the earth anchoring him down. But nothing stuck between his toes, no moss and no leaves and no slivers of insect – nothing living making its millilegged way around his ankles. This was real and it was soft and polished, clean. And it was his.

A woman in the kitchen was not his mother, although she was a mother, or something like it. He saw a curve of back, a hip, a flickering curve of bright, auburn hair. Standing in the place as if she belonged there, as if it were hers.

In a moment she would call him. In a minute. In a moment. Any minute.

'Samhain!'

The call, softly, through a fog of sleep.

'Samhain – you up?'

He came to, taking in the things close to him. Overturned waste bin, working as a bedside cabinet. Dead digital alarm clock, blank screen, no back. A pile of his mother's clothes in a wardrobe with no door.

So here he was. Mouth fuzzy with the taste of experimental, heathery homebrew. 'Yeah,' he called.

'I found these.' Flores pushed the door open, holding a set of faded floral curtains. 'Remember these? From the living room? I thought you might want them for your new place.'

Things returned to him from the previous night. Bottles of beer with lilac labels, which she said had been made by a friend. The taste of it had made him think of a coarse, sludgy brown, a colour that tasted of gorse, the ground beneath your feet. She had been glassy-eyed early; he thought she must have been drinking before he'd got there.

'You're still my little bug,' she'd kept on saying, despite everything they'd talked about. 'You're still my little bug.'

Flores didn't have a television, but she did have a battered CD player, upon which she'd kept on repeating a short CD of protest songs by a girl with a guitar and a sincere, annoying voice. She had started smoking in the house, he noticed. Everything smelled of it. The sofa, the wall hangings. The few cushions she had.

'Thanks, Mum,' he said.

'You know, I was thinking.' She, swaying slightly, grabbed the doorway, her fingers gripping white as though it were helping her stand. 'We did ok, didn't we? Me and my little bug. You know – you could have turned out much worse.' She let go of the door and stumbled into the room, the bed, where she sat down. 'Fields might technically have been your dad, but he was nowhere near being your actual dad. Panzo was much more of a father to you than he ever was.'

'I know, Mum.' He had so many questions. He wanted to know: what was he like when you met him? Was he like me? Do I look like him? Sound like him?

'Maybe I didn't get everything right.' Flores' eyes slipped, half-closing; she rocked slightly on the coverlet. She smelled strongly of last night. 'I should have told you much sooner. Maybe when you were younger. But...' she waved an arm around: 'When would it have been a good time?'

He wasn't sure whether she was asking him, or herself.

'When we came to live here? When you were a bit older? A teenager?'

'You said all this last night.'

'Did I?' Flores had put the curtains down. She reached into a sagging pocket for a roll-up which, when she found it, had already been half-smoked. 'Well, I still don't know what I should have done. When do *you* think I should have told you?' Hot strings of tobacco flared in red filaments, falling dangerously onto the carpet.

This was doubt; he remembered times, as a child, when she had fallen into it. Pits of doubt that had seemed larger than them both, and which had kept her in bed for weeks, while Panzo came around and cared for him.

'It doesn't matter now,' he said. 'Don't worry about it.'

'If you find him,' she said, 'don't bring him here. I never want to see him or hear from him again.'

'You couldn't anyway. He died last year.'

'Good. I hope whatever killed him was painful.'

'Flores...'

'Sorry.'

'No. Listen. He also had... I've got a brother. Well, two half-brothers. One a year older than me, the other a couple of years younger.'

She half-laughed, holding the dead cigarette between thumb and finger. It was a bitter thing, pinching her lips closed. 'I don't know what to say to that,' she said.

'I'm sorry, Flores,' he said.

'Like you say.' Looking around at the floor, her clothes, brushing bits of dry tobacco from her leggings onto the carpet. 'It doesn't matter.' She made to get up.

This, he recognised. Her saying things didn't matter, when to her clearly they did: things that could gain strength in numbers, like union members in a movement, and clip themselves together in her mind, weighty, immovable, until there was little room for anything else. 'It was years ago,' she said.

At the doorway, her back was a question. Asking: was he going to leave her for this new family he'd discovered, a family he'd never known he had?

'Mum,' he said. 'They're not my family. Not the way you are.'

'Huh.' She stopped, pulling at something on her tongue with curious, tapping fingers. 'That tobacco's very dry.'

'You've probably been carrying that roll-up around for months.'

'I doubt it.' Now she turned to face him fully, and he saw a cautious happiness. 'No roll-up lasts any longer than five minutes in one of my pockets.'

'One of them's in the police.'

A dry laugh. 'Figures.'

'I went to see him.'

'Why?'

Samhain started to get up. Kicking legs free, reaching for yesterday's trousers. 'I don't know. Curiosity, I guess. Wouldn't you have done the same?'

'No. I wouldn't, and I don't know why you'd want to, either.'

'I...' he was standing now, his full height. Everything in this house looked so much smaller than it had. The bed, the wardrobe, the window – everything half-sized, as though he'd remembered it wrongly. 'It's difficult to explain.'

'Then don't bother.' She was already half-way down the stairs.

'He was a dickhead,' he called. 'I didn't like him, and I won't be seeing him again.'

'Really?'

She paused, on a stair half-widthed by books. There was something on every surface in this house. The steps were part shoe-rack, part-shelf. You had to mind your step whichever way you were going. He didn't know why she kept on doing it: gathering things, magpie style, when there was nobody left in the house but her.

'Yeah,' he said. 'Get this. Graeme Stokes had fed him this bullshit story about us being cousins, and he believed it.'

'Christ.' Flores was laughing, really laughing, the way she did when Badger came round. Full peals, belly laugh, a sound that echoed around the walls. 'That's really funny.' She stopped for a moment. 'Awful, though. He's lied to them, same way he lied to us.'

'Not our problem,' he said.

'True.' She started to make her way down again, lurching, leaning heavily against the rail. Two pairs of shoes lay in a crazy pile, and she went by without touching either.

'You know Mum, you could tidy up a bit.'

'No way. I've got better things to do.'

'You could take a few things to the charity shop.'

'Salvation Army?' Flores stumbled the last few steps, and turned to look at him, in the light coming through the front door. 'Don't be stupid. Listen. I'll worry about tidying the house the day I start eating at McDonald's.'

'You won't lose me, Flores,' he said.

'I know, little bug.'

'I'm not angry,' he said. 'I'm just focusing on the future.'

'That's right. Your baby.' She turned to the book spines, poring through them. 'Speaking of tidying up. How about you take a few of these?'

Children's books. Cardboard-hard covers, with pictures of elves and princesses. Their pictures illustrated and painted by hand.

'Great, Mum,' he said. 'Thanks.'

There wasn't much where Flores lived. It was a grey, tiny place. All so much smaller than he remembered. The corner shop had shrunk to the size of a box, and the house – he worked out that the downstairs footprint had less floor space than his bedroom at the Boundary Hotel.

His feet had taken him the wrong way, past the park gates and over the motorway bridge; he was crossing the underpass and walking out of town, walking towards the bus station.

Arms weighted by the bags she'd given him. Curtains and old sheets and a huge bag of books.

'When you get everything sorted,' she said, 'can I come and see her?'

Flores had always liked Charley, and now, it seemed, she was taken with the idea of being a granny. It was the perfect excuse to start knitting again, she'd said.

'Yes, Mum,' he'd said. 'Why not.'

He hadn't liked to tell her that he was some way off seeing her himself.

8.

Dear Charley,

I'll start by saying sorry. First for the way I treated you and also for generally being a prick. You might not believe it (probably won't) but I've learned a lot lately. I'm different now from what I was. Please let me have the chance to prove it.

There's £50 in this envelope. It won't make up for everything but maybe it's a start. I didn't even know Astrid existed until about a month ago. If I had, I would have sent money before. You know I grew up without much myself and I don't want the same for her, so please take it.

You have always been so good at things Charley. I bet you don't even need my help. But Astrid is my daughter and I do want to start seeing her please. I am her father and I have rights.

I've got a job now so I'll be able to send you money more often. Also I'm moving soon. I've been looking for places with two bedrooms so she can come and stay with me sometimes.

Please tell Mart when I can come and meet her.
    Samhain.

The *I have rights* bit had been Kebby's suggestion. He had
said it a few times: that and, 'Maybe you should get a lawyer.'
But Samhain didn't see the need for that, not on his wages.

Getting a lawyer would have meant less money for Astrid,
and a bill that he'd be paying off for the rest of his life, most
likely. A lawyer would mean he'd be short on money for rent,
and that he'd have to carry on living at The Boundary Hotel
forever. He and Frankie could grow old there, living on separate
floors, gradually filling the downstairs kitchen and bar with old
guitars and fanzines, and boxes of broken electronics dragged
out of skips, while Mama Cat and Frazzles grew bad-tempered
and scratchy, upstairs: they could become a pair of burrowing
men, together.

The smell, he thought, the smell.

Nothing was too much trouble for Frankie. He planed a few
millimetres off the top of Samhain's door so that it closed
properly, re-hung it, and vacuumed the sawdust off the carpet,
all while Samhain was out at work one day. Suddenly every loo
on every floor always had toilet paper. Showers were wiped clear
and sparkling, and the kitchen became almost catering standard
clean, without Samhain having to do a thing.

Two weeks after the tour had finished, Frankie had made
the place clean enough for paying guests. Opening the front
door threw a light over a sweeping and polished staircase, a
grand, yet dilapidated entry hall; a place with swept edges and
clean skirting. Frankie had even cleaned the light fitting in the
entryway: no more cobwebs.

'When you move into your new place,' Frankie said, 'I can
do all of this sort of thing. Any sort of light fitting you want –

I'll get it. I'll make it all look nice – like this one.' Frankie let his hand drop, clasping it one way, then another, tightening his hand and seeming unable to settle it, around the screwdriver handle resting between the loops on his belt. 'For the little one, you know.'

'Astrid.'

'That's it.'

'Thanks, Frankie. I appreciate it.' Samhain didn't say that, after moving out of the Boundary Hotel, he was hoping to see as little of Frankie as possible.

One by one, the kittens went.

Marta went off to work one day with the tortie tucked inside her shirt, and came back at the end of the day without it. Frankie took the black one around to its new home in a shoebox strapped to the front of his bike, and David and Barbara came for one of the ginger ones.

'My, my.' David took a couple of broad strides into the hall. 'You've got it looking absolutely dandy in here – haven't they, Barb? Look at that.' He pointed up at the light fitting, sparkling overhead. 'That's one heck of a fine polish you've got on those bar backs, as well. Do you mind if I...' And in a minute, he was in the bar. 'Very nice,' he said. 'Very nice, indeed.'

The two remaining kittens were in their urbex playground, Frazzles jabbing and sparring his way around the drawers; his sister, more docile, was asleep in one of the drawers. Her ears were like crisp packet corners.

'Oh,' Barbara said, 'Martha said she was a lovely little cat. But I didn't realise she would be this lovely.'

'She hasn't been spayed.' Samhain lifted her out of the drawer. 'But she should be old enough for that soon, and you should get it done.'

'Oh.' Barbara accepted the kitten, warm and sleepy, in her

arms. 'Let's call her Martha. For your Martha.'

David coughed, dangling his change. 'He says she's not his Martha, love.'

Barbara's face was buried into the cat's back fluff, and she didn't reply.

'Now, let us see you right.' David got his wallet out. 'You must let us give you something for her.'

He shuffled three twenties loose, out of the back of his wallet. Barbara was trying to persuade Little Martha to go into a fabric cat carrier, and the cat did not want to go. Four limbs starfished hard against the soft entrance.

'Absolutely not,' Samhain said. 'I won't take your money.'

'Take it.'

'No. I didn't do anything. It was Mama Cat who did all the work.'

'Well.'

David looked around, apparently for somewhere to stash the notes. Glancing first at the dado rail, perhaps thinking there might be a gap down one side; but it was glued fast, Frankie must have seen to that.

'Try grabbing it by the scruff of the neck,' Samhain said.

'Seems cruel,' she said, but she did, pinching a scrap of loose skin where an older cat might wear a collar. The kitty stopped writhing and hung limp, its legs trailing like seaweed. 'Aha,' Barbara said. 'So that's how you do it.' She popped the cat into the bag, and zipped the door closed. 'Who's a good kitty, then? Who's a beautiful girl?'

'I imagine you've spent money on cat food, and so forth.' David was getting to his feet; he'd spotted an opportunity between two of the drawers, and wedged the money in there. 'We wouldn't want you to be out of pocket.'

'I'm not a breeder,' Samhain protested. He was trying to get to the money, to get it back, and force it into David's hand, but

Barbara stood in his way.

'We haven't had a pet since the dog died,' she said. 'But I just know the grandchildren are going to love little Martha. Aren't they?'

'Now look, we know you've got your job with Peter,' David went on. 'It's not as if we think you're a charity case. Just think of it as a token payment, that's all. Just to keep you in pocket for kitty litter, and so forth. It's a small price to pay, for something our girls are going to love so much. Isn't that so, dear?'

Little Martha was making a piteous mewing sound, like a cat trapped up a tree. 'Oh yes,' Barbara said. 'And you know, you can come and visit her any time you like.'

'Are you sure? About the money, I mean.'

'Don't even mention it,' David said. 'Shall we, dear?' He motioned his wife to the stairs.

'Better had,' Barbara said. 'The natives are getting restless.'

Still, that made £110 now, for sending on to Charley.

Samhain started to wish that he had waited before sealing up the envelope.

9.

'You've got everything you need in this flat.' The woman showing them around had stiff dark hair, and a face that looked as though it had been buffed to a high shine with an industrial sander. 'Kitchen – bathroom... you could put a pull-out sofa bed in the living room, and create a second bedroom.'

She gestured down the hallway. 'It's a real feature to have a separate kitchen and living area. Creates a real feeling of spaciousness.'

To say it was narrow would have been to do an unkindness to narrowboats. The kitchen had a single worktop the size of a chopping board, and the cooker only had one front leg; the other side was propped up by a tower of beermats.

'Is that safe?' Samhain asked.

'What?' The estate agent glanced at it. 'Oh, that – you could ask the landlord to sort that out before you moved in. I'm sure he'd see to it. You see, this is an ideal starter flat,' she went on.

'Perfect location – very central – only you *would* have to apply quickly, because we've had a lot of interest in this one...'

'It smells like somebody died in here,' he said.

Samhain saw: a back-to-back terraced house whose top window had a fabulous view of the nearby maximum security prison – barbed wire on top of a curved wall twenty feet high. That one had a good-sized kitchen and living room, and gold spray paint on all of the walls. 'You could redecorate if you wanted to move in,' the agent said, a middle-aged man in an ill-fitting navy suit. 'The landlord is very easy-going that way – lets his tenants decorate to their own tastes...' He looked as though he was itching to scratch himself round the collar.

'Plenty of terraced houses around here,' he said. 'All with the same layout, same number of bedrooms – but this is quite a nice one, as you can see.' He reached for the light switch, flicking it up, down, up, down. Nothing happened either way. 'Ah,' he said. 'Light bulb must have gone.'

The rent was out of Samhain's price range, anyway.

Samhain saw: an apartment in a converted Georgian house, with polished wooden floors, and a window looking out into the tops of the plane trees.

Beneath the trees, a busy road. It wasn't really near anything, apart from the main road that went to some other place. They'd had to walk ten minutes from the nearest bus stop to get here.

He looked out of the window, saw tarmac, and concrete, and steel.

'Should you have wooden floors?' he asked Mart. 'With children?'

You could take your shoes off and cross the entirety of the flat in less than twenty paces. But once you had the windows shut, it was quiet: it had a living room, two tiny bedrooms. Was she a messy child, he wondered? A girl who left toys and trucks on floors, making a plasticky safari of every room?

She tapped a foot, and her shoe made a tight echo around the walls. 'Charley's got wooden floors in her place.'

'Like it?' The agent was a slim, young Asian woman with a black ponytail, and dark jeans. She opened a door at the end of the living room. 'And look, you've got all this storage – very useful. You need that, when you've got children.' Beyond the door, a small cupboard held a big old boiler. 'And you see, we're not like the other agencies. If you ever have any problems, any emergency at all, you can always call us – 24 hours a day, not like some of the other agents. Say if the pipes burst, even on a Sunday night, you could call us and we'd have somebody out to you within the hour.'

This place was less than five minutes' walk to Charley's, Marta had said.

But to everywhere else, miles. It would be two buses to work, unless he could get Kebby to pick him up on the way in the van; half an hour's bus ride to the social club. The last bus heading this way left town at ten thirty. Moving here would mean missing the last band at any gig.

It would also mean getting a bike. 'The location's not exactly convenient,' he said.

As he said it, he caught sight of Marta's face. Eyes to the ceiling, jaw tightened as if she was getting ready to throw a punch. It was a look he'd seen before on Roxy, and on Charley, but never before on Mart. It was a face that said, you are driving me up the fucking wall.

He hadn't even known Marta could pull this face.

She took a deep breath. 'That depends on what you want it to be convenient for, doesn't it, Sam? I mean, no, it's not convenient for going out drinking. But it is extremely convenient for seeing your daughter.'

'To find a place like this, so modern, where the landlord will accept children?' the agent chimed in. 'Lucky,' she said. 'Extremely lucky. Most landlords wouldn't even have let me show it to you.'

'You're right,' he said.

The agent flashed him a veneer-bright smile. 'Is that a yes?' She was pulling a sheaf of paperwork from a folder underarm: a form, all lines and black boxes, stapled in one corner.

'Yes,' he said. 'I suppose it is.'

'Been ages since I've done this,' Samhain said to Mart.

They were in the Boundary Hotel bar. Samhain was struggling over the rental application form while Mart, over by the pumps, did something to her bike, covered in grease face and hands.

'Yeah?' she said. 'Well, better get a move on. A place like that might go fast – one that's so cheap.'

'That landlord probably owns at least half a dozen other places.'

'Probably.' She seemed disinterested. A ping, and something broke: he heard the buckshot scatter of metal flying over the wooden floor.

In a box for *References*, he started writing Frankie's name, and the address of the Boundary Hotel. 'I hate renting and I hate landlords,' he grumbled. 'Having to give this up – all of this space – to go and live in a tiny place, and pay somebody else's mortgage... pay for somebody else to get rich...'

'Yeah, well.' Her voice was sharp as a razor. 'You want to be near Charley and Astrid, don't you? And you can't keep on living here with Frankie – you said so yourself. It's called growing up, Sam.'

'I suppose.'

The two of them, he and Frankie, had a longstanding

agreement to act as one another's former employers, or landlords, in situations like these. He had been Frankie's 'manager' at least five times before himself, as Samhain Smith, MD of Smith-Wood Communications, a self-made man with a drive for success who had built up a small, but successful, telecommunications business from nothing. Samhain Smith MD had little time on his hands, and a slightly brusque telephone manner; he didn't like spending time on the phone because, as he told callers, time was money, and even though his business was telephones, he didn't like wasting time chatting on them himself.

'Think of it this way. Charley's been managing without you all this time. She doesn't need you all of a sudden. It's you who's got to fit into their lives, not the other way around.'

Last time he'd rented, it had been an escape from the Ambland Road squat, when he had lived with Charley. He'd moved into the tenancy Charley already had running, and there hadn't been any need for any of this – a guarantor form, an application to gain permission to rent. Whilst he'd been glad to get out of that squat, away from the dirt and noise, the rent had been more than he'd ever paid, and it had bound him to the crappy job he'd had at the time. Part-time work in the health food shop, for a short-tempered boss who ate meat in the back room on the sly. Some weeks, Samhain had been given as few as five hours' work. Money had always been a struggle, then.

'I know. Charley's one of the most capable people I know.'

'There you are, then.' Mart lifted her front wheel off the ground. 'So better get on with it, eh?' She pushed the tyre, making the cogs and pedals turn. 'If you want to be a part of Astrid's life, you've got to show her you can contribute something. Don't be a drain. Show Charley you can be consistent.' She did something with her hands, and let both wheels of the bike bump against the carpet. 'There,' she said, smiling. 'Fixed!'

10.

They were moving a family with two mothers. Both looked upwards of forty: the dark-haired one had lines in her face that might have been chipped from granite.

Kebby struggled out to the van with a cello under one arm, and an artist's easel under the other. 'Now I have seen it all,' he said.

The whole downstairs of the house was boxes. The family had built a city of them, different sizes, streets and mazes in the carpeted lounge. It was a house that smelled of herbal tea and rosemary; it looked like they never threw anything out.

'Shall we start with the heavy stuff?' The dark-haired mother chose a big box, and started out towards the van.

Kebby, uncharacteristically, made no attempt to stop her. He just watched, staring at her hips and arms as she went out of the door. 'Let me know if either of you ever want a job,' he said.

Samhain was next after her, with a box of books. It weighed

more than the centre of a black hole – and he marvelled, again, that people didn't clear their things out before moving. Some families packed all sorts of rubbish up in boxes to take to their new places, things they never used or looked at. This lot seemed to be that type, the sort who lived amongst dusty things. Things that had belonged to long-dead uncles and grandparents, a collection of old-timey, useless junk, as though they wanted to live in a museum of the self.

'We usually do the upstairs first,' Samhain commented, shoving his box onto the tailgate with a grunt.

'You don't want to go up there.' One mother carefully placed a side-lamp in between the boxes. 'I don't think they've even finished packing yet – have they?'

'No, and they never will. Arthur keeps putting toys in his box, then getting distracted and taking them out again to play with them. At this rate, it could take him months.' The other mother put witchy hands over tired eyes, and breathed deeply. 'I do rather think finishing the children's rooms may be a professional's job.'

'No trouble.' Kebby pulled a stack of flat boxes from the driver's cab. 'Shall we get started?'

'Please,' said the younger of the two: she took them upstairs.

In the tiny back bedroom, a boy with dark hair sat amongst a detritus of lego and foam aeroplanes, adding stickers to a book. He looked about six years old.

'Arthur,' sighed his mum. She turned to Samhain: 'I'm sorry. He's packed everything and then unpacked it again.'

Her partner appeared, sliding an arm around her waist. 'That reminds me of somebody else I know.'

Samhain started making up a new box. 'Never mind,' he said. 'Soon have you sorted.' Every new box they made was an extra £8 on top of the bill, and they were supposed to make a new one every time they came across a box packed by the owner whose lid wouldn't close, or every time they had to put a pile of unpacked things into a box: Peter made a lot of money that way. 'Here you are, Mrs Gable-Lloyd,' he said. 'Quicker we get it all sorted, quicker it's done.'

The family were moving to another part of the village, to a place less than four miles away. It was on the other edge of town, a larger place, the leafier part of the village, closer to the school.

In the van, they listened to Kebby's old band. 'Listen to this,' he said. 'A friend who knows something about computers put them onto CD for me. You hear that drum sound? They don't make snare cracks like that anymore.'

'Sounds like Motown,' Samhain said.

'Yes. We were trying for that – we thought we could be the West Yorkshire version of Stevie Wonder. I don't know if we managed it.' Kebby grinned. 'It's not too bad though, right? It gained a bit of noise in the transfer, but you can still hear it pretty well. Oh now shh, listen. This is where Eloise comes in.'

Past a church. Samhain gazed out of the window at a sign drooping on the railings. There were lights on in the church hall, and a woman was working her way along the floor with a mop.

'Hear that voice?'

Melody, pleading and strident. The girl sang as though she was angry, yet there was this beautiful, blues drawl to it.

'I don't know why she never managed to do anything as a singer,' Kebby said. 'You hear that voice? Gorgeous. She was almost as good as Aretha, that girl. Could have been famous. I don't know what happened.'

'Maybe she didn't want to be famous.'

'Maybe.' Kebby paused for a moment, indicating at a roundabout. 'It's a shame about your band, Sam.'

'Yeah, well.' Samhain shrugged. 'Had to end sometime.'

'Let me tell you.' Kebby pulled around the roundabout,

through two lanes, and up across onto the hill. 'With your little girl? You won't miss it. You are in for the adventure of a lifetime.'

'She's two now. Mart showed me a picture.'

'Two! So she'll be talking now. Just you wait. My God, the questions. "Daddy, why is the sky blue?" "Daddy, what is a different kind of bird for?" "Daddy, why doesn't my brain stop thinking in time for me to go to sleep?" "Daddy, can I have some chocolate buttons?" "Daddy, will you draw me a picture of a dog and a pig together on the same hill?"'

They were behind a builder's merchant van, its back loaded with timber.

'When you meet her, you probably won't believe it – the love you have for your children. It's so fierce, like you never knew you could feel anything like it. You would kill anybody if they tried to hurt your baby – throttle them with your bare hands. When Ayesha was a baby, we used to spend hours just watching her as she slept. Her skin. Her tiny little hands. She was so beautiful, we couldn't believe she was ours. That we had made a whole human being! Imagine!'

Shifting down a gear, Kebby chugged the van slowly uphill. 'The only thing was, when she got to the age of walking around and asking questions, she would sometimes ask things from the second she woke up, until the moment she went to sleep. She wanted to know everything, Samhain, and she thought I would have the answers. She asked about every single thing, questions you would never even think of asking yourself. Sometimes I wanted to say, For God's sake, just for a minute, can't you stop with the questions?' He took a hand off the gearstick. 'But that was only sometimes. Most of the time, you don't mind. Not really. You'll see.'

'What kind of toys do you think I should get?' Samhain asked. 'For when she comes to stay at my place?'

Greenery and tree-lined avenues, planes and falling sycamore seeds, detached houses with blackened fronts. 'Oh, everything!' Kebby said. 'You should get her everything. If you can think of it, you should get it. All sorts. Books, bricks, dolls, toy trucks, musical instruments are good, crayons and paper and paint – my Ayesha used to love drawing. They never get tired of exploring and playing and trying new things, until they start school. That's when they find out what they're really interested in, what they're really good at. They play so much, they'll play with anything and everything.' He said: 'Can't you find out from her mum what she likes already?'

'I'll get Mart to ask her.'

'Do that.' Kebby let out a low whistle. 'Man, look at this place.'

They pulled up a curved driveway under the gentle brushing of overhanging trees, to a stone house with bay windows either side of the front door. One was the kitchen, the other a living room. Broad stone steps led to a solid wooden door.

'Looks like something out of a horror film,' Samhain said.

Kebby wheezed with laughter. '"No, that huge place isn't for me, mister. Give me a tiny place any day. Because I'm a little mouse, and I want to live in a mouse's house."'

'That's not what I said.'

'I heard it in your voice.'

A large blue Volvo pulled up into the driveway behind them, with both mothers in the front seats.

'Anyway,' Kebby went on, 'when the time comes, I'll help you move. No–' he said, stopping Samhain's protests with a hand in the air: 'It's settled. I'll get Peter to let us use one of the work vans.'

He was out of the cab before Samhain could even tell him there wasn't a van's worth of stuff to move.

II.

Mama Cat had moved full time onto Samhain's old bed, leaving a moulted circle of fur around herself in the shape of Saturn's rings. Comfortable there, and declining to move.

'You really should get her spayed,' Mart said.

'Can't afford to.' Frankie had been around the hotel, gathering guest soaps. They sat, egg-nestled, in folded fresh towels, in the old Estamos merchandise box. 'And besides, she's not my cat.'

'PDSA do free spaying on a Tuesday,' she said. 'You just have to go to the place and wait.'

'How long?' Frankie put the box with the rest of Samhain's stuff, waiting by the front door.

'I don't know, however it long it takes them to see you.'

'All day?'

Mart reached down into Frazzles. He was in a box of his own, much smaller, and he moved his head, purring, under her scratching finger. 'Maybe.'

'I haven't got time for that,' Frankie said.

'You're the one who bloody let her in,' Samhain said.

'I didn't *let* her in. She just came in one day when the door was open.'

This was the largest pile of things that Samhain had ever taken in a house move. A bed frame and mattress, a double duvet off one of the beds. Sheets and pillows. Resting on these were things from the kitchen – tin opener, wooden spoon, crock pot. Samhain wasn't sure how Frankie was going to get along without these things, but Marta had put them in the pile with everything else, and talked him out of putting them back in the kitchen for Frankie.

He opened the front door. The sun gleamed into his eyes in a golden splint. 'Christ, Frankie,' Samhain said, 'I'll come back and take her to the PDSA myself.' Any minute, Kebby was going to arrive, and he wanted to be waiting when it happened. It was odd enough that he'd had to give his workmate directions to come and pick him up here, at this disinterred old guesthouse. He didn't want him going upstairs and asking questions as well. 'If you don't, she'll have another litter of kittens. Then another, then another. Who's going to look after them – you?' He was hauling his rucksack onto his shoulder; as he lifted it, he felt the old, reassuring scrape of the screwdriver handle against his neck.

'Did it this time, didn't I?'

The bag felt heavier this time, less portable than it had ever been. Weighted with spoons, with forks, glasses from the bar; it bulged with toilet rolls from the linen cupboard. 'You didn't. I did.' There was the chug of an engine outside. Samhain opened the doors wider, and waved at Kebby, pulling up in the van. 'I'll come again myself and see to it – next Tuesday, after work. Don't let her out, right?'

'I'll miss you, boyo.' Frankie came towards him, stretching out his arms. A manly hug constricted around Samhain's back in a broad elastic. The hug that Samhain had felt a thousand times – darkened bars, late nights, under deep cover of Jägermeister. In the days when he had thought he and Frankie would be best friends forever. 'Don't be a stranger, will you?'

Samhain picked up the duvet, and was transported back.

Flores, her back to him, standing in one of the yurts. Small then, his head somewhere around mid-thigh height, clutching a pillow, the only thing he was big enough to carry.

Something in his other hand, something warm and wooden. The little toy car he had loved so much.

They weren't supposed to keep toys for themselves, but somewhere along the way he had plucked this from one of the toy boxes in one of the camps, and kept it. A thing with red paint, and carved wheels that only turned some of the time.

Boys and girls were meant to play with things for a while, then return them to the shared box. But Samhain had been so attached to this car, and he'd held it often. It was always in his hand, and had been at that point. Flores gathered scraps of clothing: warm jumpers for cold, cagoules for rain, singing as she worked. She always did this when they were on the move. He hadn't asked her where they were going, not that it made any difference. Wherever they went, they were always going to the same place. Another dusty camp with tents, placards and signs and chains, to the earth and sky, the constant murmur of voices.

He'd known what a house was, because he'd built one with Lego. A house was a place where you lived forever, a sturdy thing with a roof and four walls, a door you could close when you went home.

'This all reminds me of moving when I was a kid,' he remarked.

Mart was holding Frazzles in the box. 'Better get him in the van, before we do anything else,' she said.

'Right. Just ask Kebby—'

'Somebody ask for me?'

There he was in the doorway, off-duty. Old jeans and canvas shoes, a peaked cap worn and navy.

'We said, better get the expert to move all this stuff,' Samhain said.

'That's you, but what about me?' Kebby glanced at the pile in the hall. 'So where's the rest of it?'

'This is the lot. There isn't anything else.'

Kebby grabbed the kitchen box, shaking his head. 'You're going to sit on the floor in the evenings?' He went out of the door, throwing over his shoulder: 'Let's make Peter's warehouse our second stop of the day. You need a bit more to live on than this.'

Roller blinds rattled, revealing a thicket of table legs. Tables, chairs, turned over on their backs on tops of one another, crammed helpless wooden insects.

'Now look,' Peter said. 'You've been a good worker, Samhain. So you can take whatever you want from the front part of the warehouse, within reason, but you can't take anything from the antiques at the back – I can't give you those for nothing.'

'Look, Sam.' Mart had already found a child's bed, part-concealed behind an old roll-front writing desk. It was a bunk-style thing, with a bed on top and a desk underneath. 'Perfect for Astrid's room – don't you think?'

There was an old fire surround tipped up against the ladder. 'Looks like it'll fit,' he said.

A narrow path led a crooked way past some of the tables, down into the deeper recesses of the room. Kebby was already most of the way down there; Samhain saw his baker's boy hat bob down between two sets of mirrors. 'Oh, I remember this,' he said. 'I can't believe you've still got it, Peter.' He re-emerged around the side of a Welsh dresser. 'I thought you said you were going to have this thing restored.' He said to Sam, 'Me and Simon brought this over here, well... must have been more than three years back.'

'I keep meaning to,' Peter said.

Sam couldn't see – he was climbing. Balancing with one foot on a table, and the other tentatively on a set of dining chairs. He was trying to get across to a neat sofa he'd seen, which looked purple in the darkness.

He turned, and saw Mart on the floor on the other side, a smear of dust across her cheek. 'Come on, jump down,' she said. 'I'll catch you.'

'But I haven't the time,' Peter went on. 'Thing like that – it needs a specialist restorer. I can't get anybody out to come and have a look at it.'

Samhain heard Kebby's voice, without actually being able to see the man himself. 'What? I can't believe that. If those guys could just see this place... I can't believe some of this stuff is still here. It's a crime, Peter. You should at least put some of it on eBay.'

'What's eBay?'

'Here.' Mart already had a stack going. She'd gone, magpie-eyed, around the wooden topography. 'What about this?' She led him over the dining table to an old leather sofa, then over that, further into the dark, away from the doors, to a book case and coffee table with an inlaid top. 'And what about this – any good? Do you like it?'

Then from there, with what touched his hand feeling like her skin or a piece of velvet fabric hanging loose, through legs and standard lamp fringing, to more dark, greater dust, to a desk lamp and floor lamp.

'It's great, Mart,' he said. 'How did you find all this stuff so quickly?'

'Don't know.' Things were dim here, back here, in this forgotten place so far back amongst the furniture. He could only see her teeth as she smiled. It took his eyes a moment to adjust. 'Years of scavenging, I guess.'

'You've got a great eye,' he said.

They were standing in some part of the room where, by some accident of the way the furniture was stacked, there was only just room for two pairs of adult feet, facing one another.

'So they tell me.'

She was smiling: he could hear it in her voice.

'Thanks for bringing me here, Mart,' he said.

'I didn't bring you anywhere. It was Kebby who drove the van.'

'No, but – you know what I mean. Not just for this. For everything. The flat – Charley – the... you know, the stuff with my dad.'

She reached away from him, towards a lamp with a mermaid swimming around its base. 'What's brought all this on?'

There was a cinnamon smell about her, on her hair, her clothes. 'I don't know. I guess I just looked at all the things you'd picked out, and realised how lucky I am.'

'Lucky?'

She was still smiling when he leaned down towards her: holding the lamp in one hand, sweet tea on her breath.

'Yes – lucky. I don't know what I would have done without you.'

'You would have managed.'

'Why don't you put that lamp down?'

She looked at it, smiled at the graceful creature with the fishtail, reaching her hands up towards the bulb. 'This is the best thing I've seen so far. I think I'm going to keep it.'

'Put it with the rest of the stuff.'

'Sam.' She laid the lamp down carefully, on top of a cabinet with glass windows. 'You're better than you think. You would have figured it all out. With or without me. You're smart. That's what I like about you.' The plug swung loose, and tapped against a wooden leg. 'Or at least it's one of the things I like about you, anyway.'

'There's more than one?'

'Yes, of course.'

Wondering, he looked beyond her into the jungle of furniture, at polished corners catching and reflecting the sun, at Peter's head shining with silver by the roll-top doors.

'I didn't know there was...' he began.

Then he was quietened: she closed her eyes, and pulled him close.

Kissing Mart was like eating a Danish pastry. Sticky and sweet, the kind of thing he could have kept on doing all day. Her back was a boat-sail under his arms, her hands in his hair in a light breeze.

Up close, she was syrupy, soft. All parts of her might have been made from candyfloss. He was busy trying to get to the lollipop stick in the centre when he heard the crack of somebody knocking a piece of furniture over nearby.

A table bucked sharp onto his elbow.

'Bloody thing.' Kebby's voice. 'Why is it so damn dark in here? You'd think Peter could afford to switch on the lights.'

Mart was quick, leaning to catch the falling lamp. 'Be careful,' she said.

'Sorry,' he said. 'We ought to have brought a torch. Anybody hurt?'

'No.'

'This is the last time I scratch around here for second-hand furniture,' Kebby grumbled. 'Have you found everything you need, yet? At least get a move on. I need to get home for tea.'

12.

Saturday was the most popular day for moving. The one day when everybody optimistically boxes up their things, thinking a move can be done in a single day.

But nobody settled in one day. Even Samhain knew this. It wasn't possible. He was working five days a week, sometimes six, all the hours Peter gave him, and had seen this fool's error repeated every weekend.

'We're going to get it all done today, then have Sunday to enjoy our new home.'

That was what they said. He heard it over and over.

Samhain nodded, and smiled, and said, 'Fair play to you. Let's try and get you sorted.'

He said this knowing that their Sunday would be chaos and unfamiliar light switches, turning on the bedroom light instead of the hall, wondering which switches worked and which didn't, and looking in every single box throughout the house to try and find the kettle.

A one day move wasn't possible. Nobody settled in one day, not even him, with his single bag, containing his tools and his t-shirt and his spare clean hoody.

Frazzles had a ping-pong ball that he liked to play with. He was always biting things, and trying to scrape them open with his hind legs. The cat had a favourite cushion on the sofa, which it didn't like anybody else to sit on, and it had a favourite spot under the bunk bed in the second bedroom, Astrid's room. It slept there on a faded old Estamos t-shirt, making the same circular shape as Mama Cat, in a dark spot under the desk.

*

One Sunday morning, Samhain said: 'Do you think she's ever going to let Astrid come and stay?'

He asked this while the cat scrabbled away at the door from the other side. It made a sound like winter branches on a double decker's roof.

'Should I let the cat in?' she said, but she was already up, the sun landing in a golden slant across her narrow back.

She opened the door, looked down, and asked the cat: 'Well?'

Frazzles stayed where he was, on the other side of the threshold. Looking up at Marta's face, beyond her calves into the room, with an expression that said she was a fool.

'Give it time, Sam,' she said. 'You haven't even met her yet.'

'And when is *that* going to be?'

He lay on the bed with a throb creeping up his back from everything he'd moved.

The previous day, he and Kebby and Simon had moved a whole house. An old lady had lived in it from birth until the day after her ninetieth birthday. She'd raised her children in that house, three of them, each with hobbies – cricket, rollerskating, tennis, music. They'd found dozens of broken tennis racquets. Old skates with rattling wheels. They'd found a double bass, and an upright piano hidden under a draping, dusty rug.

Her two eldest children had been arguing in the hallway. A middle-aged man, balding and hectoring, who kept saying: 'We can't keep it all, Rachel,' and: 'If you'd wanted her to leave your kids something, perhaps you should have visited more often.'

The woman he was talking to was of similar age, but with expensive blonde hair and a fancy coat; she'd kept on stopping to glance over her shoulder at Samhain and Kebby, who ceased working for nobody, and at whatever they were taking out of the house at that moment. 'That? You can't get rid of that!' And: 'I can't believe you're letting them do this.'

Kebby and Samhain had just kept their faces straight, and said nothing.

'I don't know, Sam. I'll ask her again, and see what she says.'

Mart stepped forward a little, out into the hallway. The top of her back sloped in a smooth pebble, her buttocks curving in the shape of a plum.

'Let's do something today,' she said. 'Ride bikes?'

She, it seemed, never tired of riding her bike. To and from work on it, four miles each way, then during the day, between meetings. Then what did she want to do at the weekend? Ride bikes.

He swung his feet onto the warming floor.

Mart was a red-headed, spanner-carrying angel, somebody not to be allowed to get away. 'I'll make us some sandwiches,' he said.

Samhain rode a bike with a rattling chain through puddles of light more golden than syrup. Mart was way ahead of him, along a cobbled street between the houses. She wore a long white dress, fine as parachute silk, and when she pushed her right leg down he could nearly see her knickers through the fabric.

The path didn't look like much. It was a cobbled street between the houses, which came to an end at the edge of the old mill. 'It's this way,' she said. A short metal fence with a gap, winged bows at handlebar height. 'Bit of a pain to get through.' Mart reared her bike up on its back wheel to get it through the fence.

Boats with black sides. Roses on their cabins, white and pink. On the sixth boat a woman stood on the deck, doing something with a thick rope, twisting it around and around, mooring her boat to the land.

'I had no idea this was all here,' he said. The grass by the path was high. It bowed and waved like a corps de ballet. They were on the canal tow path.

'Yeah,' Mart said. 'Not many people do. If you go that way,' she said, pointing her thumb back behind them, 'it's the quickest way to town.' She leaned right down to her handlebars, calves straining. They were coming up to a sharp hill for the locks.

The climb was sharper than he expected. Edges all green and thorny, tangled stalks with fruit coming, still aphid-green. In autumn, he and Astrid would be able to come down here, and pick enough berries to make a pie.

Gravel spat under his wheels. He looked, sweating, at the huge wooden gates at the hill's top, the levers and sluices; his bike slowed no matter how hard he pushed. Pain spiked his heart like a wire barb. She was already at the top of the hill, waiting, bicycle leaning between her legs, and the sun shining through her billowing dress like a flag.

He got off and pushed the rest of the way.

'Isn't it beautiful?' she said.

The light was against him; he heard Mart's feet on the

ground, the soft click-click of her bike as she pushed it further on the path. He blinked hard, saw her raised chin, the shape of her neck as she looked into the treetops, fingers spread out into the air.

'It's perfect,' he said.

By evening, she was gone.

Mart didn't stay over often, and never on a Sunday. Mondays were her early start, and she had said she was going to call in on Charley on the way home.

He couldn't get used to the quiet in the flat.

Nobody banging away, fixing things. No sound of sandpaper or sawdust flying all over the floor. No clink of bottles or shouts up the stairs. At this time on a Sunday, there wasn't even the sound of traffic outside.

Just Samhain and the cat, Frazzles, and whatever music Samhain put on to cover up the silence.

The cat padded in, seeming to want something. It sat on the rug, staring at him, blinking slowly. As though it had a need, and Samhain ought to know what it was. So Samhain got up to see whether the bowl was empty, and Frazzles jumped up onto the sofa, into the warm spot he had left behind.

'You tricked me,' he said.

Frazzles yawned and licked his lips, and settled himself into a soft circle.

Later, a knock.

'Now then, boyo.'

At the top of the stairs, Frankie with a bottle of Jack Daniels in one hand, and a set of shot glasses in the other.

'Brought you a housewarming present.'

Boxed glasses: Frankie had even stuck a bow on the top corner.

'For fuck's sake Frankie, if you're coming in, come in. Don't stand there dithering. The cat'll get out.'

'You and your cowing cats.' Frankie was fast – he shoved the bottle under his arm, and scooped Frazzles up with his free hand. 'Look at this tiddler. Bit bigger than when I last saw him, eh?' Inside, and Frankie kicked the door closed, slamming it with a noise fit to rattle the whole house. 'And the landlord doesn't mind you keeping pets?'

'He doesn't know.'

'That's the spirit. Anyway, thought I'd pop by, see how you were settling in.' Frankie unlaced his trainers, set them side by side by the door. 'See, I'm housetrained. Bet you didn't know that, did you?' He shook the bottle. 'Drink?'

'You go ahead. I'll get the kettle on.'

Now loose, Frankie's feet gave off a smell that could flatten a tower block. 'That's not like you.' Frankie crept flat-footed forward, peeking his way around the living room door. 'Got it looking cozy in here, mind. Marta help?'

'Yeah. I've got an early start tomorrow.' Kebby was calling for him at seven thirty, so they could make a two-hour drive to some guy's storage unit in an industrial estate, to move a load of old tractor and car engines. Then they were driving another two hours to put it in another storage unit in an industrial estate somewhere over the Pennines.

Frankie put the bottle, and the cat, down on the kitchen worktop.

The cat, who had never been up there before, started sniffing its way towards the cooker top.

'Yeah?' Frankie slapped a hand over his freshly shaved head.

'For God's sake, Frankie.' Samhain grabbed the cat, and put him down on the floor. 'He'll burn his little paws.'

'It isn't switched on.'

'No, but it was earlier, and he won't understand... never

mind.'

'This is a nice place.'

Frankie was poking around, hidden from sight, but not more than a metre or so away. He was in Astrid's room, the bathroom; he had his nose in Samhain's room, where the duvet was probably still on the floor.

'If you stand in the right spot, you can see all of it at once,' Frankie went on. 'Kitchen – bedroom – living room – bathroom – second bedroom.'

'That's right.' The kettle clicked off. 'No grand staircases or hidden back corridors.'

'You should come back and visit,' Frankie said. 'Old place isn't the same without you.'

Steaming water, bloating tea bags, hot mugs. Peppermint tea bags floated like bubbling swim shorts. 'Don't know when I'll have time,' Samhain said.

'Well.' In the living room, Frankie was fiddling with the record player. 'You just come whenever you can, that's all.' His old friend was staring at a set of needles on the amp. 'You got this working yet?'

'Record player works,' Samhain said. 'Buzzes like a motherfucker, though.'

This stereo had come to him through several pairs of hands. Ten years ago, to some person, it had been new. Eight years ago, Marta had found it in a charity shop. She'd used it for a while, and then it had spent some years in a box at the back of a cupboard, when she and Jeff had moved in together. Last month, she'd found it again, and brought it here.

When Samhain had hooked it up, he'd seen why nobody wanted to keep it any length of time. Something about it rattled like a faulty lawnmower, and the record player seemed to bust a driver every sixth or seventh record.

'It's a piece of crap,' Samhain said. 'I think I need to get–'

'Soon have this sorted.' Frankie had produced a screwdriver and soldering iron, and was jemmying the casing loose with a screwdriver end. 'Can't have you going without your music, can we?'

13.

The old arts college wore within it a fading spectre of its past self. Everything was sixties, rectangular. Doorways and corridors and rooms climbed off one another at right angles.

It was all joined by a single corridor, a square skeleton which boxed in the large downstairs studio. Every staircase and doorway came off this hall.

'I'm Aiden.' A wiry man in his sixties with long grey hair, wearing navy dungarees, came out of the studio door. Like all the doors, it was a peculiar turquoise colour which, you could tell, had once been bright. 'Come in. Everything's already packed.'

The sun landed on huge boxes in the centre of the room; rows of easels leaned against one another like tripping goalposts. 'I promised the students all an A if they packed up their own studios.' Whiskered carp swam up both his forearms.

Each box was named. Phaedra Vanderbelt. Rose Hart. Thomas Porter-Woodsley.

'Right then,' Kebby said. 'Shall we get to it?'

Those were the names of kids who'd never done a hard day's work in their lives. Putting their own things in boxes had probably been the toughest thing they'd ever done, and now here were Samhain and Kebby, doing all of the real work.

'Ah'll get these.' Aiden picked up a stack of easels. 'Honestly, can't believe ah'm doing this. Didn't think ah'd be here this long.' He spoke softly, with a Boro accent. 'When ah first came, ah said to meself, just do a couple a' years, then get somethin' else.' The easels cracked against each other gently, as they stepped outside. 'Never did ah think ah'd still be here, thirty years later, moving things out so they can refurbish the place.'

'I didn't even know this place was here.' Samhain shoved boxes onto the van back. They were lighter than they looked: it was going to be an easy day's work.

'Well, that's the thing, you see. People don't – unless they really want to study art... this is the place to come if you want to study illustration or ceramics.' Aiden turned, and gestured at the doors. 'See here, they'll put new doors in – automatic ones – to make it easier to get in and out. For the students in wheelchairs, see. Or if you're carrying a piece of artwork. And ah found this old feller in Ather's Edge who specialises in restoration signs and lettering – that's all he does – and he's going to do the sign over the door. It'll be perfect when he does it, it'll look right bonny.' Aiden jumped down off the truck back, and towards the college doors. 'Ah get a bit excited when ah think about it, how good it'll all look when it's done.' His voice sped up as he talked. 'Have ya been inside an art college before? Come, ah'll show you 'round.'

The lower floor was all classrooms. Big things, linoleum floors. Fake tiles worn to white by hundreds of successive pairs of feet: shoe, after shoe, after shoe, after shoe. The windows were a single glaze, jittering in their cases.

'That downstairs is the lower teaching studio,' Aiden said. 'Where we teach printmaking and lifedrawing and all that sort of thing – and upstairs...'

A wooden staircase at the back led to another two, maybe three, identical corridors, around similar looking classrooms, all with the same, sick tropical colour doors. 'Print room,' Aiden said. 'Individual studios. Ceramics studio. Dark room...'

They passed all these rooms, with their doors partly open, and all their contents already boxed. Samhain couldn't see what any of them were. It left him quite disoriented.

'And there,' Aiden said, 'is our garden.' A back window looked out over an interior garden. A slight square of herbs and shrubs, with cigarette butts all the way around the path.

In the upstairs room, space opened out like apartments not yet built. Glass on two sides to the north and east, with a view over the city. Marks had been left on the floor by temporary studio walls.

The whole room smelled faintly of turpentine and solvents.

'Some view, eh?' Aiden commented. 'This is what's kept me here all these years.'

'It's not half bad,' Samhain agreed.

Samhain's phone beeped; he could hear Kebby's footsteps coming up the stairs.

The message came up as Unknown Number. *Hi. Its Charley. Mart came 2 c me. thnk u 4 money. Used 2 buy Astrid shoes n coat.*

Aiden strode across the long, empty floor, followed by his own blurry shadow. 'Ah was a joiner when ah first came here. Used to make tables – cabinets – with these carvings in the edges, more for myself than anybody else. Ah was making these cabinets and they looked a bit plain, so ah said to myself, Aiden, why not carve a ladybird running up the joist? And it got to be a bit of a running joke that ah had with myself.'

Samhain stared at his phone screen, watching it fade to black. Something, he didn't know what, had changed her mind.

'We should have started up here,' Kebby said. 'We always start upstairs,' he said to Aiden.

'Right,' said Aiden, moving towards the classrooms. 'Empty this room first?'

Samhain followed, following Aiden's faint smell of sawdust. A tiny feeling nibbled gently at him, the same feeling of calmness that came from walking out of a stuffy, beer-soaked squat, into an evening of cool air and sparkling stars.

'You alright there, mate?' Aiden asked. 'This building does funny things to people. Ah know it did me, first time ah came in.'

'I'm fine.' Samhain grabbed a box. Crinkling with newspaper, clunking with plates.

'Careful – that's fragile.'

'We always are careful,' Kebby said.

'He's right, you know. We are.'

'The stairs are quite steep–'

'We can handle it.' Kebby was already halfway down.

'Anyway.' Aiden had another of the boxes. 'Back to my cabinets – ah wanted to know, what was the most ah could get away with before someone came back on me and said, "Here, this wardrobe's got a mouse running along the top!"'

'So what happened?' Samhain felt his way down the steps, elbow to the handrail, foot tracing the stairs' edges. 'Did anybody ever come and ask for their money back?'

'Naw. They got t'like it, didn't they? Ah ended up with a waiting list six months long, just f'r fitted wardrobes.'

'You should get into that.' Outside, Kebby packed boxes into the van. Shoving things a little harder than was strictly necessary, and Samhain knew, even though he couldn't see Kebby's face, what sort of a mood he was in for having had to come upstairs looking for them. 'Knocking bits of wood together – that's your sort of thing, isn't it?'

Samhain passed up the box. 'Frankie did most of the work in our old place.' But he had the angle slightly wrong, and sent a set of easels tumbling down towards the gate.

'You leave this to me.' Kebby pulled the box away, crash-quick, and straightened everything out. 'You're better off inside – where you can't cause any trouble.'

'Is he going to be ok?' Aiden asked. 'Ah don't want things getting broken.'

Inside, Samhain grappled with a fake studio wall. It was nowhere near as heavy as it looked, and lifted away from the floor easily as a ballerina. The surprise lost his footing, and he stumbled back a couple of steps. 'No. He's fine. It's me who's on the wrong end of things today.'

'Ah'd never been in an art college either, when ah started. Then the old Dean ordered a bit of furniture from me, and said, Aiden, you should come and teach at the college, these students could learn a lot from you. I said to her, Padrice, what are you talking about, ah'm no artist. And she said, well, ya just can't stop it, can you? Carving all those little insects and mice on every bit of furniture you make. If that's not art, ah don't know what is.'

Kebby swept past, and picked up three walls at once. 'We need to keep moving,' he said.

'I thought you were outside.'

'Well, I was. And then I came inside.' Kebby grunted, angling his walls out of the doorway. 'This is a three-man job. Peter should never have sent Simon off alone on that one-man-and-van job.' He went out, still grumbling. 'It's a good job we've got the client here to help us, otherwise we'd struggle.'

'So you haven't even got an art degree?'

'Ah have *now*. They wouldn't let me teach if ah hadn't.' Aiden wasn't even lifting his walls. He pushed them, still on their feet, towards the exit. 'But ah started in the seventies, and things were different then. Not like it is now.' He reached the doorway, and pushed his walls out into the corridor. They stuck on the carpet, and, drawing his breath, he started to try and wriggle them free. 'Well, this was a stupid way to do it,' he said.

Kebby's arm appeared. It reached for the edge, lifted the walls off and away and out of the door.

Outside, the air was bright with the smell of warmed sugar and marmalade, from the jam factory downwind. 'We need to get a move on,' he said.

14.

The amount of things Astrid needed was staggering. Charley had sent a list, and it was a lot for a little person. Nappies, changing mat, spare clothes, baby bottles and tippy cups, a high chair, baby food and fruit juice, toys and books and bricks and puzzles: he'd had no idea, he realised, reeling, how much there was, and how much of it she had already done without him.

He wanted to say sorry, and soon, he was going to get the chance to.

'Card.' It was the table-chested man with the thick beard. 'There's a computer free now, if you hurry up. Here's your code – it'll only work today. So, no point trying to use it to try and log in again tomorrow. Computer 14.' He raised an arm at the bank of computers in the corner. 'If you get stuck, just give me a shout and I'll try to help.

'Oh – also,' he said. 'There's a note for you, from upstairs.'

Guest

Fox-Eyes' writing. *Come up and see me*, it said. *Did you manage to find them?*

Samhain clicked around all of his usual websites. MySpace, Yahoo! Mail, Red and Black News:

Call out for action in the G8!

Join us for dissent and protest at next year's G8, to be held in Seattle. We say NO to neoliberalism. NO to a world that benefits corporations and the wealthy. NO to global warming, global poverty, and NO to exploitation of the working classes.

Contact us here if you are planning an affinity protest.

Samhain looked, and was exhausted. Days in a camp. Beards and dogs. Going out with a rucksack packed with gaffer tape, goggles, and tools and scissors and market pens, all the things you'd need on a protest. Leaving your passport back at the meeting point in case you were arrested.

He could stay home instead. Where it was comfortable. Where there were cushions, a duvet, a kettle. Where there was no danger of being arrested or sprayed with tear gas.

But he wanted to do *something*. He closed the tab, and browsed over to the social club website.

Cafe volunteers wanted!

We always need people to help out in the cafe. Can you cook or wash up? Would you be willing to give a few hours every week to help run our vegan cafe? Get in touch!

This was something he could do. Something useful, close to home, and without the element of danger.

The entry was dated two months ago. He started typing

an email:

Stef,

Are you still looking for volunteers for the cafe? Reckon I could do one evening a week. Is it still on a Tuesday? I'm not the best cook but I can do a not-bad punk stew. Also can wash up. Could you text me back? I'm working a lot at the moment and don't get to check my emails all that often.

Samhain

Upstairs.

She looked different today: pinched cheeks, slack striped dress, drooping on one side.

'Sam!' An exclamation given quietly, the most excited you were allowed to get in a library. Face brighter than a warm cake.

'Hey, Alice,' he said.

'It's been ages.' She turned a little away from him, rummaging under the desk. Looking, he supposed, for the small key on the large fob that opened the door into the back. 'How'd you get on? Aha!' Lifting it, its teeth twinkling, she got out of her chair. 'I was thinking about you,' she said. 'After that last CopWatch meeting. Wondering what you'd done afterwards.'

She climbed from behind the desk as though competing in an obstacle race. Everything got in her way. The chair, the desks. The returns shelf, a metal trolley on wheels.

'They should have been a bit more accommodating,' she said. 'People going to the meeting are bound to have issues. They're supposed to be for anybody.' Fox-Eyes was heading for the back of the room. The rack of leaflets, the concealed door. She already had her hand on it before he could stop her.

'Hold on,' he said.

'I thought you might want to look some more stuff up,' she

said. Her hand dropped to her side.

'Don't need to.' They were standing by the last desk in the room, which was empty. Highly polished wood, a copy of the day's Daily Mail on a stick. The yellow-jacketed Council Vacancies booklet on the desktop beside it. 'Let's sit here.'

He dropped his books on the desk. Covers with smiling babies, and titles like *Development: A Parent's Guide* and *Growing Up: What To Expect*.

'Are you taking a course?' she asked.

'No. These are for me.'

'Huh.' She seemed less certain now, sliding into the seat opposite. 'What for?'

'So I can look after my little girl,' he said.

'Huh.' She spun the books around, glanced at their covers. 'Didn't know you had a daughter,' she said. There seemed to be something uncomfortable about the bench on her side: she shuffled around on it, one side to another, one side to another, as though being poked.

'Well, I do.' Samhain took the books back, and straightened them into a pile. 'Haven't met her yet, but that's only a matter of time.'

'I'm sorry about your dad,' she said. 'That he passed away before you got chance to meet him.'

'Yeah, well.' Samhain levelled the corners of his books. 'I don't think we would have got along.'

'You know, you could go back to CopWatch,' she said. 'Challenge their decision. Ask them to let you go to their meetings. They're looking for people to help bring a case against the Met—'

'No.' Samhain was shaking his head.

Behind them, a clearing throat. The accusatory rattling of a newspaper page being turned loudly, pointedly, signalling the act of being interrupted.

Samhain whispered: 'I don't want to bring a case. I've got other stuff to think about.' He said: 'Thanks, though. You did everything you could.'

'Yeah, well,' her cheeks burnished. 'It's wrong, what the police have done. To people like you and your mum.'

'It did help,' he said. 'And I got to meet my brother, which I couldn't have done otherwise.'

'Really?' she said. 'Samhain, that's great. Are you going to keep the contact going?'

'No,' he said. 'He's a total dick.'

Silent giggles. Shoulders juddering like an old car trying to start. 'Sam!'

'You can't have everything.'

She was pretty when she smiled, the way her whole face opened.

'Listen,' he said. 'It didn't totally work out, and I'd never say this to my mum, but I'm glad I got to know who he was. At least I've got a picture of him. To know his name.'

She leaned back. 'Well, that's great, Sam. And if you ever want to find out anything more...'

'I know where you are.'

Sam got up, lifting his books, propping them under his arm. 'Thank you, Alice. For all that you've done. I'll see you.'

He went downstairs, and got on his bike, and cycled all the way home, rain falling lightly on the backs of his hands.

15.

'Why do anarchists drink herbal tea?'

Stef crouched, sandy hair wavy as spaghetti, wearing a jumper you could use to drain pasta.

Click, click. Eyes level with the cooker knobs, one thumb on the ignition. 'There's a trick to this. In a minute, it'll...'

The nearest gas ring flared and spluttered. A bloom of fire exploded, clouding close to Stef's eyebrows.

'There,' he said. 'That's it going. Did you hear the click?' Stef stood, and opened the nearest cupboard. 'You have to keep pressing and unpressing the ignition, then when you hear the click, turn the cooker knob about halfway up – but not too fast. That's the only way to get the rings lit. It's a bit temperamental, but you'll soon get used to it.'

'Is it because all proper tea is theft?'

'Hmm?' Stef inspected a bent tin of kidney beans.

'Why anarchists drink herbal tea – is it because all proper

tea is theft?'

In response, a quizzical look. 'Didn't I tell you that one a minute ago?' Stef felt around the worktop. 'Tin opener. Tin opener.'

Samhain took a scourer, and ran the tap over it. People left the cafe in a real mess. He'd only been here an hour, and already found spilled beer, sticky and dried, in cloudy brown patches all over the serving hatch side. It had taken him half an hour of scrubbing to get it up, and he'd had to throw the sponge away afterwards. 'Back pocket,' he said.

'Hmm?'

'The tin opener. It's in your back pocket.'

'Yes. Of course.' Stef whipped it out, grinding its blunt teeth against the can top. 'Now.' He frowned over the top of his glasses. 'Is this your first time making a bean burger?'

'No.' Open cupboard doors: Samhain took boxes and packets down, to wipe down the insides. They kept – and to him, this was the most impressive part – a whole cupboard full of herbs and spices, and eighteen different kinds of herbal tea.

'You've made bean burgers from a packet, I expect.'

'Yes.'

'This is different. You may *think* you know how to make a bean burger. What's that?' Stef reached across, and plucked apart an old, dusty packet of star anise. 'Look at the date on that. 1996. This should be in a museum.' He flicked it into the bin. 'Well, what I'm about to teach you today is going to blow your mind. Or something. You see, here, on gig nights, we never make burgers from packets, no. Today, Samhain, you are going to learn one of the best kept secrets of the club – how to make a Social Club Beanburger. It's only ever made here, using a recipe closely guarded by a select group of anarchists, and only ever handed down through anarchist hands.' Stef rustled through a plastic bag of new ingredients. 'It's also in the club cookbook,

but whoever wrote it down made a mistake. They forgot to say...'
drawing out a bag of flour, of millet; beetroot, newly purple and
fresh from the ground, still wearing wet soil on its skin: '...they
forgot to mention the cabbage.' Stef tossed the beetroot into the
sink, rubbing the earth from his hands. 'It's better with it, but
sometimes you have to manage your best without.'

Samhain sliced potatoes for chips as the band arrived. Six
of them, dirty-faced, with sleeping bags and banjos, came in
looking as though they were trying to find their location on a
map. The smell coming off them was something far stronger
than you got from a week on the road: he watched them walk
through the cafe with their bags and their cases, vests hanging
loose from their shoulders, and tried hard not to slice his fingers.

Frying onions gave off a hearty, caramelising smell. Pan
clattering and hammering on the ring as Stef poked them with
a spoon. 'Wait until they're lovely and brown,' he said. 'How are
you getting on with them potatoes?'

'Perfect.' The last of the boys went through the gig room
door, tote bag in hand, guitar leads trailing from the zipper.
Samhain laid raw potato carefully in strips on kitchen roll,
sprinkling them in a glittering snowfall of salt. 'Stef, do you ever
miss touring?'

'What?'

Pushing glasses back up his nose, glancing at the closing
door to the other room.

The smash of cymbals falling, a shouted curse. The door
opened and two of the band came out again, eyes blackened and
heads hanging, hands empty. 'Did you bring the guitars in yet?'
one said to the other.

'Still in the van – and the bass cab,' said the other. 'Pete
better not leave it all to us this time.'

His companion rolled his eyes, scurrying after.

'Miss it?' Stef nodded at the two lads. 'No way. I like sleeping in my own bed too much.' He grinned. 'Are you thinking of leaving us already?'

'I don't think so.' The smell of the onions was making him hungry, and Samhain found that he didn't much mind.

He noticed he was humming.

Lemmers came in, carrying a big plastic box full of microphones and DI boxes.

'Hello,' he said, putting it down on the serving hatch.

'Hello.' Samhain was grating carrots, a whole bag of them, like Stef had told him to.

'Well.' The box lid loose on one side; Lemmers tried to squeeze it closed. 'Haven't seen you for a while. Are you volunteering in the cafe now?'

Lemmers fiddled with switches and knobs, turning things on, off, up, down. Adjusting levels on a rack mount that wasn't even plugged in.

'Seems that way. This is my first time.' Samhain put the bowl to one side, and rubbed knives and forks clean and dry with a towel. 'We'll have to see whether they'll have me back a second time.'

He seemed very interested in the knobs, staring at them even while Samhain shredded the carrots, even while he put two wooden spoons into the salad bowl to turn the leaves. 'I bet they will,' he said. 'People are always needed in the cafe.'

'Lemmers.' Samhain laid knives and forks down in the cutlery tray. 'I'm sorry I ruined the tour.'

'Yeah, well.' Lemmers hesitated, tipping one corner of the box up, then the other. 'I don't think anybody really blamed you. We all knew you were going through some... you know. Nobody minded.'

'But what about Ned – wasn't he...?'

'Oh yeah, Ned. We had to take him to Dutch A&E at four

in the morning. That wasn't great. His girlfriend went mental – she wanted him to go straight home, but he stayed. Not that he could play anything for the rest of the tour, not with all the stitches. Still...' Lemmers picked up his box. 'It got him out of carrying anything heavy for the rest of the way around.'

'And Romey?'

'What about Romey?'

'Wasn't he pissed off?'

'Ah, no.' Lemmers grinned. 'Romey forgot about the whole thing after a couple more drinks. I think he was just glad to be out of the house. Good to see you again, man.'

Later, Samhain cleaned the cooker. Washed every mug, put all of the spoons and forks and everything else away, ready for the next person to come and mess it all up again before he was next in.

It was late. The band were still banging and scraping away in the gig room, making their noise over the speakers, even though half the audience had already left. They had gone yawning, or running to catch their last bus.

Samhain was packing his bag when the text came through.

So how come ur cooking now? U never used 2 do that wen we were 2getha!

Charley.

He switched the cooker off at the wall, and turned the lights off in the kitchen. Left the damp tea towel hanging over the oven door handle.

He texted back: *I must have changed!* He added: *Stefan taught me.*

Closed the door, pulled the latch over the serving window. Called out: 'Night, Rawlplug,' to the barman.

'Night.'

Charley replied when he was around the back of the club. Outside in the dark, unchaining his bike from the rack.

U can come Sunday pm 2 meet Astrid if u like. We'll be at my mum's. Come @2.

He texted back: *I'll be there.*

He wondered whether her boyfriend would be there too. She'd got this guy called Tom, somebody she'd apparently met through work, or so he'd heard. People said he was a great guy. Very clean, very straight up. Tidy clothes and short back and sides. Looked ordinary, but he was anything but. Samhain knew this, because he'd been asking around about Tom for a couple of weeks, and nobody had a bad word to say about him.

So this much he knew: Tom was steady, Tom paid his bills on time and never owed money. Tom had once spent a year in the former Yugoslavia doing good works that nobody could exactly name. He still went back sometimes to give a lick of paint to the school or hospital he had helped build. He did some kind of voluntary work with asylum seekers that was maybe giving legal advice, or something to do with housing. Samhain was not sure how he'd also had time to get together with a woman.

This was something nobody knew, what exact date to put on Tom and Charley's relationship. 'I don't know, a couple of years maybe?' one person had said; another, 'Must be about a year. No, maybe nine months. No wait, it might be six.'

The boyfriend he knew about, but not how long the boyfriend had been the boyfriend. They could have been together when Astrid was small. When she was still a red-faced, crying thing with weak legs and strong lungs. This Tom might have held her while she still needed her neck supporting, rocking her when she screamed, changing her nappies. May have been there before she was even walking. When Astrid hadn't fully gained vision yet, before she could even have known the difference between one large pink human-shaped blob and another.

She might even be calling him 'Dad.'
He texted a second time: *Does she know I'm her father?*
No reply. For hours and hours and hours.

16.

Charley's mum lived in a stone cottage, a place of grey stone and black edges, a place with two floors and a low chimney. The doorstep had rosemary and mint in terracotta pots, scenting your steps as you walked to the door. It was the sort of home you could almost fit in your jeans pocket.

Three houses similar in the row, looking softly out into the cul-de-sac. She had new neighbours since the last time he'd been here – they'd painted their front door a smart, shiny black.

He arrived by bike, up to the fence. Mart's bike was already chained up, shackled by the unbreakable D-lock.

The path to the front door was short. Paved, the lawn next to it shorn closer than a spring sheep. A pink plastic trike lay on its side in the grass.

He walked, pulling the rope lock off his shoulder. It was a heavy, treatment-coated thing, that somebody from the bike club had got for him. The casing was supposed to be unbreakable.

'Well, a thief could break it,' they'd said. 'But they'd need about seven hours and a blowtorch.'

Maybe he didn't need to lock his bike, not around here. Not if they were happily leaving Astrid's – his daughter's – trike laid out there on the grass.

She was old enough, big enough, to ride a scooter. Samhain pressed his bike against Mart's, looping them both with the chain. Not that anybody would want to steal his bike. It was an ungainly, bumpy old thing, with sticky gears and a too-hard seat, with the seat post rusted slightly too low for his height. This bike must have been around the block a hundred thousand times, and probably been left out in the rain fifty nights out of a hundred.

'I'm going to count to three...'

Charley's voice. He looked up: the bathroom window was open.

That voice. It took him back. Unmistakeably Huddersfield. With a friendliness that made you want to do what it commanded, and a shortness that made you afraid not to. Hearing it took him back to the Sunday afternoon cafe, the way she used to deal with bumblers holding up the queue, the ones who weren't sure what they wanted. 'Make your mind up, love, this isn't *Who Wants to be a Millionaire.*'

'*No*,' she said. 'You're not going in Grandma Best's bedroom. Stop messing about now – put your trousers on, like a good girl, or there'll be no Thomas the Tank Engine.'

'No!' came a determined baby voice. 'No, no, no, no, no, no, no!'

Samhain smiled. That was his girl. A spirited thing, naked from the waist down and doing what she liked, refusing to do as she was told. He came to the door, fist poised to knock. Not out of nappies yet, and already Astrid had the makings of an anarchist.

Mart's voice came through the open living room window:
'You alright up there?'

'I'm fine,' Charley shouted back. Then more quietly, to
Astrid: 'Quickly now, before Samhain gets here.'

He stopped, cold. The same way he had sometimes out on
protest, when he had realised he was in the wrong spot, and the
police were coming. This was the way he'd been introduced –
Samhain, 'Mummy's friend,' a stranger.

A face at the window. Mart waving, the speed of a child's
windmill caught in high winds. 'Hey, Sam! You're there.' She
called upstairs: 'He's here!' Then again, to Sam: 'Why didn't you
knock, you doughnut?'

'I just–'

'Never mind. I'll let you in. Oh...'

Perhaps this other man, this amazing Tom guy, he of the
sterling competence in all areas of life: putting shelves up,
having a job, cooking and tidying and washing up; remembering
birthdays and buying unexpected presents, and doing everything
else a perfect boyfriend should do, including being amazing in
bed, making cups of tea in the morning; getting up early to
deal with Astrid, and taking her to the park when Charley was
tired, taking them both on days out to the seaside and funfair,
opening doors and rubbing feet, and doing all sorts of things
that Charley had claimed not to care about when they were
together, but now clearly did, and had found them all in this
man who had a car, and a job, and prospects, and did everything
he was asked to and much more without even being asked to,
he'd probably even said, 'I don't mind if you let her call Samhain
Dad,' so comfortable was he already in the knowledge Astrid
already thought of him as her father.

'Now then.'

The door swung open. Samhain stood there, on the step,
one corner of his bag scraping his spine. Mart had said he could

bring presents: he was being dug by a set of wooden bricks.

'You must be Samhain.'

A cheery, friendly-faced man his own age, with short curly hair, and uneven stubble. 'You'll have to excuse the mess,' he said. 'Everything's chaos today.' Tom had a smile like a new shirt being opened, and a hand the size of an oven glove; he looked liked the kind of man who'd have a go at building a raft, even though he didn't know a thing about it.

Unfortunately, Samhain liked him straight away.

'It's fine. I brought you a present...' Samhain dug around for the small box of not-too-fancy chocolates for Charley, ones he knew she'd share with her boyfriend, with a nice bottle of beer, sitting on their comfy sofa, in their lovely flat. He had thought that if the boyfriend was anything like Samhain, he'd go for all the best ones first, before she even got a look in.

But Superman Tom, in his newish red jumper that looked like it had only been worn a few times, wasn't anything like Samhain. He could see that now.

'You shouldn't have.' Tom took the box.

'Hi!'

Mart's voice. He peered around the doorway, and saw her in the living room. She was wearing lipstick, the same shade she put on when she had to go to an important meeting.

'I knew you wouldn't be long.' She spoke as though being charged by the word. 'We were just saying, as it's such a lovely day, perhaps we should all go to the park?' When he really looked at her, that was when he saw how tightly she was holding the cup, how closely she was sitting to the edge of the sofa.

'Whatever you all think,' he mumbled. 'I'll go along with whatever you think's best.'

The click of the bathroom door.

'Come on,' Charley said. 'Hold my hand.'

Samhain looked up.

At the top of the stairs settled a tiny pair of shoes. Pale blue and round-toed, with Charley's feet beside them in her battered old Converse. Laces grey and tattered.

He saw the front of the shoes. New, bright, clean. And Charley's: the shoes that had done a hundred thousand miles. 'Is that you, Samhain?' she said. 'Give us a few minutes. We're just coming down.' To the girl: 'Come on, Bibbledy Boo.'

One step down, the top of the stairs. Baby legs to whom the stairs were a full leg-length. Holding on tight to her mother, stretching up like a shirt on a line. 'One step, Bibbledy Boo,' Charley said. 'Two step, Bibbledy Boo.'

'This part always takes ages.' Tom turned around, twinkling a smile up the stairs. 'They could be an hour or more, doing that.'

'Yeah, sorry.' Charley's laughing voice down the stairs. 'Doing the stairs is always a bit of a mission. Tom, why don't you bring Samhain into the house?'

Samhain kept on looking. The rest of her was coming into view. Bendy legs, stout as a pig's. Sturdy torso, broad as a young tree, wearing a pink floral top.

'Shall I just carry you the rest of the way, Bibbledy Boo?' Charley said.

'No!' Tiny foot stamping, hitting the floor with the weight of a half-mouse. 'I do it.'

'Sorry,' Charley's laughing voice. 'We could be a while.'

'That's Astrid for you.' Tom grinned, stood aside. Pushing the door all the way back, opening a welcome up into the house. 'She won't be told. Come on, don't stand out there on the step. Why don't you come on in?'

Acknowledgements

First of all, thanks to my editor Nathan Connolly, for believing in this book and for all of his help and encouragement and support. Without him, you wouldn't be holding this book in your hands now.

Huge thanks also go to Nick at The Print Project, the sadly late and much-missed Protag, and Cathy. Perhaps without them even knowing it, conversations with them around the time of the Mark Stone case being reported led to the ideas that made me write this book in the first place.

Many thanks to Martin Cornwell for lending me books that helped with the research, for letting me stay at his house that one time, for reading and commenting on early drafts, and for the conversations whilst I was writing it. Also, huge thanks to Peter, again for lending research books, for letting me stay at his house, and for being one of the most fascinating people I know. Thanks to Caroline for being such a welcoming host. I couldn't have done it without you.

I'd like to thank all of the workers, volunteers, and members at Wharf Chambers, for giving me an insight into how flat organising works in practice, and also for the amazing beer.

During the course of writing this book I've had some great support and the opportunity to be involved in some wonderful projects, so I would also like to thank: Gianni and Jennifer at December magazine, Barney Walsh at Litro, and Russell MacAlpine at Disclaimer magazine for publishing my stories, and in Barney's case, for reading early drafts and sending some very useful comments; to all staff at The Leeds Library, for letting me sit quietly in a corner tapping away at my laptop; to Fiona Gell at Leeds Big Bookend for her enthusiasm and support; to the Northern Short Story Festival volunteers, and to Linzi at Carriageworks; to Max and Sai at Remember Oluwale;

and to Max Dunbar for many, many drinks and interesting conversations. Massive thanks also to Rachael Rix-Moore and Alice Rix-Moore for their friendship, hilarity, and dedication to making great art projects happen. The two of you continue to be a huge source of inspiration, encouragement, and laughs, even when things go bad, so thank you. I would have been lost without your help.

I couldn't have written the middle section of this book without having toured the UK in the back of a van, and I couldn't have toured the UK in the back of a van without my old friend and bandmate Nicky Bray. Thank you to her for all of the good times and memories which inspired this part of the book. Also, a side thank you to Jon Nash and the rest of Tigers!, Human Fly, Wakey Steve, Mike in Grimsby, Dom, Dan and Roo, and to that guy in Sheffield with the glitter cannons, you know who you are.

Almost last but certainly not least, a special thank you to my Fictions of Every Kind co-organisers, Jenna Isherwood and Claire Stephenson. Your friendship and support has meant so much, and without it I wouldn't have had half so many laughs, or have finished this book, so thank you.

Lastly, thanks to my family, a great source of support, fun, kindness, and inspiration, throughout the past few years; especially to my husband, Ricky, for supporting my writing by asking after the book's general health, for looking after me when I'm so busy I forget to eat, and for making cups of tea whenever it looks like I need one (all the time). You are the best and I couldn't have done it without you.

SJ Bradley

SJ Bradley is a writer from Leeds and one of the organisers behind Fictions of Every Kind. She won the Willesden Herald Short Story Prize and was shortlisted for the Gladstone Writers in Residency Award. Her debut novel, *Brick Mother*, was published by Dead Ink in 2014.

Publishing the Underground

Publishing the Underground is Dead Ink's project to develop the careers of new and emerging authors. Supported by Arts Council England, we use our own crowdfunding platform to ask readers to act as patrons and fund the first run print costs.

If you'd like to support new writing then visit our website and join our mailing list. This book was made possible by kind contributions from the following people...

R Adam
Mediah Ahmed
Jenny Alexander
Nick Allen
Lulu Allison
Rj Barker
Teika Bellamy
Seth Bennett
Alex Blott
Naomi Booth
Florence Bradley
Carrie Braithwaite
Julia Brich
Gary Budden
Edward Burness
Daniel Carpenter
Gina Cattini
Sarah Cleave
Ellie Clement
Ian Cockburn
Tracey Connolly

Nyle Connolly
Rachel Connor
Martin Cornwell
Catriona Cox
Stuart Crewes
David Cundall
Rachel Darling
Claire Dean
Steve Dearden
Vanessa Dodd
Jack Ecans
Su Edwards
Laura Elliott
Lee Farley
Max Farrar
Arlene Finnigan
Naomi Frisby
Harry Gallon
Peter Gallon
Heidi Gardner
Trina Garnett

Sarah Garnham
Fiona Gell
Martin Geraghty
Dan Grace
Alan Griffith
Vince Haig
Paul Hancock
Tania Hershman
A Hill
Harriet Hirshman
Richard Hirst
Simon Holloway
Darren Hopes
Rebekah Hughes
Nasser Hussain
Jennifer Isherwood
Sadiq Jaffery
Laura Jones
Avril Joy
Benjamin Judge
Haroun Khan
Lewis King
Wes Lee
Simon Lee
David Martin
Margaret McCormack
Heather McDaid
Chloe McLeod
Carmel McNamara
Kiran Millwood Hargrave
Stephen Moran
Andrew Myers
Marc Nash

Ruth Nassar
Chris Naylor
David Newsome
James Oddy
Sophie Hopesmith
Elizabeth Ottosson
Ruth Pooley Ford
James Powell
Hannah Powley
Sarah Pybus
Faith Radford-Lloyd
Mal Ramsay
Jane Riley
Liam Riley
Alice Rix
Matthew Shenton
Alex Shough
Nicky Smalley
Vicky Smith
Richard Smyth
Julie Swain
Catherine Syson
Mia Tagg
Morgan Tatchell-Evans
Michael Thomson
Sally Vince
Barney Walsh
Allan Whalley
Emily Whitaker
Sara White
Sandy Wilkie
Eley Williams
James Yeoman

Also from Dead Ink...

Every Fox is a Rabid Fox
Harry Gallon

'Every Fox is a Rabid Fox is a harrowing and brutal read. But I fell for its incredibly tender heart. I loved this book.'
   - Claire Fuller, author of Swimming Lessons and Our Endless Numbered Days

'Beautifully executed tale of innocence, tragedy, and the family traumas we all carry with us and many times fail to leave behind.'
   - Fernando Sdrigotti, author of Dysfunctional Males

Robert didn't mean to kill his brother. Now he's stuck between grief and guilt with only ex-girlfriend Willow and the ghost of his dead twin sister for company. Terrified of doing more harm, Robert's hysteria and anxiety grow while Willow and his sister's ghost fight over him: one trying to save him, the other digging his grave.

Every Fox Is A Rabid Fox is a brutal yet tender tale of family tragedy, mental illness and a young man searching for escape from his unravelling mind.

Another Justified Sinner
Sophie Hopesmith

It's the eve of the recession, but who cares? For commodity trader Marcus, life is good: he's at the top of the food chain. So what if he's a fantasist? So what if he wills his college sweetheart to death? So what if it's all falling apart? This isn't a crisis. Until it is.

As misfortune strikes again and again, he goes to help others and 'find himself' abroad – but it turns out that's not as easy as celebrities make it look on TV. Another Justified Sinner is a feverish black comedy about the fall and rise and fall of Marcus, an English psycopath. How difficult is it to be good?

Sophie Hopesmith is a 2012 Atty Awards finalist and her background is in feature writing. Born and bred in London, she works for a reading charity. She likes comedy, poetry, writing music, and Oxford commas. All of her favourite films were made in the 70s.

About Dead Ink...

Dead Ink is a small, ambitious and experimental literary publisher based in Liverpool.

Supported by Arts Council England, we're focused on developing the careers of new and emerging authors.

We believe that there are brilliant authors out there who may not yet be known or commercially viable. We see it as Dead Ink's job to bring the most challenging and experimental new writing out from the underground and present it to our audience in the most beautiful way possible.

Our readers form an integral part of our team. You don't simply buy a Dead Ink book, you invest in the authors and the books you love.